HEAVENLY

BY JENNIFER LAURENS

Grove Creek Publishing

A Grove Creek Publishing Book
HEAVENLY
Grove Creek Publishing / June 2009
All Rights Reserved.
Copyright 2009 by Katherine Mardesich

This book may not be reproduced in whole or in part without permission.
For further information:
Grove Creek Publishing, LLC
1404 West State Road, Suite 202
Pleasant Grove, Ut 84062

Cover: Sapphire Designs
http://designs.sapphiredreams.org/
Book Design: Julia Lloyd, Nature Walk Design
ISBN: 978-1-933963-84-6
$13.95
Printed in the United States of America

For Cooper

2004 - 2008

HEAVENLY

ONE

I opened my eyes and found myself in a dark room. In a strange bed. My head throbbed. I tried to lift my arms, to rub my face, but my limbs were so heavy I could barely move. A sour residue thickened the inside of my mouth. Where was I? What had happened? Images pulsed through my mind: Faces. Laughter. Shadows.

How did I get here?

It took all my strength to lift my head so I could look around. Black corners. A shadowy door. A draped window.

I still wore the jeans and long sleeved red tee shirt I'd put on before the party, but the cool air on my shoulder drew my fuzzy gaze to a jagged tear in the fabric, leaving me exposed.

On a groan, my head fell back against the pillow. Something was wrong. I was smashed, yet I hadn't had anything to drink. *What happened? Where am I?* Panic rolled through my system. I drew in a deep breath, determined to rise up to my elbows so I could make out this place, but the act was like lifting a cement slab.

That's when I saw him.

Felt him.

Like the sun raging behind a storm.

He sat in the chair like a warrior after battle. His long legs extended arms out to his sides, palms up—as if battle had drained him. But that was impossible. The source from which his energy flowed was Eternal. The comfort

I was accustomed to when he was in my presence was out of my reach, dancing around him in a soft glow. The only light in the room emanated from his being, beneath the soft ivory of his clothes. He didn't say anything. His clear blue eyes were fierce, locked with mine. A shiver trickled through my limbs.

His gaze held mine in piercing intensity, cutting my soul open as if he would dissect right then and there if I was innocent or guilty of the night's activities. I opened my mouth to defend myself, not sure what retribution I would face but my throat froze. Had I put us in danger? Would the heavens thrash and roar? Would he leave me? The thought filled me with a dread so black, my arms trembled. I nearly crumpled into the mattress.

"What happened?" I rasped.

His lock on my gaze held me captive, a blinkless stare I couldn't escape. Memories of the night dripped with a slow leak into my conscience and shame forced me to close my eyes.

Why did you go inside, Zoe?

I heard his question as clearly as if he'd spoken to me. But he hadn't. We could read each others' thoughts, that was the beauty, the miracle of our relationship.

I was angry. I'm sorry. I shouldn't have. It was wrong. I'm sorry.

Silence. Thick. Hot. Sticky.

Look at me.

I can't. Tears rushed behind my eyes and burst through my closed lashes. He'd saved me tonight. Whatever had happened had been treacherous, the magnitude something I could only measure by the intensity in his countenance—like the sun tearing through black clouds, claiming possession of the sky.

※ ※ ※

➤ ✦ ⋐

hey

My fingers tapped out a reply text message on my pink cell phone:

what's up?

nothin

yawn i'm bored.

where r u

park w/abria

ooo, so sorry

yeah… I looked up to check on my little sister. The swing where she'd been sitting was empty, and lulled to a stop.

I looked right, then left.

Nothing.

I jumped from the bench, breath frozen in my chest and whirled, scanning the skeletal park to see where she was.

Nothing.

I ran to the bulky cedar climbing gym and peered into the round holes that were supposed to be windows. "Abria?"

"Abria!" The second scream from my throat left my arms and legs trembling. I ducked low, looked underneath the slide, then I ran around to the other side of the wooden mass.

The play area was empty.

Panic rushed up my throat, clutching it in a tight fist. I stood in the sand, my gaze scanning the outer reaches of the park for her small form. Spread out east was an empty baseball diamond. To the west: grass and sleeping aspens, spindly from winter's breath. Overhead, furious black clouds collided with dark gray vapors, filling the air with rumbling thunder. A covered pavilion with tables and benches was behind me. It, too, was empty except for a discarded white paper plate that drifted from one table to the next, carried on the light breeze.

I couldn't swallow the knot in my throat. I couldn't stop shaking. A feeling of heaviness, one that I was well familiar with, settled over my shoulders like I'd been buried alive.

Abria had disappeared before, but you never got used to a five year old vanishing into thin air. She had autism. My parents, younger brother, and I often wished we had eyes in the backs of our heads.

Today was my day to watch her.

My pounding heart sunk to my feet as I scanned the park but still saw nothing. I wanted to run, but my legs were lead. The vast park stretched out in front of me, bare trees trembling, green grass turning gold. No one else was here. It was too cold to be at a park.

So why had I brought her?

Visions of my little sister running without care down the middle of a road, wandering into someone's backyard or getting lost in the thick forest covering the nearby mountains clogged my head.

Finally, I moved. *Please, God, wherever she is, keep her safe.* I started in the direction of the pavilion to make sure she wasn't behind the building, though I was certain she wasn't. When she ran, she was like a feather in the wind. She didn't stop.

My tennis shoes squeaked on the cement floor of the vacant pavilion. "Abria?" Her name echoed then disappeared. A rush of tears veiled my vision.

I shouldn't have taken my eyes off her. I knew better. I should have stayed home, kept her inside. I could have sat her down in front of the TV and put on a DVD…That was the easy way, and I'd done it too many times to count. Taken the easy way because it meant I could do whatever I wanted: talk on the phone, get online while she sat stupefied in front of something brainless.

Bringing her to the park may have sounded like a selfless act on my part, but it wasn't, and that was why guilt weighed so heavily, suffocating me now.

"Park." Was one of a handful of words Abria knew. She chirped it like a baby bird.

"Take her, Zoe," Mom told me not less than an hour ago.

Babysitting was the last thing I wanted to do.

⋙ ⚹ ⋘

"I'll give you ten bucks if you'll take her out for an hour," Mom finally sighed.

So here I was.

The bill was in the front pocket of my jeans.

A bitter wind bit my cheeks and I drew my brown hoodie closer around me. I should have brought a coat, but I hadn't planned on staying long. I'd planned on ten minutes at the park, fifteen minutes driving in my car with the music blasting.

Driving was the second easiest thing to do to anesthetize Abria.

"Where are you?" I screamed. She'd never answer. She wouldn't respond by poking her head out from a hiding place like a normal kid. If she was like any other kid, this wouldn't be happening. She'd answer me. She'd play with me. She'd be a real sister and not like some alien from another planet who I couldn't talk with, didn't understand, loved half the time, and resented the other half of the time because my life hadn't been my own since she'd been born.

Even with all of our differences, I'd always felt an unusual connection with Abria. Maybe because I'd been a second mother to her, felt the depth of my parents' concern for her life, happiness and safety as if she was a part of me.

I stood still, closed my eyes and listened, hoping I'd hear her light giggle on the breeze. Hoping somehow, I'd know where she was. *Abria, where are you?*

Wind whispered through empty branches—a hissing of condemnation and guilt.

I circled back around the side of the pavilion just as the clouds crackled and boomed. I had to call Mom and tell her, but I was avoiding it.

I came around the corner of the brick wall and stopped. There, standing before me was a young man. He had Abria by the hand. The pounding in my chest notched up. I'd been absolutely positive we were alone in the park.

Where had this guy come from?

He had the most piercing blue eyes. They locked on mine, unwavering. "Hello." His voice was deep and calm, like warm water pouring.

"Uh, hi." I stepped forward and scooped Abria into my arms, then stepped back. "Here you are." I quickly checked her from head to toe. Had he touched her? Hurt her? I'd never know, she couldn't tell me, her voice locked inside of her somewhere.

Knowing that she and I were alone with this stranger caused my nerves to crimp. My heart banged harder and the nervousness I felt crept up my throat and practically strangled me. "You found her. Thanks," I muttered.

He smiled then, and it was as though a stream of sunlight surrounded us, raising the cool winter air to a comfortable temperature. His crystal blue eyes were sharp, yet as calming as peering into the creek that ran behind our house, the soft sounds of which often soothed me when I could take no more.

"She was running," he said.

"Yeah, she does that." I shivered in spite of the warmth surrounding me. I wondered how he could be out in the biting cold in an outfit that looked like he'd just stepped off the beach: ivory slacks and a white shirt out of the same silky material. But his skin wasn't tan like he'd been at the beach, rather more pale than mine and unblemished as freshly fallen snow.

"Um, thanks."

"Not at all."

"How did you find her? I mean, I didn't see you." What if he had been hiding, watching us, waiting.

"I saw her running."

I stepped back again, even though I knew I couldn't outrun him. He was lean under those caressing clothes, and he wasn't that much older than me. He'd have us both in a second, and then he'd let Abria go while he did whatever he'd come to do. I squeezed her against me.

"Well, thanks again," I said, slowly moving away. Abria hated being held, and she squirmed and grunted on my hip. Her weight strained my arms and I felt her slowly slip from my grasp.

He didn't move, just stood with a pleasant smile. But I wouldn't be fooled. How many times had I seen faces just like his on the news? Well, maybe not just like his. He was better looking than the average psychos. I almost gave into the calmness that tried to spread into me whenever I looked into his eyes.

"Goodbye, Abria." He gave her a small wave and she granted him a look, though she was still busy trying to wriggle from my arms.

"How do you know her name?" I asked.

Confusion flashed on his face. "I heard you calling her."

"Oh. Right. Thanks again. She doesn't know any better. She has autism."

He seemed to ponder my words, his expression thoughtful. He didn't say anything, but his gaze stayed on Abria in a kind, sympathetic way. Most teenagers I explained Abria's handicap to eyed her with fascination and pity, along with a good measure of horror. He must be older than he looks, I thought, because there was none of the awkward discomfort so many of my peers expressed when they saw my sister.

At last Abria wiggled to freedom, but I snatched her wrist. "No, you're not going anywhere."

She let out a high-pitched howl. I cringed. Surely the stranger would be aghast. His face remained calm, collected, and what surprised me the most was the compassion I saw color his eyes a deeper shade of blue. I was so transfixed by the shades changing in his gaze, I stood still, staring.

Abria grunted and writhed against my hold. She wanted to run again because that's what she did in wide open spaces like this. One fierce yank brought me out of my daze, and I jerked her against me, flushing with embarrassment and fury that he stood so composed while I struggled not to blow a gasket, whack her butt, and haul her to the car.

"Stop it. I'd better go. Thanks again," I said.

"Of course."

She howled and tried to bite me. I started off in the direction of the car, hating that she behaved like a wild animal. Her tantrums always left me feeling exposed— naked—as if all the anger and resentment I carried inside for her could be seen by a judging audience who would laugh at me and say, 'Poor you, look what you're stuck with!'

"Come on." I urged her alongside of me, not caring what he thought or how crazed and furious I looked. She'd stolen my pleasant afternoon. Part of me always relished scolding her in public. Like I could stand with the rest of the world and laugh at her, too. Feel sorry for her. Distance myself from her.

Pleasure lasted only seconds. Inevitably, shame trickled in. Her innocent expression was caught in an oblivion no one, not even I, understood. And I couldn't rescue her from that foreign place either. Like everyone else, I stood helplessly outside.

What would the stranger think of my juvenile display? Surely there would be sympathy on his face, understanding that my plate was full and I couldn't take another second of this challenge. When my frustration at last ebbed away and was replaced by curiosity, I chanced a look over my shoulder.

He was gone.

TWO

The perks of having a sibling who couldn't talk were few, but as I drove home, creeped and confused by the experience with the guy at the park, I was glad Abria wouldn't be saying anything about my negligence to Mom and Dad.

I looked at her through my rear view mirror. She sat, strapped in, flapping her hands. I hated it when she flapped. "Quit flapping. You look like a bird."

"Bir. Bir."

Yeah, whatever. My mood was at a detcon ten. Yet she sat there smiling, happily gazing out the window as if the last fifteen minutes had never happened. For all I knew, for her they hadn't. Either that or she loved putting me through the terror I'd just experienced.

I flicked on the radio, blasting something rock. I had to get my mind clear and the only way I knew how was to drown in music. She hated loud music for yet another reason none of us understood except to say that many children with autism have hyper-sensitive hearing. Often, even a classical piece left her whimpering.

I looked at her again. At least she'd stopped flapping. Now, she sat perfectly still as if listening to a strain of the music I couldn't hear, and she stared out the window like a statue.

Good. The victory was sweet but bitterness soon followed. I couldn't, in good conscience, leave the music assaulting her ears so I turned it down and watched her reaction. She blinked, and started to come to life again.

I sighed.

We drove, me listening to the music and her babbling. I thought about the guy at the park. His blue eyes, both soothing and electric, were etched in my memory. I tried to remember the details of his face. I hadn't even noticed what color his hair was. I couldn't conjure up any feature but his eyes. "A lot of good I'd be if I had to go in for a police line-up."

Abria chattered nonsensically in the backseat.

"How did you find that guy, huh?" Mom believed that if we talked to Abria enough, someday, she'd talk back. So we'd been trained to carry on these one-sided conversations that left—at least me—feeling stupid. Still, at that moment, I wished I could peer into her brain and rewind what had happened at the park.

Ours had been the only car in the parking lot. Out of habit, I thoroughly checked any place we took Abria, because the less people around, the better. She didn't do well in crowds and I hated how people stared.

No one was at the park, that was a fact.

I'd taken my attention off of her to text Britt and she'd vanished. I knew how fast she could run, but I would have seen her backside disappearing, I was sure of it.

I'd been texting. *Texting.* The disgrace of that forced my heart into another fit of shame. I should be able to text for one second and not lose my sister in the process. Yet I couldn't explain how she got to the pavilion in a half-a-second's time.

"Who was that guy?" I frowned. Maybe he'd been hiding, waiting to come out, and the minute I'd taken my eyes off Abria he sprinted, grabbed her and dashed to the pavilion. But that sounded as ridiculous as Brad Pitt falling from the sky.

"I wish, just for once, that you could tell me what happened at the park."

"Park! Park! Park!"

I'd said the blasted word. Now she was chirping like a parakeet. Crap. I looked at her through the rear view mirror. She was flapping again.

The oddity of the situation at the park didn't leave me, even when I saw the safety of home. Our grey-brick house with black shutters and white trim used to be my refuge from any and all things I couldn't deal with. But lately, peace was harder and harder for me to find—even at home.

We lived on a street slivered out of the mountain bench, in a neighborhood sprinkled with pines and aspens at the fringe of forest behind us. Luke, my brother, was out front, his blonde head of hair buried beneath the hood of his latest car, an ancient blue Suzuki Samurai.

I pulled into the driveway, parked, and got Abria out. As was her custom when we arrived home, she ran to the door, pushed it open and vanished.

Though I tried to forget the brush with the stranger, I couldn't, and not telling my parents about the incident left me feeling like I was keeping a secret. But then I was, and Abria and I were the only ones in on it.

"How's the car, bud?" To get my mind off the incident, I strolled over to Luke. He was greasy from fingers to elbows. A black smudge slashed across his cheek where he'd probably scratched himself.

"I can't figure out where this cable goes." My brother's voice was so low it scraped the street, a characteristic that made him sound years older when in fact his round, baby face and big blue eyes made him look like a little boy even though he was just two years younger than me.

"Better wrap it up soon, looks like it's gonna rain," I told him. The clouds over head were so angry; I shivered at the ominous layers and devouring formations.

"Can I borrow your car if I can't get this thing fixed?" he asked without looking away from the puzzle of wires and cables. "I have some plans."

I started for the house. "Only if I don't hang with Britt."

Silent, Luke continued to work. His patience amazed me. I could never obsess over details like he did without yanking my hair out.

I went inside.

The house smelled of baking bread. Rather than be thrilled by the aromatic scent, at the Rachael Rayness of it all, my stomach turned. Mom only punched her fists in the dough when she was under stress, which meant I needed to find a way to get out of the house as soon as possible. I turned around and made a beeline for the door.

"Zoe!"

I stopped, sighed.

"I heard the alarm Zoe, don't ignore me." Out of necessity we'd had an alarm system installed to monitor Abria's comings and goings so that every time she tried to open a door or window, we'd be alerted. Never mind that the rest of us felt trapped.

"I could have been Luke," I told her, sulking into the kitchen. Abria was at the kitchen table with a giant bag of potato chips.

"He's been out front for an hour." Mom wiped an already spotless counter. Stress drew a line between her brows and deepened the creases at the sides of her pinched mouth.

I didn't want to ask her how her day had been. The lame day was written in the surrender in her eyes, the tense way her body moved in a jagged effort to appear normal. Our family hadn't been 'normal' since Abria was diagnosed.

Abria's light mutterings drew my frustrated gaze to where she sat— eating—in her usual oblivion. She caught me watching and began to climb on her chair.

"Get down!"

"Don't yell at her," Mom snipped.

Abria climbed on anything and she climbed over and over again. It didn't matter how we told her not to: patiently lifting her from harm's way or yanking her down. Screaming or whispering. Begging or demanding. She went back to climbing as if driven by an unseen force.

"Oh, so you can but I can't?"

Mom stopped wiping the counter and closed her eyes as if praying for patience. "We've all done our share of yelling, but that doesn't mean we have to continue."

"So when are *you* going to stop?"

Her eyes met mine; weary and hopeless. I hated that look. The Mom I remembered before Abria was diagnosed was lively, determined, strong, and never gave up. This Mom I'd seen gradually worn down, sanded away until only tissue paper remained.

Abria was still standing on the chair. Her perky eyes looked off into nowhere as she muttered endless no-nonsense phrases.

At that moment, I wanted to stuff her back into her seat. My fingers squeezed into fists. With Mom so obviously tense, I turned to leave before I did something I'd get in trouble for.

"Where are you going?" Mom demanded.

"I can't stay here anymore."

"Well you can't walk out either," Mom snapped. She didn't want to be alone in her misery. "Set the table. Dinner's almost ready."

I muttered curses under my breath and crossed the kitchen to the cabinets. Robotically, I pulled out a red and white tablecloth and laid it out. Abria, still standing on the chair, now stepped onto the table.

"Get down!" I strode over, yanked her down and plunked her into the chair.

I shot a glance over my shoulder at Mom, afraid she'd disapprove of my harsh treatment but she was wiping down the other counter. Her back remained turned.

I didn't have dinner, too angry to eat. I couldn't wait to get out of the house and hang with Britt. We'd planned on driving around, blasting music and maybe picking up some hot guys if we came across any. Britt's parents didn't care if we brought kids back to their house to watch movies or raid their fridge.

We never went to my house.

I put on a short black skirt and tight white shirt. Mascara defined my green eyes. Blush and sparkly lip gloss colored my pale skin and lips to a soft, rosy hue. I left my dark hair long, a tempting flow around my shoulders, then I headed for the front door. Upstairs, I heard Mom's raised voice, "Time for bath, Abria."

Abria shrieked. The sound of her running footsteps, followed by Mom's frantic pound of feet followed. "Stop running away from me!" Mom shouted.

I went out the door.

Two seconds later, the front door opened. I whirled around, ready to scream that I was not going to stay. Luke came jogging after me. He had on jeans, a tee shirt and a long sleeved striped shirt in blue and white that made his eyes bluer than afternoon sky. When he saw me dressed up, he slowed and sighed. "Man. So you're going out? I was hoping to use your car."

I continued on. "Sorry, bud."

"Can you drop me somewhere?"

Sticking the key in the lock, I grinned at him. "What? Can't take another moment of home sweet home?"

Luke snorted and opened the passenger door. "Save me."

I got in. "So, what have you got going on?"

He slid in, shut the door and shrugged. "Nothing. Getting out of the house is my only plan." He buckled his seat belt and I started the engine.

"I hear ya," I said, pulling onto the street. "Abria's been on one for days. I can't stand to be around her."

He nodded, looking out the window at the houses we passed. Night blackened the sky. Lights from houses cast golden beams onto lawns and streets.

"I don't know why Mom and Dad don't look into putting her in one of those special care places. Do you know how much easier that would make our lives? Not just Mom and Dad's but all of ours."

Luke didn't say anything, just kept staring out the window and into darkness.

"They take care of those kinds of people, you know?" I went on, my voice rising. "We're not equipped to take care of her. She's so out of control, breaking everything, crawling on everything, making holes in the walls, running away. You know, it isn't going to get any easier as she gets older. She's so strong now. Dad can barely control her when she has a spaz. Imagine what it will be like to have someone your size, or my size, throwing a fit in the mall or something." I crammed my hand into my hair and let out a groan.

Luke kept his face averted. "Yeah."

"I mean," I shifted gears, revving faster down the street, "It's embarrassing. We can't go anywhere together. What are we going to do, break up our lives into shifts forever? You go with Dad to dinner first, then Mom and I go later? As it is we can't go on any trips together. We're stuck with Abria and that sucks. She hates going anywhere. I feel like I live in prison."

Luke reached into his pocket and started tapping out a text to someone. "Can you drop me at Sam's?"

I glared at him. "He's a loser, why do you hang out with him?"

"I don't know."

I did, and my anger shifted. "Is he selling you weed?"

Luke stared out the window.

"You'd better not come home high. That's the last thing Mom and Dad need right now."

He didn't say anything.

"I'm not taking you to a druggie's house," I spat, turning toward Britt's street. I didn't know what I'd do with him, but there was no way I was going to escort him to druggie hell.

"We won't smoke," he protested.

"You can pull the wool over Mom and Dad's eyes but I've seen you wasted. They have enough to worry about, Luke, without worrying about you. Grow up."

We came to a stop sign and he busted out of the door, slamming it behind him. He took off across the street in a jog without looking back. I pounded the heel of my hand on the horn. Luke didn't look back.

Forget it. I screeched off in the direction of Britt's, my blood at a roar.

15

I was fairly sure my parents didn't know about Luke's marijuana habit—they were far too preoccupied and the constant severity of Abria's affliction provided a perfect curtain to veil Luke and me from their vision.

I was, by no means, without my own secrets. But I'd never touched drugs or smoked cigarettes, both habits I deemed for losers. Deep inside, I hurt. Luke wasn't a loser. However, I easily swept him into a corner with the rest of the world hooked on disgusting habits.

I checked my rearview mirror to see if he was anywhere in sight. I closed my eyes a moment, swamped by guilt, knowing I'd basically abandoned him to Sam and an evening of getting high when I should have taken him home.

He's sixteen, I thought. *He can take care of himself. Just like I can.*

THREE

I pulled up next to Britt's house and texted her that I was outside. She was never ready on time, and I waited, the heater and music blasting. Her parents liked to think they were progressive allowing Britt and her friends to come and go whenever, but I'd lived long enough with my parents and the fragile situation with Abria that I never assumed an open door really meant walk-in-any-time. Every family had stuff they didn't want the world to witness.

Soon, Britt came out, her tall leggy form in glove-fit jeans, baggy sweater with fringe on the arms, her long straight blonde hair swinging to the rhythm of her runway model stride.

She stopped, posed and laughed. I laughed, too, realizing how good it felt—the first laugh I'd had all day.

"I'm so ready for tonight," Britt said, once inside the car. She tossed her retro suede bag into the backseat and brought the door closed.

"You?" I pulled out onto the road. "I'm ready to kill somebody."

"Your mom again?" Britt pulled down the visor. The mirror lit and she gazed at her angular face in the mirror.

"Everyone. Mom was sulking around like someone was going to die if she didn't die first. But I'm totally disgusted with Luke. He's hanging out with Sam Penrod."

"The drug guy?" Britt looked at me.

"Yeah."

She slapped the mirror shut. "Man. What is it with Luke, anyway?"

"Who knows? I'm sick of trying to figure him out."

"Sorry you've had a lousy day, hon." She patted my shoulder. "I know just the thing to cheer you up."

I doubted anything could blast me out of my foul mood. "Is it male? Cause that's what will cheer me up, that's what I need right now. Where am I going, anyway?"

Britt laughed and cranked up the music so we'd have to shout. "Weston Larson's house."

My eyes met hers. I grinned. "No way."

She nodded, pleased to have delivered good news.

"How did you swing that?"

"Apparently Weston's wanted to meet me for some time now." She batted her lashes.

"See? I told you he had it for you. I saw the way he watched you at the assembly. Still, how did you get us into his party?"

"I got sick of waiting for him to get up the nerve to talk to me, so I cornered him outside his locker yesterday. You should have seen his face. I swear he swallowed his tongue."

We laughed.

She had someone for the night, but that didn't help me any. My mood still reeked. I drove up Mt. Cherry Drive toward the sprawling white brick house every girl at Pleasant Grove High School knew belonged to Weston Larson and his world-traveling parents. I suppose Weston's jock-player-partier good looks and money made him famous.

The house sat even closer to the forest than ours did, cradled deep in aspens and pines. A large, semi-circular driveway made the grounds grandiose. Every light was on and music pounded from windows open in spite of chilly winter temperatures.

Even though dozens of cars lined the street and the circular drive, I pulled my silver VW right up onto the grass and up to the front door.

Britt grinned. "Love the way you park, girl."

"That's the beauty of driving a bug." I got out and locked the doors.

We hooked arms and entered the pulsing place. Lights were low. Candles made everything smell like fruit and cinnamon, the flames creating flickering shadows on every wall. A shiver sent thrills through my body, thrills that reverberated with the pounding bass beat.

Couples stood locked in corners, kissing. Hands groped. I watched, jealous it wasn't me being ravished, more determined to be ravished before the night was over.

A deep male voice plunged through the loud music, and Britt came to a stop next to me.

"Hey." The voice belonged to Weston. He stood in a tight white tee shirt skimming every hard curve of his chest, back and arms. Jeans hugged his built legs. In his right hand, he held an amber bottle. His dark eyes smiled at Britt.

"Hey, Weston. Nice party."

"Now that you're here," he said.

I rolled my eyes.

Britt's arm slipped from mine and I was on my own. She inched toward him, lit up from head-to-toe. "How about you show me your house?"

His All-American grin deepened. "Can I get you something to drink on the way?" He slid his arm around her waist and was about to usher her away when she turned back toward me. "You going to be okay, Zoe?"

I gave her a confident nod. "Yeah, of course. Go."

They took off. I tried not to be annoyed by the fact that he hadn't even looked at me, not said hello or acknowledged my presence. I'd been friends too long with Britt to be jealous of her. Besides, she'd been collecting boys since ninth grade.

Determined to ditch my bad mood, I decided to find myself a guy and headed into the crowd. Faces eyed me and heads leaned into whisper as I passed. The game was so trivial, yet here I was, once again throwing the roulette wheel into motion. But the game was the only way I knew to really ditch my worries, even temporarily, of Luke, my parents, and the losing battle of Abria, not to mention my own rollercoaster ride. These people had no idea how heavy my shoulders were. Part of me hated them because they had such easy lives. Another part of me knew everyone had their problems, but surely none crushed as deeply as mine.

I crossed to one of the ice chests propped invitingly open, packed with bottles and cans of beer. I plucked an icy bottle, twisted off the top and drank. Though beer wasn't my drink of choice, it worked fast enough, deadening what I didn't want to feel inside anymore, enabling me to slip into sludge mode. I could handle one drink.

Unlike Luke, I wasn't addicted.

I cruised the place, greeting those I knew. Eyeing couples locked together, my own hungers intensified. I'd done this. I knew what I was hunting for: hot, easy and fast. Names were fine, but bodies were all that mattered. Within minutes, the beer was gone. I was still empty inside. I got another, closed my eyes, and forced the sharp bubbles down.

"Whoa there. You thirsty or what?"

I opened my eyes and looked into the pudgy face of a guy I didn't know.

"Or what," I answered.

He laughed and his rounded belly jiggled underneath his blue plaid shirt. "Okaaay. Is that your first or fifth?"

"Neither." He looked like Santa's son—definitely not my type and I faked a fat yawn, looking around for a trash can.

"Want to talk about it?"

I lifted my lip and glared. A nice buzz dulled my compassion. "Um... not right now." Then I passed him, tossing my bottle into an overflowing waste basket and I stumbled into the living room where I could search for hotter prospects.

Here, the music broke my eardrums, the pulsing beat resounding through my body in a guttural rhythm that made me search each single guy with the urgency of a cat in heat.

I'd always been partial to guys with dark hair and a cluster of mop-heads stood next to the fireplace with bottles in their hands. I made my way over, nearly tripping on some chick's leg as she lay prostrate on the couch with some dude, her left leg blocking the only clear path.

The guys in the huddle all seemed to twitch when they saw me heading their direction. I grinned. "Hey," my voice had dropped a few octaves, and sounded like a rusty engine, just starting up.

"Hey," they said.

"Anybody wanna dance?" One was totally my type: dark hair, dark eyes, white teeth and lanky build. I brushed up against him. "How 'bout you?"

He appeared taken aback, but he shot his buddies a smile then lifted his shoulders. "Sure."

I took his hand and we wove through dancing bodies until we found a tiny spot open and wedged in. I slid my arms up around his neck, snuggling close, taking a deep breath. "Mmm. You smell good," I said against his neck.

He was like dancing with a surfboard. I didn't care. Most guys softened up after a while, I was sure he would eventually. Then we'd find a nice, cozy corner and ravish each other.

"Tell me your name." I looked up at his face. Nice face. He glanced at me.

"Tyler."

"Ty—ler. Mmm. I like that."

I laid my head against his chest, wanting to hear his heartbeat but couldn't over the pounding music. Then I jerked back. "Don't you wanna know my name?" I never gave my real name at these hunting parties. Anonyminity was crucial to saving face. Besides, what teenager doesn't like to pretend they're somebody else?

"Sure. Okay."

"Clementine." He nodded. "Say it," I said. "I wanna hear you say it."

"Clementine."

"Good. See? It wasn't hard to say, was it?"

He shook his head.

I rested my head on his chest again and held on tighter. He felt so good, so strong. Male. I wanted him to kiss me. I wanted to feel his hands on my back, not stuck—like they seemed to be. His grip hadn't relaxed any. I was pricked by his lack of interest. I lifted my head and looked at him. He stared off over my shoulder.

"Don't you wanna dance with me?"

His eyes met mine. Even in my dulled state I didn't miss the flash of discomfort crossing his face. "Uh. Yeah. I do." He looked away.

I might not have been Britt, all legs and confidence, but I could hold my own. And I was there to hook up, not baby-sit. "You look bored."

"Why do we have to talk about it?"

He was right. I was ruining the dance. Still, when I snuggled against him again and he didn't soften any, the discomfort he was feeling transferred to me.

We continued to dance, like corpses stuck together. Finally the music stopped and without a goodbye or even a thanks, he was gone and back in the safe circle with his friends.

"That's it?" I shouted over the music, but he was too far away now and the music was too loud. He didn't hear me.

I plunged through the bopping crowd in search of another guy. By this time I was pretty dazed, knocking into people with the finesse of a bowling ball rolling downhill. I said hi to those I knew, moved on from those I didn't until I found myself at another cooler of bottles.

Another wouldn't hurt me. I plucked one out, but the top was so tight, I couldn't twist it off.

Sticking the metal cap between my teeth didn't help—and I cursed, ready to hit the bottle top against the nearest surface in order to break it. Turning, I swerved smack into the chest of Santa's son.

He grinned, his rosy cheeks shiny in the dim light. "Want some help with that?" he took the bottle from my hand and easily twisted it open before handing it back to me.

"What're you doing," I mumbled. "Stalking me?"

He laughed. "Yeah, but you're too wasted to notice, right?"

"Not drunk." I shook my head, tilted it back and drank, eyes closed. Then I let out a satisfied sigh. "Well, maybe a teensy."

≥✴≤
22

"Hey, you wanna go upstairs?"

I cocked my head and sneered. "I'm not *that* drunk." After another deep swig I headed away from him. "Creep." He was so desperate. *Pathetic.* I scanned the bopping living room for another potential hook up.

Moving up the stairway was Britt, holding Weston's hand. She didn't see me, too enamored with him to look at anything but his face. But, host that Weston was, his quick see-if-anyone's-watching-me glance caught mine and held. A funny feeling trickled through me, one that left me wondering why he was staring at me while he held the hand of the school's most beautiful girl.

I tossed back the last of the beer in my bottle as if to send him an I-don't-give-a-rip-about-who-you're-with-Weston look and when I was finished, the two of them had disappeared upstairs.

A lonely echo pounded through my heart. How many times had I felt alone, torn between jealousy and joy watching Britt get whatever she wanted while I stood on the sidelines? I closed my eyes, forcing back tears of self pity and threw the bottle on the floor before continuing on my quest for a hottie of my own.

My gaze connected with a few single guys but none of them cranked my soused libido. Everywhere I looked couples were locked together.

The scent in the room thickened to a lusty soup. My gag reflex kicked in. I headed for the front door. I had seconds to make it outside where I could heave without anyone seeing me.

My puke covered the bush to the right of Weston's front door, turning the green plant into a shimmering, orangey, sludge-like fungus. The sight made me heave again.

When I was certain my stomach was empty, I stood upright. My abdominal walls ached.

Storm clouds overhead broke, sending hard pellets of water to the ground. I dove for the safety of the covered porch. Light-headed, I looked for something to wipe my mouth with. There was nothing, so I lifted the hem of my shirt for a fast swipe. I closed my eyes, sighed, and waited for the stars spinning behind my vision to slow. I'd done this to myself. I really didn't need to even ask why. The answer always hovered over me – I hated life, had for a long time.

Music pulsed into the night from the open windows. I looked at everyone inside, smiling, laughing, lost in licentious oblivion and wondered why I couldn't have gone in there, found somebody and done the same. Why did I always end up outside, looking in?

I stumbled back indoors, determined that this night would be different from all the others. Britt wouldn't be the only one getting what she wanted.

Standing in the foyer, I scanned the place. There was only one problem. I didn't know what I wanted.

FOUR

I always slept in late enough that Mom and Dad never found out about my drinking. Awake, I lay with my brain in a puddle of mental mush. What happened last night? I remembered barfing. Going back into the house, looking for an easy hook up. Beyond that...the rest of the night slowly came clear to me, as if emerging from a dense fog. Dance. I'd done more dancing. A dark room. Groping hands. Skin and lips. Veiled faces swished through my memory in gray and black smoke.

With a groan, I sat up. Robotically, I went through the motions of getting dressed for church so I could further my charade. Mom and Dad rarely asked questions when I walked in step with them through motions of expectation.

Outside my bedroom door rattled the sounds of the shower, Abria screaming as Mom tried to coerce her into wearing a dress—something she hated because her legs were left bare—and the soft music Mom played from the stereo on Sundays—her effort at bringing some serenity into the house. I'd suggested we let Abria wear whatever she pleased to church, *that* would add a dose of serenity, but Mom held on to the fragile thread of hope that someday, Abria would finally submit to wearing something appropriate.

Who cared what the kid wore? She was going. What more could we ask?

Hearing the shower brought my mind to Luke. Had he gotten stoned last night? I'd know soon enough. No red eye, dull, listless look got past me.

With that, I checked my own hazy reflection.

Thank heaven for makeup.

After I dressed, I headed downstairs, holding the banister tight. My head was still a little light, and swam every third step.

The scent of waffles nearly made me wretch. I avoided the kitchen, plopped down on the couch in the living room and closed my eyes. Why did I party when I hated myself the next day? I couldn't even remember what had happened last night except for the crap: heaving, rejecting losers, *being* rejected and watching Britt and Weston take off.

I groaned.

You're the loser.

I heard soft breathing, felt the presence of someone and opened my eyes. Abria stood staring at me.

"Go away," I muttered, curling up on the couch. Sleep. I needed more.

Her soft voice sang a nonsensical tune, up and down, all around. Jumbled words. Some made sense, others did not. I often wondered if she thought in such fragments. If she did, it was no wonder she behaved erratically.

"Leave me alone," I said, louder. I needed complete silence to disappear.

"Everybody in the car." Dad. I could tell by the nearness of his voice, he was in the hall and no doubt watching me.

I stretched and stood. His discerning gaze held me as he finished tying the knot in his tie. "I didn't hear you come in last night, Zoe."

"I was super quiet."

That look of *yeah right* crossed his face. I was dressed and ready to *baaah-baaah* my way to church. What more did he want?

"Abria?" Mom's tone was frantic as usual when my little sister was out of her eyesight. "Where's Abria?"

"In here," Dad and I spoke in unison and I grinned, hoping to break the ice I felt between us, but it didn't. Dad stood, hands on his hips, eyes still searching mine, no hint of humor in his gaze.

Mom appeared, dressed, though disheveled. Her perfect appearance had

26

slowly unraveled. Hair like a skewed broom, circles under her eyes no amount of concealer could cover and she'd dropped jewelry and accessories because Abria was fascinated with all things glittery and off limits like earrings and necklaces and belts. She'd rip them off faster than a thief in a jewelry store.

Again, resentment scratched at me. I didn't look long at my mother. It hurt too much seeing her wither before my eyes.

"Where's Luke?" Mom glanced around.

"Here." Luke's bass voice slid down the stairs. I moved in for a closer look at him. He, too, was thrown together, his sandy hair mussed, shirt wrinkled, pants baggy. Yep. The lazy look in his eyes told me he'd gotten high last night. When our gazes met, I rolled my eyes at him. He gave me a heavy blink.

"Can I drive with you?" Luke asked me.

"Can't we all drive together?" Dad's tone was irritated but I knew why Luke wanted me to drive over: he didn't want Mom and Dad too close, they might get a real good look at him. And his car was still busted.

Dad threw his stare between Luke and me, but dropped the fight. I glanced at the coat tree by the front door, not sure if I'd hung my purse there last night. When I saw my denim bag, I reached over and grabbed it, digging for my keys. .

Abria started running upstairs, so Dad snagged her into his arms.

"Let's go," Mom snapped. "Abria's getting antsy."

Of course. *Let's bow to Abria. All hail Abria, queen of the moment, ruler of our lives.* I let out a loud sigh so Mom and Dad would hear my displeasure, then turned and went out into the bright, sunny Sunday morning.

Winter air nipped at my exposed skin, and I shuddered, wishing I was back in my toasty bed, sleeping.

In the car, Luke leaned his head back and closed his eyes. "Man, I'm so tired."

"No doubt residual weed in your blood," I smirked. "You wanted me to drive so you could squeeze in as much time to sober up as possible."

Luke sniffed. "I wouldn't get too close to them if I was you."

I cupped my hand over my mouth for a whiff of my own breath. Sure enough, the sour stench made my face crinkle.

Luke looked over with a lopsided grin. "Lush."

"Okay, so neither one of us is perfect."

"Thankfully."

"But I'm not addicted, there's a difference," I said.

"I'm not addicted. I smoke socially."

"Yeah," I laughed, "but it becomes addicting when all your friends do the same thing."

"So you're saying Britt and all your friends don't drink?"

"No, they do. But not every time we're together."

"Then they're missing out." He closed his eyes again.

"No. They know when it is and is not appropriate. You and your friends on the other hand only need a lighter and you light up."

"Because we know how to relax. That's your problem, Z. You're too uptight, even with the booze."

"I am not uptight." Frustration bubbled in my veins. "You don't know anything."

"Whatever."

I flicked on the CD player and raw guitar licks grated the air. So much for Mom's efforts to bring peace to Sundays. I peered through my rearview mirror, saw Mom and Dad in the car following us and felt anger and guilt collide inside of me. They'd die if they knew I drank. Die. In their eyes, I was the oldest child and the rock. I was the rock, all right. The rock everybody else climbed all over. *Zoe, do this. Zoe, help with that.*

I may have felt distant from them now, but my childhood had been full and lovely, with lots of sunny days and complete immersion in adoration. Clouds had shadowed our lives only after Abria came onto the scene.

Why did she have to be in our family? This question nipped at me continually, an ugly, itchy rash that never went away, just moved to another part of me. Countless times I'd been unable to answer the question with what reason resided in my head. "One of God's mysteries," our Pastor had once murmured—in what he thought was comfort—to my teary-eyed mother.

Mystery? It doesn't get much more mysterious than a child who doesn't have any sense of danger. A child who eats poop because it's there. Who can't stand having her hair brushed, or won't wear anything but tight-fitting clothes even in the burning heat of summer. A kid who can't stop mumbling nonsense. Or one who can't speak at all, as some are inclined. Kids who scream and tantrum for no apparent reason. A child you can't reason with. A kid whose brain is wired to do nothing else but self stimulate with repetitive behaviors that make them look like loons.

A child who doesn't understand what *I love you* means.

I blinked back tears. Layers of my heart peeled away. I pictured my mother's face and the sorrow she wore because her baby wouldn't look at her, would never know her name—not Mom, not Debbie—nothing.

And she would never say *I love you, too.*

Church was on the opposite side of the street and I pulled into the center lane, signaled, and waited for traffic to clear before driving into the packed parking lot. The white building with its steeple reaching heavenward should have brought me some relief but I only got angrier. Why had God done this to us?

I parked the car into a spot and killed the engine, waking a snoozing Luke who jerked upright then rubbed his hands down his face.

"We're here." I got out and looked around the lot for Mom and Dad's car. My searching gaze finally caught Dad's head when he got out of the car a few dozen rows away. Then I heard, "Abria!"

Luke jumped out. I leapt into the empty aisle, eyes wide, looking for Abria who could dart out at any moment, or get lost in the maze of parked vehicles, or worse, run into the busy boulevard.

"Where is she?" Mom shrieked.

Abria was too small to be visible over the rows of shiny cars. Luke took off one direction, me another. I didn't see where Mom and Dad went. We were Pavlov's dogs trained to hunt when Abria ran. I bent down and looked underneath the cars, hoping to see her tiny feet scurrying. Crouched over, I raced along, aware that my dress hiked up in the back. The cool breeze I felt on my underwear told me I was on display, but I could care less.

My back began to ache, so I stood upright and continued my search, glancing back to see that Mom, Dad, and Luke were on the other side of the parking lot.

My heart pounded. Where was Abria?

I ran to the edge of the lot, the edge that bordered on the busy street, and stood ready to tackle her if she emerged from the rows of cars. I looked left, then right. Then I saw him. The same guy I'd seen at the park. I'd just looked and not seen anyone, I was sure of it. Yet there he stood, dressed in similar sherbet-colored clothes I'd seen him in yesterday, his toffee hair a striking contrast against his fair skin and clothing. He had Abria by the hand and she walked calmly alongside him.

Shocked, I couldn't move. I blinked. He was still there, still coming toward me. He smiled. His lips moved, as if he was talking to Abria, but there were too many cars swooshing by, I couldn't hear what he was saying.

Mom was nowhere to be found. Dad was too far away to hear me, even if I screamed. Luke's sandy head popped up between cars now and then as he searched. Clearly, I should tell them I'd found Abria. I should ease their fears. But when I opened my mouth, nothing came.

Within seconds the stranger stood in front of me, smiling down into my eyes, the cool gray of his mesmerizing.

"You…" My voice trailed off. I was taken in by a feeling warm, comforting and safe. The sensation spread out from my heart, filling my arms and legs as if I'd swallowed the sun and now its light pressed through my skin. Moments stretched. Any fear I'd had about him was gone, evaporated by the reassuring aura radiating from him.

This feeling, this surety had to be my own foolishness. He was a stranger. A stranger I'd seen twice in two days now, and Dad had always told us that anyone we saw more than twice was following us. Yet, even those thoughts didn't pierce through the light comfort I was bathed in at the moment.

His gaze penetrated, as if he saw straight into my heart. I wanted to shrink even though a voice somewhere inside of me whispered not to be afraid.

"Hello." I'd heard him speak yesterday, but fear had deafened my ears. If lying under a morning sun had a melody, his voice was that melody, a strong incisive tone with the clarity of a fervent prayer. "It seems I found Miss Abria again."

"Yeah, imagine that…" I reached out and took Abria, lifting her onto my hip. She started to cry. Why was she cooperative with this complete stranger and the minute I picked her up, whining like a baby? "Do you know how worried Mom is? She's freaking out because you ran off. Bad girl."

A flash of discomfort, like he didn't care for my disciplining tactics, colored his gray-blue eyes.

"Look, I appreciate you finding her—again—but do you have a handicapped brother or sister?"

Abria squealed and wailed. "This is hard for you," he said.

"You have no idea."

His eyes pierced mine before shifting to Abria. "Shh. You're fine now, little Abria." His voice was softer than a caress. He reached out and his long fingers touched the top of her head, lightly fluttering over the silky strands of her hair. Abria went silent.

"Fine now," she said. Clear. Concise. Perfect.

I stared at her. She'd never said more than one coherent word at a time. And she'd just spoken—coherently—to this stranger. She'd used two words. Yes, she'd repeated what he'd said, kids with autism were known to do that, but she'd never repeated more than one word. And she'd calmed the instant he'd touched her.

"I can't believe…she's never done that before. I can't believe she spoke to you." Abria rested her head on my shoulder. "Who are you and how did you do that? Why do I keep seeing you everywhere?"

"My name is Matthias." He kept his hands in the front pockets of his slacks, his gaze on Abria, a slight smile on his lips. Full lips, I noticed for the first time. A great mouth. Unnerved at my reaction, I took a step back. Then I heard the frantic cries from my mother, and I looked out over the parking lot.

"She's here." I turned and waved until Mom, Dad and Luke saw me and started in our direction. When I turned back to face the stranger, he was gone.

I whirled around. Looked north. East. Out into traffic. Back into the parking lot. He'd vanished as quickly as he'd appeared. The warmth I'd sampled in his presence was gone now, and I shuddered from the cool air. I clutched Abria close, took her face in my fingers and asked, "What happened? Who is that guy? Talk to me."

I started toward Mom, whose face was contorted in terror. Her arms reached; as if by sheer will she could suck Abria out of my arms and into hers without the necessity of taking the steps that would bring her closer. Sobs broke her shoulders into wracking spasms. She snagged Abria out of my embrace and squeezed her, weeping on Abria's shoulder. At her side, Dad silently patted her back. Luke and I exchanged relieved glances.

Without another word, we started for the building.

Luke and I hung back behind Mom and Dad. I leaned toward Luke. "Did you see anybody suspicious?"

"What do you mean?"

"I mean, did you see anybody lurking around?"

He glanced over his shoulder. "Now?"

"Now, yes, or earlier when you were looking for Abria."

"No, just some church people."

That made me think; maybe Matthias was a member of our parish. Someone I hadn't seen yet. "You know anybody named Matthias?"

The far off look in Luke's eyes told me the wheels were spinning through the leftover tangle of weed in his head. "Matthias? What's he look like?"

"Tallish, caramely hair, really blue eyes."

Luke grinned. "I know a guy named Matt."

I pictured Matthias. Something ethereal about him told me he was definitely not a pot-head. Luke wasn't your most observant guy; there was a chance that Matthias was a new member of our church. Pastor Perrigan kept a special eye out for Abria. Maybe he'd found some social worker somewhere he thought could covertly keep watch on her.

That idea felt pretty good and made sense. Something akin to wonder jangled in my blood and streamed through my system. I'd felt this curious excitement before: when something thrilling was about to happen. But how could Abria's safety issues link to something thrilling?

Throughout the service I couldn't think about anything but my odd encounter with the stranger named Matthias. Maybe that wasn't his real name. How could I know?

When Abria started to squirm and make noise, drawing curious and annoyed glances, I stood, gathered her into my arms, and slid silently out of the pew. Mom's hand touched my arm and our eyes met for a brief moment, just long enough for me to read, "Thank you," in her gaze.

Out in the foyer, I set Abria to her feet. She raced for the door. In her lacy white dress with a big blue sash, ties long undone and hanging at her back, she looked like a cherub trying to escape. I laughed. *How ironic.* Like a shadow I followed her out to the large patch of grass and shrubbery that cradled the building.

Telling her to stay nearby was like telling a puppy not to explore, so I continued following her. The day was bright and I was glad to be outside, feeling the rays of the sun cut through the cool air and warm my skin.

Maybe I'd see this guy again, since he seemed to pop out of thin air wherever Abria was. I swept my surroundings, but didn't see him. Who was he, really? How did he come and go so quickly? What did he really want with Abria? Was he some doctor studying children with autism? That had to be it. Maybe there was a hidden camera. Maybe we were part of a reality show following children with autism and their families, documenting the slow insanity that comes over everybody when they live with kids like Abria, the inevitable death that occurs as a family is torn apart under pressure.

I let out a sneer. Like anybody cared.

"Sometimes it's really lame you can't talk to me," I said. She babbled back. "You could tell me who that guy was." *And tell me why I don't feel afraid around him.* His face came into my mind. I hadn't been so creeped out this time. Nope. And the reason was clear now. He was a hottie. What kind of girl looks at a complete stranger, one who could very well be stalking her little sister, and sees him as an object of desire? I shook my head.

"Well, if I see him again, I'm going to tell him to leave us alone or I'm going to call the cops."

Abria stepped up onto a decorative boulder and squealed with delight. Grass surrounded the rock, so I let her enjoy the indulgence.

My thoughts drifted back to Matthias. *The first cute guy I see in a really long time and he comes and goes like a dream?* Did Abria have to be in mortal peril for him to appear? Our family had learned to be dobermans where my sister was concerned—following, guarding, protecting like she was a priceless treasure.

Abria lifted her small arms heavenward and started giggling.

The drive home Abria rode with me and Luke. She stared out the window, seeming to enjoy watching the buildings go by. At home, I offered to change her into some play clothes so Mom could take a breather, and Abria cooperated.

Mom's 'special' Sunday music played lightly in the background.

Dinners were usually a fight with Abria to keep her from crawling and standing on the table while the rest of us ate. Not tonight. Tonight she sat, watched, seemed to listen, and ate—I hated to think the words, but couldn't help it—like a normal little girl, minus the little girl talk about kittens and dolls and everything sugary. Her mumblings and songs were in her very own language.

About halfway through dinner, I looked around the table. Mom's face didn't look quite as defeated. She even smiled. Laughed twice. Dad noticed her lighter mood, because his gaze met mine and in his eyes I saw a sparkle I hadn't seen there for a long time. Luke was typically uninterested in anything but eating and splitting the scene. I wished he'd lift his head from his cell phone and texting long enough to witness the miracle happening.

"I'm done. Can I go now?" He rose and took his empty plate to the kitchen sink.

"Where are you going that can't wait until tomorrow?" I asked. I sent him an *it better not be Sam's house* look, which he ignored.

"Kevin wants to hang out. He's gonna fix my car."

"It's Sunday, Luke. We talked about making Sunday a family day," Dad said.

"I need the car fixed."

Dad eyed Luke for a long moment—as if weighing the battle— then finally nodded.

Luke strode out without another glance at me or anyone else. Inside, I hoped fixing the car was all he was planning to do.

"Abria's being so good today," Mom said as she and I cleaned up the kitchen. It was good to see her smiling.

"Yeah, she is." I glanced over my shoulder at Abria, standing on her chair now, flapping her hands. "Abria, sit down. Sit."

She giggled and flapped more furiously, her eyes wide, mouth puckered in one of many odd facial expressions in her repertoire.

"Kind of gives me a peek at how she'd be if she didn't have autism." Mom's eyes glistened like they did sometimes. Random moments I could never predict. Tears would simply be there. Mom's tears always pulled a chord deep inside of me.

I wanted to hug her, but we hadn't hugged for so long, except for obligatory hello/goodbye hugs, I was afraid I'd somehow ruin the moment. I continued loading the dishwasher.

"Get off the table, Abria." Mom's voice was patient as she crossed to my sister, standing on the table, laughing. Mom pulled her into her arms and hugged her. My mind flashed a memory of hugs just like that when it had been me in her arms, being squeezed so tight breath left me. I missed those hugs.

"Want me to get her ready for bed?" I asked, closing the now full dishwasher.

Mom looked over. The surprise in her eyes didn't settle well with me. I'd been ignorant of helping her for too long.

"That'd be nice." She brought Abria to me and passed her into my arms. "Thank you, honey."

"No problem." I started out of the kitchen, catching Mom's glance to Dad.

Abria loved bath time. She splashed like a baby. The tiled walls were drenched, the floor had puddles and my own clothes were splattered. Her fine hair curled around her face, accentuating her rosebud lips and round cheeks. When my heart was full and ready to burst with caring for her, I reminded myself to remember times like this. *See, you do love her.* When aggravation reached a boiling point, I'd ask myself if I really loved her. *Would I care if anything happened to her? Of course I care. Look how I took off today, racing after her in the parking lot.* Just thinking she might be harmed by one of those speeding cars sent a shudder through me.

Then *he* had shown up.

Matthias.

"Matthias." When I said his name, Abria looked at me for a second then went back to splashing. Did she remember him? He'd only spent a few minutes with her. But he'd spoken to her with that tranquil voice.

I closed my eyes, seeing the graceful curve of his fingers, the way they'd fluttered over her hair before finally laying on her head for the briefest moment.

She'd been calm since.

Could her changed behavior really be linked to his touch? The idea was outlandish, yet streaming warmth and comfort filled my soul, like the feelings I'd had when I stood in his presence.

I let the water out of the tub, hoisted Abria out and dried her, all the while she sang and chattered. I tried to reason why something so impossible was not real. And yet, there was no other explanation except that with autism, behavior was unpredictable.

Abria liked to sleep in one of my old tee shirts, and she had a spaz if she couldn't. Mom always made sure there was a stack of them in my drawer, because after her bath, Abria ran naked into my bedroom and stole one.

I slipped the shirt over her head, carefully ran my fingers through her hair because she hated it when the bristles of a brush touched her scalp, then I picked her up and held her on my hip, looking into her distracted face.

"Matthias," I whispered.

Her eyes widened. A tingle raced through me. "Who is Matthias, Abria?"

She seemed mesmerized by either my voice or his name, how could I know which? Her eyes rounded, focused on my mouth. The room was quiet. All I heard was the soft rapid beat of her breath. I hugged her close, snuggling against the softness of her body. "Time for bed," I said.

Abria let me put her into bed, and she looked into my eyes intently for a few seconds—a brief miracle I savored before she stared up at the ceiling and started flapping.

I stood back, relief filling my inner core. She was safe. Home, in bed, and safe. If Matthias really did come only when Abria was in some sort of peril, I wouldn't be seeing him any more tonight.

FIVE

Morning came, and I showered and dressed for school in jeans and a baggy white hoodie. I'd busted my butt for three years so I could have a semi-relaxed senior year. My first period started at second period, which enabled me to sleep off whatever I'd done the night before.

I added some color to my cheeks, plus a little eye shadow and mascara. I threw my dark hair up in a pony tail.

The house was unusually quiet. How had Abria done through the night? I hadn't heard her get up. Had her changed behavior lasted?

I went downstairs to the kitchen where Mom, dressed in a black suit for work at the real estate office, sat over a bowl of fiber cereal. She looked more rested today than she had in a long time. Abria sat behind a plate of apple slices, toast, and a banana.

"Morning, sweetheart."

"Hey." I went to the fridge, opened it and stared at its contents, then glanced at Mom. "You look nice."

"I do? Oh. Thanks."

I shut the door and decided to forget about eating. The clock over the microwave read eight-twenty. "Want me to take Abria out and wait for the bus?"

"That'd be great." Mom took another bite of her cereal. "But aren't you going to eat something?" Her gaze skimmed me from head to toe. "There are blueberry muffins in the pantry."

"Costco?"

She nodded. That didn't sound too bad. I went over, got one, and grabbed a napkin. "So how did Abria do last night? I didn't hear her get up."

"She didn't." Mom glowed. "I don't know what happened yesterday, but I'd like about a thousand yesterdays to happen again. It was wonderful."

I nodded. "You were such a good girl yesterday, Abria. Good girl."

Abria flapped and made one of her animated, goofy faces.

Finished, Mom took her bowl to the sink then kissed Abria on the cheek, wiping my sister's hands with a napkin so she was clean. "It's time for school, sweetheart."

"Come on." I took Abria's hand, grabbed her backpack, slung it over my shoulder and headed out the garage door so we could wait on the driveway for the bus.

Abria was enrolled in a special school for the handicapped. Her bus came at eight-thirty. Typically, we were distracted by the gargantuan effort it took to get her ready and she missed the ride. Then Mom would have me drive her to school.

Today, the same smoothness we'd enjoyed the day before seemed to linger. I was glad. Mom and Dad deserved a little break from the twenty-four hour stress that was living with a child with autism.

Abria broke free of my arms, antsy. She wanted to run up the street. "Stay here. No running." She giggled and ran back and forth on the icy sidewalk.

Winter's air nipped my cheeks and lips. I eyed the blueberry muffin and took a bite. Nothing was worse at school than a quiet classroom and a growling stomach.

When the bus finally ambled to a stop, I chased after Abria, who was halfway down the street in the opposite direction now, gathered her into my arms and hauled her, and her backpack, onto the bus.

"Mornin' Abria." Her driver was an older, jovial, bellied man named Dan who always greeted her with a twinkling smile. His helper Marla, a grandma-type, assisted the children into the seatbelts some handicapped children needed to stay put for the drive.

"Morning," I said, setting Abria down inside the bus. She tried to take off down the aisle, but Marla stopped her with a laugh and a fast grip.

"Not so fast little missy." She plopped Abria onto a bench and began strapping her in.

Smiling, I looked at the distracted faces of the other little children on the bus, some staring into space, others focused out the window.

Then I saw Matthias.

He sat at the very back of the bus, alone. Smiling.

"Hey!" I pointed at him.

Preoccupied with strapping Abria in, Marla didn't look where I was pointing. Dapper Dan had stolen the opportunity to sip the Starbucks waiting for him in his drink holder.

"You know that guy?" I asked, looking at Dan.

Dan set his cup down and craned around. "What guy?"

"That one…in the back." I pointed at Matthias who sat angled in the seat, one arm resting on the bench in front of him, the slightest smile on his lips. I was sure he could hear me; the bus was a short compact model.

Dan looked through his long rearview mirror, then turned around. "I don't see anybody."

A rock lodged in my throat. "You…don't?"

"Just the kids. You ready there Marla?"

"I'm having a hard time with this buckle," Marla grunted.

I made my way around her bent-over backside and in six fast steps stood in front of Matthias. I stopped, staring down into his gray-blue eyes. That reassuring calm I'd felt yesterday oozed into the air around him, the soothing warmth settling into my very bones. My mouth opened but nothing came out.

"There." I heard Marla say. "All strapped in and safe, little missy."

Abria squealed.

I wanted to ask Matthias what he was doing, and how was it that only I saw him. But I couldn't find my voice. His brows tweaked, as if he knew I was tongue tied, and he settled back against the window with a glittering grin.

"You'll need to get off the bus now, honey." Marla's voice was right behind my shoulder.

"He's there. In the seat," I said, pointing at Matthias again. "You see him, right?"

I tore my eyes from Matthias, afraid he'd be gone if my gaze left him for even a second, to see Marla's reaction. Her face was blank.

"There's nobody there, honey. Maybe you didn't get enough sleep last night?" She patted my shoulders and, with her hands gently on my arms, turned me and escorted me down the aisle.

I kept glancing back at Matthias. Questions raced through my head and jumbled into a mess I couldn't sort. I realized then, there was a very good possibility I really was overtired and hallucinating.

Slowly, I took the steps of the bus down, confused, fascinated, pausing for one last look at him. He was still there, still watching me, still smiling. He waved. I didn't dare wave back; I'd look like a whack job. Marla finally had to nudge me out so the doors could squeak and flap shut.

On the sidewalk I stood, staring at him through the window. Then a thought occurred to me. I turned and ran into the house

"She get on the bus okay?" Mom asked when I flew past her. I scrambled for my purse.

"Yeah, fine. Bye, Mom." I saw the purse on the entryway hall tree, snatched it and was back out the door, racing to my car before I could take another breath. The bus' back end, with Matthias in it, was just pulling away from the curb.

I ran to my car, unlocked it and hopped in. "You can't get away from me," I snickered, tossing the muffin and my purse into the empty passenger seat. I started the car, yanked it around and rode the tail like a cop after a criminal.

How could only I see him? He was right there. *Right there in the back of that bus.* My eyes weren't playing tricks on me; I'd been close enough to see him breathe. Close enough that I'd been swamped with that warm blanket aura of his again.

Matthias didn't notice I was tailing the bus, he remained sitting forward, facing the children. I almost honked the horn. I couldn't wait to see his face when he realized I was onto him. He wore that same outfit I'd seen him in yesterday and the first day I'd seen him. What was that all about? Was the guy fashion challenged?

At a stoplight, I tried to maneuver myself for a peek at his shoes through the emergency exit door, but only saw the tip of his right foot—an off-white pair of casual looking old man style shoes. *Blech.* He was definitely fashion challenged.

"I'm not letting you out of my sight, Mister Matthias," I said, then let out a snort. "I'm going to get to the bottom of whatever it is you're up to and I'm going to do it today. No more of this slinking around. I want to know what you're up to and what you want with my little sister and a bus load of handicapped kids."

The bus started on its journey again and I stayed glued to its behind. I turned off the CD player. I started to sweat.

A few minutes later, we were at Abria's school. The drop off was lined with buses. I couldn't follow suit in the special unloading lane, so I parked on the street, got out and boldly strode right to the back so Matthias would see me. He did.

He stood, looking out the window at me.

I set my hands on my hips and slit my eyes at him. "That's right. I'm watching you," I said, pointing at him, speaking loud enough I was sure he heard me above the rumbling diesel engines. "And you better not think of doing anything to these kids."

He held up his hands, as if to surrender. His whole face smiled: his eyes, lips, even his teeth shined bright. How could Marla and Dan not see this guy? I glanced at the front of the bus, saw the two of them unloading the children one at a time. Were they old *and* blind?

When I took my attention back to Matthias, my heart dropped. He was gone. I ran to the front of the bus, but only Dan and Marla were there, along with the children and their teachers who greeted them and escorted them inside every morning.

Dan looked at me, confusion on his face. Heat flushed my skin. I sent him a quick wave and jogged around to the other side of the bus, searching for Matthias.

I saw him standing under a tree at the edge of the parking lot. I hadn't seen him get off the bus, and I'd watched everyone line up and exit, one-by-one.

My head emptied of thoughts.

Who is he?

Driven by curiosity, I took slow steps until I was within five feet of where he stood. His soft curls gleamed in the sunlight. The fair color of his skin nearly melted into the silky fabric of his shirt and slacks which radiated a soft, electric-like glow. I wrung my clammy hands over and over. Swallowed. Searched for words, but nothing came into my mind.

"Hello again," he said. The moment his voice filled the air, the wrinkles in my anxiety smoothed out.

"This isn't funny," I sputtered. The pleasant look on his face vanished. His eyes narrowed in confusion. "You following Abria," I continued. "It isn't funny and it has to stop." I stepped closer, courage pumping through my system. "I bet you didn't think I'd come after you."

He took a deep breath. Good. He breathes. He's a human. I felt a little rush of relief but I still had too many questions to completely disregard his behavior. A quick scan of his arms: feathered hair. At the opening where his shirt was unbuttoned: smooth skin. But a lot of guys waxed nowadays. I stared at his chest, just to make sure I saw it rise and fall. Definitely human.

My gaze lifted to his. A crooked smile lifted his lips. Heat flushed my cheeks and I averted my gaze, gathering dignity and composure. The same comfort and feeling of safety once again settled around me, and, in my heart, I knew everything was going to be okay. In fact, his expression was so pure, I felt guilty having accused him of something I wasn't sure of.

"I was certain you'd follow me," he said.

"You were?"

"You love Abria. You'd do anything to protect her."

"She's my sister. Of course I'd protect her. Which brings me to you. At first I thought it was just a coincidence—you know—when you found her at the park. But now I'm starting to think you've got an ulterior motive."

He shot me a lopsided grin. "You're mistaken."

"Then why are you following her—me, or whatever it is you're doing? I don't know you. You show up and disappear. Do you *like* doing creepy?"

"Doing creepy?"

"Being all criminal and that?"

"Do you feel afraid?"

The feelings that overcame me whenever he was near left no room for fear, but I couldn't admit that to him—stranger that he was.

His blue-gray eyes locked on mine. "In your heart, you're not afraid, are you?"

I wet my lips, swallowed. "No."

"I'm not here to hurt Abria or you," he said.

I shifted. "You're just saying that because I caught you."

"You're a feisty little bearcat, aren't you? No, I'm not just saying that. Test a man's temper why don't you?"

Bearcat? The word caused me to stumble. "Then why are you here?"

He looked around, as if in thought, took in a deep breath, and then his sharp gaze once again focused on me. "I watch out for Abria."

"I knew it!" I let out a nervous laugh. "Phew. I thought I was going nuts. Who hired you? Was it Pastor Perrigan? He's really fond of my parents, and he knows how hard it is to live with Abria."

Matthias seemed amused by my deduction. "No, it wasn't."

"Then...who was it?"

"Someone...else."

"Now you're doing creepy again. Tell me who hired you. No, better yet, you tell whoever it was they can take their CSI job and shove it for all I care. We don't need a pity party. We've done just fine taking care of Abria on our own. Besides, I don't want someone watching her who doesn't have the guts to show his face."

His eyes widened. The air around us suddenly tensed like it did before a lightning storm. A shudder slid down my spine. He threw back his head, breaking out in a rich, hearty laugh, cutting the tension in the air until it was gone.

"My-oh-my," he said. "You are lively."

"Look you flamer, whoever you think you are, you've chosen the wrong family to stalk, because we won't stand for it."

He crossed his arms over his chest and rocked back on his heels, enjoying the tail end of his laugh. "You've got it all wrong." His firm tone penetrated me to the bone. "I'm not here to do anything but protect her."

"What do you mean? Explain yourself."

"Gladly." His eyes lit on something behind me, and I turned. Marla was heading my direction.

"Oh, no. You...don't move." I shot him a warning look. "No more of this disappearing thing you conveniently do whenever somebody comes along, understand?"

A slow smile spread his lips wide. He was gorgeous, no getting around it, and my female heart fluttered. "I wouldn't dare."

"There you are honey." Marla came right to me, her brow furrowed. "Are you all right?"

"Yes. Yeah. I'm fine. Just getting a little fresh air and talking to this joker."

Marla's eyes widened as she looked around. "Talking?"

"This is the guy I saw sitting on your bus. His name is Matthias. Although I'm not sure that really *is* his name. But I'm going to find out." I gestured to Matthias, who, thankfully, had not pulled one of his vanishing acts. He stood with his hands clasped behind his back, his mouth turned up at the edges.

"Honey, I don't see anyone." Marla's voice quavered. She put her arm around me. "Let me help you back to your car."

I couldn't move. She tugged, but I refused to budge, panic bouncing in my stomach. I could excuse her age for her faulty eyesight on the bus, but here we stood five feet from Matthias. How could she miss him?

"He's right there," I said, pointing to where he stood.

She looked right at him, but the deep crease in her brow told me she thought I'd lost it. Again she gently urged me with her arm wrapped around my shoulders. "Why don't you come this way? There's a nurse on staff at the school and I'm sure she'd be happy to—"

"No." I yanked free of her embrace. "I'm okay. Really." I pressed my fingertips to my temples and closed my eyes. Then opened them. "Look, Marla." I took her by the arm and led her smack up to Matthias's chest but he took a step back, hands up.

"No touching." He shook his head. "No touching if she isn't my charge."

"Your *charge*?" I snickered. "Marla, you heard what he said, that he couldn't touch you?" I waited for some glimmer of recognition on Marla's concerned face, but it never came. In fact, she turned white.

She leaned close to me, so close I thought she was coming in for a kiss. She sniffed my breath. "Maybe you ought to let Dan drive you home," she whispered.

I let go of her arm, and stared at Matthias, his eyes like a hawk, pinning me in place. This woman really could not see him. My mind emptied. Marla muttered something, but the words were buffered by my dulled senses.

"I...need...to...sit." I collapsed to the grass in a daze.

"You want me to get a doctor?" Marla asked.

"No. I'll be...fine...I think." I glanced up at Matthias. The instant my eyes met his, peace spread through my insides, thawing the stony cold shock in my system. I couldn't tear my gaze away, drawn by a magnetic force I couldn't resist.

"Should I get you some water? Maybe some food? Have you eaten? You're a tiny little thing. You're not anorexic are you?"

I let out a light laugh. "No." I buried my head in my hands. "I'll be

HEAVENLY - JENNIFER LAURENS

okay. I think I can, I think I can, I think I can."

"You won't get behind the wheel until you're good and sure in the head, will you?"

"No, I won't." I met Marla's concerned gaze. "Thanks."

"You're welcome, honey." I watched her start back for the bus and when she was out of hearing range, I shifted my gaze to Matthias again.

He sat down next to me. His nearness sent my pulse into a whirl. He leaned back on his hands, his gaze fastened with mine. I had so many thoughts, even more questions. I didn't know where to begin. All I knew was that, twice now, I had seen him when no one else could. That either meant I was seriously exhausted, a walking zombie dreaming all of this, or I was imagining him.

"You have questions," he said, his voice soft. "Don't be afraid to ask. I'll answer you."

The way he said, *Don't be afraid*...was like being tucked in bed at night, warm soft blankets from heart to toes. I took a deep breath. "Am I dreaming?"

"What does your heart tell you?"

I closed my eyes. I already knew the answer, but I kept my eyes shut, embarrassed to meet his gaze and admit the truth. "My heart tells me that I'm not dreaming."

"What else?"

I swallowed a knot. "That...you're really here, even if no one else can see you."

"Yes."

Whispering into my mind was the idea that he was someone different. Someone special. Someone to believe in. But common sense waved red flags. *This isn't happening. You're hallucinating. This is the hangover of all hangovers, Zoe.*

"What else does your heart tell you?" he urged.

"I—I don't know."

"You do. Your heart is where the voice of truth speaks, Zoe."

My eyes flashed. "How do you know my name?" But even as I asked the

47

question I knew. This guy understood much more than I did. I felt as though I stood in front of the earth, watching it whirl and spin, and if I looked close, I would see beyond the surface to the pumping red heart where all my questions would be answered. The reassurance I experienced was total, complete, submerging.

"Who are you?"

"A friend."

"Friends, by definition, know each other. I've never met you. And if you say you know Abria, I'm going to slug you because she doesn't have friends. She has autism. She doesn't know what friendship is."

His eyes slit briefly. "You don't know what you're saying."

"Excuse me, but I do. I'm sure you mean well, but I really don't appreciate people who pretend to know what I'm going through or what my family is going through, and sit all comfy on the sidelines. You can't possibly know what it's like." My voice had risen, and the silence left in its aftermath crackled with ugliness. I looked away.

"Your wounds are deep." His tone was gentle. "But they won't always be. I promise you that."

I closed off the tears welling in my eyes. "Don't say things you don't know."

"I don't."

I glared at him, but the potent conviction in his countenance warned me to tread carefully.

"You won't let yourself have faith in what you see, that's your problem."

"I thought faith was believing in things you *can't* see."

"You can't see the future."

"Neither can you," I shot. Then, "Can you?"

He tilted his head, his smile teasing. "It's going to be fun, being with you."

"*Being* with me? I've got news for you." I pushed to my feet. "You're not going to *be* with anybody until you answer my questions. I'm not letting you near my little sister."

He stood and in one long step, placed himself close enough for our arms to nearly brush, but they didn't. A craving wound tight in my gut. I wanted to touch him. See if he was real.

"Tell me how you know my name. And why do you show up whenever Abria's in some kind of danger? It's like you're waiting—"

"I am," he said matter-of-factly. "Listen to what's inside of you."

I took a deep breath, focused on the serene color of his eyes, shaded by thick, dark lashes. His irises, slashed with gold and agate, rimmed with ocean blue, lulled my anxious heart into a steady, calm beat. A trembling breath eased from my chest. I emptied my head of doubts and opened the stiff door of possibility.

One voice in my head hissed that this was unbelievable. Another, stronger voice whispered that what he was saying was true. He meant Abria no harm. But did I believe him because he was beautiful and convincing? Who wouldn't want a hottie as their protector? But he wasn't my protector, he was Abria's.

At that moment, my heart and soul were not my own. Whoever he was, he was capable of reaching inside of me and taking them both. And I was helpless to stop him.

I took a step back hoping distance would clear my head. Again, he brought his body nearly flush with mine, staring into my eyes.

"I told you not to be afraid." He lifted his hands, as if debating putting them on my shoulders. My insides hummed. My gaze darted from his hands, now less than an inch from my arms to the tumultuous expression tightening his face.

A knot surfaced in his jaw. He lowered his hands back to his sides. "It's your choice."

"You never told me how you know my and Abria's name."

"Because you went off on a tangent."

"So I'm off the tangent. How?"

His eyes lit with amusement. "My...*boss*... tells me everything I need to know to do my job."

"*You're getting paid for this?*"

"In a matter of speaking, yes."

"Wow." My heart took a hit. "Well, that kinda takes the whole charity element and shoves it out the window now doesn't it?" I made sure my tone was laced with plenty of disappointment and disdain. Here I was, trying to buy the fantasy that he was some guardian angel and he was lining his pockets with my deflated dreams.

I headed for my car.

I'd walked away from plenty of uncomfortable situations: home and Abria, lame guys, witchy girls. A voice inside whispered, *walking is weak. Face him, head on. Get to the bottom of this or you won't know for sure.*

I stopped, and did an about face. Matthias stood where I'd left him, and he was watching me. I marched back.

His hands moved in the depths of his front pockets. His lips lifted into a wider grin. "I was hoping you weren't done with me."

A thread sizzled through my body. Whoever he was, he had spunk. I liked that. I stopped inches away from him and looked up into his smiling face. A soft breeze lifted his toffee-colored waves, showing off flawless, smooth skin, except for a light scar above his left brow which I hadn't noticed before.

"I'm definitely not done with you," I said, planting my feet. "How did you get that scar?"

He touched the line on his face. "Long story."

"I'm already late for school. Tell me."

"Another time. Shouldn't you be on your way?"

"You said you'd answer my questions."

"And I will. Any question but that one. For now, anyway."

"Hmmm." The mystery would nag at me until I knew. "So if you're Abria's special friend, why aren't you in there watching her?"

His gaze shot over my shoulder to the school. "Because she's in good hands here."

"How do you know all this, anyway? Your boss must have done some serious investigating." It startled me that someone could know so much about us without us noticing we were being watched.

"You could say he's the chief of all chief investigators."

I was awed. "I'm still deciding whether or not I like the idea that 'big brother' is keeping tabs on my family."

"It's not like that. You've still got privacy."

"I should hope." A cold shudder slid down my spine. Had any of my impatience with Abria or my lies to my parents, times I'd gotten drunk—anything I was ashamed of—gotten caught on tape?

"So, is there like a film crew or something?" I glanced around.

His warm laugh filled the air. "Zoe, you've got a healthy imagination. You'll have all of your questions answered to your satisfaction in time."

"Is that your way of saying, bug off?"

"Not at all. Layer upon layer. How do you explain romantic love to a child?" His gaze penetrated my heart, sending a warm flush through my system.

"You can't, it's impossible."

"But a teenager, that's a different story."

"They're still too young to understand romantic love."

His gaze skimmed over my face, pausing at my mouth before lifting to my eyes. "Someday, I want you to tell me about Zoe Dodd and romantic love," he said.

Wow. My whole body heated. I liked that he talked to me without any condescension. I liked that I felt safe and secure in his presence. I liked that he listened to me, saw who I was, and didn't look at me with judgment in his eyes. "As long as I get to hear about Matthias and romantic love."

"Deal."

I stuck out my hand to shake on it. His eyes shot to my extended hand, his jaw in a tense knot. He didn't move. "We don't need to shake on it to be a covenant."

I blinked. "A covenant?" I let out a light laugh. "Gee, I can't remember the last covenant I made. Just a shake, Matthias."

"You have my word," he said hands in his front pockets.

"I guess your word will have to do then." I withdrew my hand. "You'd better not go back on it, or this—whatever is going on here—is over."

He gave me a quick salute and grinned. "Your wish is my command."

"It would be totally cool if that was true."

"You'd like a genie, wouldn't you?"

"Three wishes for anything in the world I want? Absolutely."

"What would you wish for?"

This time, my brain was so full I couldn't sift through my dreams fast enough. "I'd want Mom and Dad to be happy. They're happy, but…they deserve more freedom." My gaze shifted to Abria's school. "I'd wish that Abria was…normal. And I'd wish for Luke, my brother, to stop using. I hate that he uses. He doesn't know how dangerous it is. Not just for him, but for everyone."

Compassion glistened in Matthias' eyes. He nodded, looked over at the school, then back at me. "Those are good wishes. Life isn't meant to be easy," he said.

"Yeah, I'm figuring that out," I sighed. "But what's with the people who float through life like it's an endless party? Why didn't I get an invite?" I'd done my share of immersing in the fun house in hopes that the distorted mirrors would reflect an image of myself I could embrace. That I could forget my troubles with enough laughter, and pointless games, deafen reality with loud music.

"Believe me when I say, the party isn't what it appears to be," he murmured.

Did he have troubles of his own? Where did he come from? How did he grow up? "Spoken like someone who knows."

He lowered his head. The mood around us shifted, becoming fragile.

"Did I say something wrong? You looked like…like you were remembering something awful."

I hoped he was going to share something of himself with me. My curiosity grew—a hunger that churned deep inside. After a moment, his shoulders went erect. "That is neither here nor there."

"Then where the eff is it?" I blew out. The corner of his lip lifted and his eyes twinkled. I continued, "I can unload but you can't? That's not going to work for me."

"Demanding. Feisty. And I'll add sassy to the growing list."

I grinned. "What happened to bearcat?"

He laughed, and pushed his hands through his hair. Suddenly, his gaze locked on the school. His hands came out of his mussed hair and slowly fell to his sides. "It's time for me to go," he said, an anxious expression tightening his features.

"Is everything all right?" I followed his gaze. He started toward the school and I trailed after him.

"Everything's fine."

"Should I be worried?"

He walked backwards, urgency in his steps. "What does your heart tell you?"

My heart told me not to worry. I glanced around the empty parking lot, hoping no one had witnessed my "discussion" with him. The buses had since gone on their way and the lot was vacant except for the faculty cars.

Who was he really?

My heart beat steady and calm in my chest, and I turned, intent on asking him again, but he was gone.

SIX

I'm not sure how long I sat in my car waiting for Matthias to come out of the school, show up, or something. I couldn't get him out of my head. I still had questions. As though someone had moved inside of me and was pushing me his direction. Beyond curious. Bordering on obsession. My cell phone buzzed over and over but I ignored it, too fixated on the school—watching every movement, every person who entered and left the place.

Was this what it was like for the people watching us? The voyeuristic quality was kind of cool. I'd never followed anybody before. Certainly, I'd never watched anyone this intently except for Abria, and she was predictably unpredictable.

When my stomach growled, I glanced at my cell phone to see what time it was. Noon. I gasped. *I'd sat here for three hours?* Missed most of my classes, not to mention texts and phone calls.

"You're seriously losing it," I muttered, turning the key in the ignition. Matthias was no where in sight, so I headed to school.

Disappointed, I read my texts as I drove. Britt.

where r u???

Britt still hadn't told me what had happened between her and Weston Saturday night. I was pretty sure they'd hooked up. Britt had wanted Weston for a long time, and she always got what she wanted.

Luke: **got any money?**

Yeah right, like I'd support your habit. Just what I didn't need: to worry about Luke out there on the prowl for the next high—an alley cat scouring the gutters for a dead mouse. I shoved the thought away, deleted Santa's son's text, and readied to answer Britt, waiting until I came to a red light.

sorry late where r u & what happened Sat?

When the light changed, I continued in the direction of school.

at purple turtle

order me a salad, k?

k.

I drove to the Purple Turtle, a burger place close to school where half the student body congregated for lunch. The purple and stone bungalow was the current place to be seen by Pleasant Grove's population of teenagers.

Busy as a beehive, cars zoomed in and out of the parking lot, teens hanging out car windows, laughing, shouting to outdo each other on the attention meter. I squeezed into a place on the street and searched the parking lot for Luke, on the off chance he was hanging there. I didn't see him. Why didn't he do what every normal teenager did? If he'd been at the Purple Turtle I could have introduced him to my friends. I could have tried to help him see that there was a lot more out there than the dark alleys his friends hung out in.

I jogged to the door, passing some faces I recognized with a nod and a wave.

I found Britt sitting with Weston along with some of his guy friends. Britt waved me over. Awkward. I didn't want to interrupt what was obviously the beginning of something for Britt, since she was eating lunch with Weston and his gang.

"Hey." Britt stood and hugged me. "Where've you been?"

"I was late. Abria."

Brady, one of Weston's pals scooted over so I could sit next to her. I debated staying. I wasn't in the mood for idle chit-chat with Weston and his group. I wanted to get to the bottom of Matthias. But when would that happen? Abria was safe at school. I sat anyway and Britt slid my salad toward me.

Britt leaned close enough so she wouldn't be overheard. "I was worried about you after the party."

So worried she hadn't texted me until this morning? "Thanks for driving me home, by the way," I told her.

She cocked her head. "From the party? I didn't drive you home."

"You didn't?" My breath stalled in my chest. "Are you sure?"

Her eyes twinkled and she leaned close. "Positive. I was with Weston in his bedroom."

As shocked as I was that she and Weston had hooked up so fast, I was stunned to learn I'd gotten into my car and driven myself home and not remembered one second of it. "Wow," I murmured.

"It was awesome," Britt whispered. She didn't get that I wasn't referring to her and Weston. "Did your parents find out you were wasted?" she asked.

"No." But it didn't help that most, if not all of these guys at the table had seen me smashed. No doubt some of them had witnessed me stumbling to the car. Why hadn't anybody stopped me? I could have killed myself. *Or someone else.* The reality sunk my appetite. I stirred my salad with disinterest.

"Well." Britt plucked a fry. "I'm glad you decided to join us for lunch. You've been too serious lately."

I shrugged. Britt, for all of her fun, easy-going qualities, could never relate to the impossible life I led. She was all about guys, looking good, and making it through each day scoring with those good looks.

"I had stuff to do." I wasn't ready to tell anybody about Matthias. I wasn't sure who he was, and I didn't want to sound like a lunatic, rambling about my sister's invisible buddy. I lowered my voice. "So you hooked up. Cool."

Britt glowed. "It was awesome. I'm way into him."

"From the looks of him, he's into you, too." I stole a peek at Weston, who could barely keep his eyes off Britt. The sparkle in both of their eyes spoke volumes of lust. A pang of longing erupted with joy inside of me. Would anyone ever look at me that way?

"You missed that test in history," Britt said.

"Oh, no." I slapped my forehead. "Eff. I was ready, too. I'll have to go by and see if he'll let me make it up. How was Brinkerhoff's mood?"

"Seemed okay. I think I aced it, except for the essay about prohibition. Which means my essay is screwed."

I laughed. "Has Brinkerhoff ever given you anything but A's?" I made a mental note to look over everything I could about prohibition so I was prepared to write a killer essay.

"No." She laughed. For the first time, her flippancy annoyed me. The fact that she could smile her way into a good grade made her easy breezy, flip-my-blond-hair life seem like a walk on the beach. "Anyway, Weston is so hot," Britt lowered her voice. Her lashes batted Weston's direction. "That mouth. Mmm."

I glanced at Weston's mouth, moving in a slow circle as he chewed. Yep. He had a nice one. For some reason, I thought of Matthias, of when he'd looked at my lips. A warm tingle slipped through my insides.

"You're smiling." Britt eyed me.

"I am?" Heat flushed my cheeks. "Yeah, but not about Weston."

"You don't think his lips are lush?"

"Yeah, I do. But I'm not looking at him like *that*."

"Oh, I know," she said, as if he'd be more interested in the study of volcanic ash than me. "He likes blondes, anyway. And you're way too intense for him."

That pinched. I swallowed and played with the chicken in my salad. "So you're dumbing down for him?"

Britt's smile vanished. "No, I am not. I don't do that."

"Sounds like it to me." Why was I being mean? Britt was the one person I could be myself with. She knew my highs and lows, my heartaches and dreams. She knew how I felt about Abria. "Sorry," I said. "Just don't dumb down. He's not worth it. I don't care if he is Weston Larson."

"Easy for you to say." Her tone was sharp. "You've had—what—zero boyfriends this year?"

"Because I'm focusing on grades and my future, not on getting some with every guy who comes along."

Britt's eyes widened. "You've gotten around a lot more than I have, Zoe."

The truth cut deep. I couldn't sit there with Britt and those guys with my ego exposed. I slid the salad away, stood and walked out of the place. Anger and humiliation prickled every hair on my body. Why had I walked out like that? I should have stayed and verbally beaten Britt at her game. I'd been brittle inside for so long, I wasn't sure what held me together anymore.

I stormed to my car, glancing around the lot one last time for Luke. Nothing. My cell phone vibrated in my pocket. I plucked it out, hoping it was Britt. It was. Good, we can apologize and forget what just happened.

u owe me for the salad!

I shoved the phone deep in my pocket, got into the car and turned the engine. Rage soared through my system. I pushed my foot down on the gas pedal, waited for a spot to open up and speared into traffic. Pressure built inside of me like water filling a balloon. I crammed my hand through my hair. I wanted to explode. At the same time, I yearned for the comforting sureness I had felt when I was with Matthias.

I let out a snort. "Wish I had a Matthias of my own," I muttered, jealous of Abria for the first time in my life.

The temptation to go back to Abria's school and simply sit, wait and watch was strong. I wasn't an addict, but I'd heard Luke talk about cravings. The gnaw inside of me was fierce. I couldn't miss anymore classes. I had to go to school. But that tranquil feeling…I tried to feel it, my soul searching for serenity, but I came up empty.

Disillusioned, disappointed, I drove to school and parked near the football field where no one parked, as far away from the buildings as I could get, so I could cry my eyes out without being seen.

At that moment, I was ready to run as far away as I could without saying goodbye—take responsibility, family, and future, and toss them out the window.

I dried the tears on my cheeks and caught sight of three guys sitting around the base of one of the goal posts. I would have recognized Luke's mop of blonde hair in a crowd of a thousand. I got out and marched over.

They noticed me when I was halfway across the field. Two got up and made a beeline for the classrooms, tamping out whatever they'd been smoking on the way. Luke stood, hands diving into the depths of his front pockets.

Sweet smoke gave away their vice, that and the glazed look in Luke's eyes. "What are you doing? Smoking on school property. Are you nuts? You could get arrested!"

"Quiet down."

"Oh, you're afraid of being caught but you choose to light up out where everyone can see you? You really are stupid, you know that?"

He lowered his head, didn't say anything. The slump in his shoulders said more than words ever could. That pained me. Why he gave in to stupidity when he'd been the brightest, happiest little boy was another painful mystery I yearned to solve, just like the mystery of Abria and autism, the elusiveness of both the root of the helplessness I carried.

"Leave me alone." He started toward the building, head hung, shoulders caved. I had the fleeting wish I could tell him about Matthias. Share with him the calm peace I'd felt. But he'd think I'd just smoked a joint of my own.

I let out a sigh. I wasn't sure what to do, but the usual fury I carried inside when I caught him doing something brainless had already vanished. Replacing the turbulent feelings was the need to make him feel better.

I caught up with him. "I'm sorry. I shouldn't have called you stupid. I've been on one today. Britt…Abria…stuff…"

"Yeah."

"I really didn't mean it," I said, wanting him to acknowledge my effort at apologizing.

"It's okay."

He'd always been quietly agreeable, but inside I knew I couldn't possibly bandage the wound my words had inflicted. "You want to go do something? We could skip class."

"I've already skipped this morning."

I laughed. "So did I. Maybe that isn't a great idea."

He looked over. "You never sluff."

"Yeah, well, I'm not as perfect as you think I am." I joked but he didn't smile. I was pretty sure he saw my faults as blatantly as I saw his.

We walked in silence into the closest building, the gulf between us frighteningly wide, deep and seemingly impossible to cross. A gulf dug with years of differences in age, friends and choices.

Luke was no more than a stranger with my last name.

He walked off toward his class, his blond mop hanging, his jeans unapologetically haggard, riding as low as his self image. I cringed when he didn't say goodbye. What was his next class? I didn't know.

With a sore heart, I headed for history.

Mr. Brinkerhoff's room was full with a class starting in a few minutes. I went to his desk and he looked up from the papers he was shuffling through. "Yes Zoe?"

"Sorry I missed class today. I wondered if I could come after school and make up the test and essay."

"Sure. But be here on time, I only have an hour."

"It won't take me that long," I smiled, trying my own brand of charm.

He grinned. "No, it probably won't. See you after class."

I went out feeling momentary power. Britt wasn't the only one who could wrap a teacher around her finger. I wasn't a teacher's pet by any means, but I was smarter than the average student behind the desk, and I had the respect of all my teachers because, in spite of my partying mentality, I always made time to learn.

I headed for Journalism. Our next issue of the Gazette was already at the printer, so I snuck the time to study, rereading the chapters in American History, and researching prohibition again so the wild period of history was fresh in my mind for the essay.

Mr. Brinkerhoff's favorite pastime was to point out paradoxical stories in history. He was passionate about the fact that twists of irony were the rebar that held earth and space in fair alignment. Maybe he didn't believe in a higher power, but the whole irony idea seemed kind of twisted to me.

I checked my cell phone for new texts. None. Britt and I usually never stayed mad at each other for more than a couple of hours. But with Weston in her life now, I had no idea how long she'd be pissed at me.

With nothing in my life but my problems, the next few days looked unbearably long. But not so unbearable that I wanted to be the first to apologize. I always apologized first. Today, I'd apologized to Luke. But then, I'd been the one to call him stupid. I cringed. Why did the nastiness I locked away in my heart sneak out when my tongue started to whip? Inevitably, I hated myself afterwards.

I sat back and sighed. Other class members laughed and teased each other. A paper airplane flew over my head. I envied the other students. The girls spent their free time taunting the boys, who flirted back. Chase Webster and I were the lone wolves, always on the hunt for the next hot story.

Chase was an intellectual outcast. He had the whole Clark Kent thing going on with his glasses, khaki's and polo's. I liked talking with him because he actually thought about things. I could see his brain working behind his round brown eyes.

Like now. He sat, tipped back in his metal chair, studying whatever it was he was looking at on the computer.

I wondered what he'd think of the whole Matthias thing. He happened to look over and I looked away. *How embarrassing.* It's not like I liked him. I just happened to be looking at him and he happened to look over. Simple.

Chancing a second look, I caught him still watching me. I smiled, got up and went over. My direct approach took him off guard. He looked up too fast, lost his teetering balance, and toppled backwards in the chair.

The clattering brought all noise in the room to a stand still. Then the class broke out in applause. I dropped down and reached out to help him. "Oh my gosh, are you okay?"

61

His face was red.

"Way to go, Chase," someone snickered.

Chase scrambled to his feet and set his chair upright. His glasses sat askew on his nose and he pushed them into place, straightening his polo shirt. "I'm fine. Thanks. Hi."

"Hi." I pulled a chair closer and sat.

Wide-eyed, he stood staring at me, as if deciding whether or not I was really there. Seconds passed and he finally sat down. "Can I help you?"

"Um." I glanced around, made sure everyone was back to their useless time wasting. "Maybe you can, actually."

"Sure. Okay."

"Do…do…" How to phrase this and not sound like I had one hen lose in the barn. "Do you believe in angels?"

Behind his spectacles, his big eyes blinked. "Well. Metaphysically or spiritually?"

"Both, I guess."

"Good answer, Zoe, because both are possible. It's just that some people's beliefs are born of spiritual roots, while others are born of scientific. Do you have a preference?"

"I just want to know if you think they exist."

"I'd like to think they exist. In fact, my roots come from an experience I once had when I was seven years old. My great aunt passed away. We went to her funeral and I saw her, lying in the coffin. It was the first time I'd ever seen somebody dead before. Creeped me out."

"Yeah." I nodded. "I bet."

"That night, as I lay in the motel room, I think it was a Motel Six, not a Best Western, because the towels were pretty soft. She was there, standing by the bed, looking at me. She didn't speak. She just watched. I felt…" he glanced around, leaned closer and in a lowered voice said, "I felt calm. Peaceful. I wasn't scared even though I knew she had died and was…a ghost."

I swallowed. "Wow."

"But I don't like calling her a ghost. In fact, I never did. But she didn't look like us. There was a transparency to her body and clothes. Faded colors. And she wasn't wearing what she'd been buried in, either."

"What did she have on?"

"In the coffin?"

"No, when you saw her."

"She dressed like a gypsy most of the time. When I saw her, she had on a gauzy dress in soft yellow, and she was barefoot."

I nodded, processing the information. No barriers went up. No red flags or whisperings came, challenging his words. I accepted what he told me as truth.

He sat back, staring at me. "You think I'm nuts, don't you?"

"No." I reached out, touched his knee and his eyes locked on my hand. I withdrew. "That's why I asked you. I knew you'd have an intelligent opinion on the subject."

"You...did? Really?"

I nodded.

"I haven't told anybody about that," he said. "Except my family. They thought I was hallucinating. They thought that I had food poisoning from the funeral potatoes served at the family dinner the neighbors put on for us."

"That's lame," I said. "I definitely don't think you were hallucinating." I debated telling him about Matthias. But since I still wasn't sure who Matthias was, I decided against it.

"So have you had any...sightings?" He pushed his glasses back up his nose.

"No. Kinda. Maybe."

"Tell me about it."

"I can't...yet."

He nodded. The sober expression on his face told me he believed. My shoulders felt a little lighter.

"When you're ready," he whispered. Then he pulled out his cell phone. "Can...I have your number? You know, just in case we want to talk about this again?"

63

"Um." His hand, holding the phone, trembled. I fought a chuckle. "Sure." I gave him my number.

"Do...you...want mine?" he sputtered.

"Oh. Sure."

I entered his name and at his insistence, his email addy into my cell phone. I felt connected to him now, in a mysterious way. It'd be nice having someone understand what I was going through, even if he didn't have the same puzzle piece I did: a handicapped sister.

I noticed our little pow-wow had caught the eye of a few of our classmates, and I stood. "Thanks, Chase."

"Yeah. No prob. Be in touch." Chase tipped back in his chair again and I went back to my desk.

※ ※ ※

After school, I went to Mr. Brinkerhoff's room feeling like I could ace anything.

I took the test, popped out the essay and was done in less than forty minutes. Mr. Brinkerhoff smiled when I handed him the papers. "Beat your last record, Zoe."

"You keep track?"

"I've never had student plow through work like you do. You're one of my quieter students, but, like Brittany, you're also very popular. There's irony in the fact that you're a stellar student and you're socially acceptable."

More of Mr. Brinkerhoff's irony. I grinned.

I left the building and checked my phone for texts. None. My good mood popped.

If Britt was waiting for me to apologize first, it'd be a long wait. As I walked to my car, greeting faces as I passed, I realized I was right: she had Weston. The hole I'd left behind in her life was in *his* shadow.

But I had Chase now.

64

I got in my car, started the engine. I didn't really *have* Chase, not like Britt had Weston. But he was someone I could talk to. Mr. Brinkerhoff noticing I was on Britt's social level amused me. How many other teachers had taken the time to deduce the same?

Britt and I had been friends since 9th grade—four years now. Sure, her face and bod had opened a lot of social doors, but I had friends of my own. Doors opened for me because I told them to open.

Then it hit me like a lead ball to my chest.

Who were my friends?

The last four years of my social life flashed before my eyes, dwindling with every year. The diminishment had nothing to do with Britt or our tight relationship; rather the spiral into social exclusivity my life had taken after Abria was diagnosed. Ashamed, embarrassed about Abria, I'd weeded out friends I knew would raise their eyebrows at her. That had left a few acquaintances—like Chase—who didn't know Abria existed. And Britt.

No wonder I felt alone.

My spirits crashed. To my horror, tears rushed behind my eyes. I blinked them back. I needed to do something fun. Party, get my mind off my skeletal social existence. Normally, Britt and I hung on week nights when we had the time. I doubted she had me in mind for that evening. If I wanted to see her, I'd have to suck it up and apologize.

A flash of desperation struck me. I texted her, my heart thumping.

i was out of it earlier, sorry

I drove with my gaze volleying between the road and the phone. Minutes ticked by. Five. Seven. Would Britt dump me that easily?

I was home, pulling up next to the curb when ten minutes had passed without an answer. Britt's normal return time was under ten seconds.

Her past boyfriends had never gotten in the way of our friendship. Like accessories, she'd worn them until she was bored and then tossed them. Clearly, her pattern was changing. If she was willing to neglect me because of Weston, that was not something I had to take.

Frustrated, I stormed into the house and slammed the door. No one was home. Mom worked at the real estate office until five most days and Dad got home around the same time. It was my job to be here when Abria's bus came. I made sure she had a snack and watched her until Mom and Dad got home. When he was around, Luke shared in the responsibility. I had a few minutes before Abria's bus pulled up. A few minutes to calm down, figure out why Britt was ignoring me and indulge in plenty of self pity.

I flopped on the couch, staring at my silent phone. If she abandoned me, the crevasse of loneliness inside would widen into a valley.

Sucking my pride, I texted her again.

u there?

yes

So she had read my text. I shrunk. Fought biting her head off. Took a deep breath.

u still mad?

kinda

i said i was sorry

i'm sick of you walking away, u always do that when it gets tough

what was i supposed to do? weston was there

we could have talked about it

we are talking about it

i guess. i have to go

u wanna hang 2nite?

can't

weston?

yeah. maybe 2morrow.

sure

i'm serious. he's got bball

Sure. k. talk later

I clicked off the phone and stuffed it in my pocket. At least I knew where I stood: behind Weston. We both put guys in first position when the opportunity arose. Zero friends was my fault. No. Not my fault, Abria's. My time hadn't been my own since Mom had covertly assigned me to be Abria's second mother, a job I'd savored when Abria was an infant—before we knew she had autism. Once the devil autism had invaded her, being second Mom relegated me to a glorified an animal trainer.

I turned on my side, emotions pressing so heavily upon me I closed my eyes. Fought off angry tears. *If I could sink into the couch for a few minutes…*

The blare of a school bus horn woke me. I bolted to my feet, wobbled, then made my way to the door, waking up along the way. I couldn't believe I'd slept.

I opened the door and Abria flew past me. Marla frowned. "We weren't sure anyone was home."

"I was asleep. Sorry." *You'd hate it if I didn't answer the door and you had to spend five extra minutes with her, wouldn't you lady?*

"We're only allowed to wait three minutes at pick up and drop off. It throws off our schedule otherwise," she said.

"Oh, so you'd have taken her home for the rest of the night if I hadn't answered?"

She cocked her head.

What had gotten into me? "Thanks," I said, then shut the door in her face. Abria. Home. Ugh. Her sing-song voice came from the kitchen. I found her standing on the table, flapping. I rolled my eyes. "Get down you flamer. What do you want to eat?" I went to the refrigerator, opened it.

"I'd love some milk if you can spare any."

I whirled around. Matthias stood at the table, next to Abria. His blue eyes twinkled. My heart flipped and spun in my chest.

"I didn't scare you, did I?"

Stunned was more like it. Words locked in my throat. I shook my head. Looking at him eased my entire being from an angry fist into an open hand. Every worry, every care was gone, drowned in his aura now filling the room.

"You…want milk?" I asked.

He nodded. "If you've got some."

"Doesn't every family?" I couldn't take my eyes from him, refused to for fear he'd be gone when I looked back. Blindly, I reached for the milk, closed the refrigerator door and felt my way to the glass cabinet.

"What do you want to eat, little miss?" Matthias gently lifted Abria into his arms. My body buzzed. I imagined myself there, his comforting embrace around me, soothing and strong. My knees trembled and I grabbed onto the counter.

"You all right?" he asked.

"Uh. Yeah. Milk. I was pouring milk." Still afraid he'd vanish, I kept my gaze glued to him, opened the cabinet, felt for a glass and poured milk to overflowing. "Oops."

He chuckled. "I'm not going anywhere, Zoe."

Please tell me he can't read my thoughts. Oh no. No. NO. He'd have heard me thinking about being in his arms...*crap.* I cringed and reached for a towel to wipe the spill. *I'm going to go with the thought that he can't hear what I'm thinking. It's the only way to save face.* I carried the glass over.

His twinkling gaze steadied on my hand, wrapped around the glass. "Please put it on the table. Thank you."

I set the glass down.

Matthias. Four feet—no three—away. Close. *Breathing.* He gingerly helped Abria sit in a chair. "What about Miss Abria? What does she want to eat?" His eyes lifted to mine.

I swallowed, opened my mouth. A pathetic squeak came out.

"Zoe?"

"Oh. Abria, what do you want to eat, sweetie?"

She kept looking at Matthias, batting her lashes and turning away as if she was playing coy. "She's...I think she's flirting with you."

His smile was genuine. "Something she picked up from her sister perhaps?"

"I can handle flirting, sure," I teased. "In fact, I'm the best kind of flirt: covert. You won't even realize I have you until it's too late."

His crystal blue gaze locked on mine. He lifted the milk to his lips, the color in his eyes deepening, but he didn't say anything. Slowly, he sipped, as if savoring. I'd never seen anyone drink milk as if it was an intoxicating elixir.

⇒ ✦ ⇐
68

He drank the entire glass down at once, closing his eyes as the last of it slipped into his mouth. A warm tingling down low in my belly caused my cheeks to heat.

"You want some more?" I asked, reaching for the glass.

Again, he watched my hand, and carefully placed the glass between us on the table. "No, thank you. That was nifty."

"Nifty?" I laughed. "Where do you come up with these words?"

He tilted his head, confused. "Don't you think milk is nifty?"

"I hate milk. I know it's one of the four food groups, but not in Zoe's pyramid."

"What's in Zoe's pyramid?"

Booze, I thought, but wouldn't say. I chose my favorite alternative. "Rockstar. Proteins, carbs, fruits, veggies. And more Rockstar."

"Ah, yes. One of those new energy drinks I've heard so much about."

"Ever tried one?"

He shook his head.

I started toward the refrigerator. "I have one hidden in the lettuce crisper."

"No." He held up a hand. "The milk was dandy. Thank you." He turned his attention to Abria. "Abria still hasn't had nourishment."

"Nourishment?" I squelched a laugh. The innocence on his face mesmerized me. For a hottie, he sure talked strange. "Where are you from, anyway?" I grabbed a banana because it was close, and took it over to Abria, dropping it in front of her.

"Originally I'm from New York City."

"Nice. I've never been there."

"I hear it's changed since I lived there."

"When...exactly...did you live there?"

"It's been a few years now."

Abria picked up the banana and tossed it to the floor. Still afraid Matthias would somehow disappear, I locked my gaze on him, bent over sideways, retrieved the banana and dropped it in front of her again.

69

She tossed it.

"Hey," I snapped.

"I don't think she wants the banana," Matthias observed.

"Yeah, well, we don't always get what we want." I shut my mouth. Accustomed as I was to spouting off, the habit was coming back to bite me.

I didn't feel any judgment vibes. Matthias simply stood patiently. Again, I plucked the fallen banana from the floor and put the bruised fruit in front of Abria. She picked it up and stared at it.

"Ba-nan-a," I said. "*You love* bananas."

Matthias chuckled. "That's obvious."

I cocked my head at him. "Why are you here again?" I teased. "Abria's home, with me. How much safer can she get?"

A taunting smile curled the corners of his mouth. "You were asleep, were you not?"

"Did…you…wake me? Or was it something else. Like…" I looked around. "You know something I don't, like there's a stranger in the house."

"No strangers, Zoe."

"That's good. So, explain to me one more time how this…*you*…thing works. If Abria's not in danger, then why are you here? Not to be rude and not that I mind—you're welcome here any time. In fact," I shifted, hemmed, "I like it when you're here. I just…I guess I still have questions."

"Understandable." He gave a sharp nod. "May I?" He gestured to one of the chairs surrounding the kitchen table.

"Of course! Jeez. Sorry. I'm such a flamer. I really do have manners." After he was seated, I sat across from him. He was a vision in his powdered blue shirt and creamy slacks.

"Flamer." He tilted his head in thought. "You've used that term before. I've never heard it."

"It's just one of my words."

"You have your own vocabulary?"

"Sometimes, yeah, usually when I'm frustrated or pissed."

His eyes shot wide. He sat back in the chair as if he'd been knocked by a gust of wind. His cheeks flushed to a crimson hue. "So...pissed...doesn't mean a man urinating?"

I enjoyed a robust laugh. "No, Matthias. Well, yes, it does mean that, but it also means angry." I propped up an elbow, leaned my chin on my fist and stared. "You're...really not from around here, are you?"

"What's your impression of me?"

Whoa. Sweat popped under my armpits. I glanced at Abria, amazingly engrossed in her banana. "Um. I'm still trying to figure that out, actually."

He sat back, crossing his arms over his chest. "What have you got so far?"

I'm getting a huge crush on you, I thought. *HUGE.* "So far? I think you're...different. There's something special about you. I can't put my finger on it, but I feel it. I feel it whenever you're near."

Thick silence stretched between us.

"What do you feel?"

Like I'm wrapped in a warm blanket, held and protected from every care and worry. No pain. No sorrow. Joy, sweet and pure engulfs my soul. I cleared my throat. "I feel good."

Was that understanding I read behind his crystal blue gaze? He gave a nod.

"I'm glad I make you feel good."

"Is that how Abria feels you think? I mean, are you here to make her feel that way?"

"I ensure her safety. How she feels? I've heard the feeling described in a similar fashion."

"How many times have been a bodyguard?"

Amusement lit his face. "You think I'm a bodyguard?"

"Well..." *Bodyguard* didn't feel right. But it was the closest way to describe how I saw him.

He leaned forward, his clasped hands at his mouth, his piercing eyes unwavering. "What does your heart tell you?"

I swallowed the fluttering in my throat but it wouldn't go down. "I..."

my voice trembled. "My heart tells me…" I closed my eyes, thinking if I wasn't looking at him, I'd be able to access lusty, raw reason. But the sweetness in the air seeped through my skin, into my senses, and I couldn't find anything but pure truth.

"Your heart, Zoe," his voice trickled into my conscience.

"Tells me you aren't real," I lied. "You can't be." I opened my eyes. His were focused tight on mine. I'd never had anyone look at me like that before— as if he saw through my soul and, even with its scars and imperfections, he cared about what was there. "Who are you, really?"

"Someone who cares about Abria."

How I wanted someone to care like that for me. Of course I had family who cared. But my eighteen year old heart longed for someone more.

His unblinking gaze was too intense to endure any longer. I looked at Abria, finished with her banana and now rubbing banana slime in patterns on top of the table.

"This is a record for her," I said.

"Because she ate the banana?" he asked.

"Because she's so calm." I met his gaze. "Whenever you're around her she's calm. She's more aware. It's like you carry a frequency she can tune into."

"Nicely put."

"I write for the newspaper at school."

"Then you come by your gift of vocabulary naturally."

"Are you trying to change the subject?"

He smiled and the room lit. "No. I imagine Abria feels what you said you feel and that eases every pathway inside of her."

That made sense. "I've heard about pathways in the brain. Some doctors told us that if we do certain kinds of exercises with her, her broken pathways will mend. Do you think that's possible?"

"I'm sure of it."

Outside of my parents and a few zealous autism enthusiasts, I'd never heard anyone so convinced of something. Yet his words, delivered with a powerful surety, convinced me deep inside that he truly believed that mending pathways was true.

"We've jumped on every wagon that's passed by promising a miracle cure and…I know it sounds stupid, but when you're desperate, you'll do just about anything. It's really hard to believe."

"Not a lot of young women would sacrifice all that you've given up for their family."

Tears threatened to fill my eyes and I looked away, ashamed that I was so easily stirred to self pity. But that he could see, know, and understand that—yes—I had given up a lot, moved me.

"She's my sister." I watched Abria, quietly wiggling her fingers. She'd sat in the chair for at least five minutes. It was a miracle.

"Zoe," his tone was serious, "your kindness doesn't go unnoticed. Your parents, your brother, Abria, each of them whether they tell you or not, appreciate what you do."

"But…sometimes it's so hard. And I…" What would he think if I admitted my Jekyll and Hyde feelings for Abria? What if he found me disgusting and never came back? The thought was quickly pushed aside as the tranquility in the room worked its way into the recesses of my mind. "I feel guilty. Sometimes I don't know how I feel about her."

He nodded.

"I mean, at first, she was so much fun. She was the sweetest little baby. She's still sweet, don't get me wrong, but when the autism happened, it took over. Whoever she was got locked away inside of her somewhere. It's so unfair." My voice scratched. "How can that happen? What did she ever do to anyone?"

His eyes glistened but he held my gaze steadily.

"I get really angry about it," I said. "What kind of person allows this kind of injustice? Wouldn't it be nicer—easier—if everybody in the world was on an even playing field? Instead, there are tons of people at a disadvantage. How unfair is that?"

He steepled his fingers at his mouth, thinking. "Easier for whom?"

"For everyone! People who can't deal with handicapped people would just go on their merry mean way tormenting normal people who can at least defend themselves! Life's hard enough."

"Do you think Abria is bothered by these mean people?"

"Well…no…she doesn't really notice one way or the other, but don't throw that card at me, Matthias."

"But tormenting is okay between people who are not handicapped?"

I clenched my fists on the table. "No, of course not. I can't believe you think that, either."

"I'm trying to help you understand your thoughts."

"I understand my thoughts just fine, thanks. I'm angry!" I couldn't believe I was arguing with him. Oddly, the air around us was still peaceful, as if our words floated like clouds merely passing through the sky without the threat of a storm.

"Your anger is understandable." His tone was gentle. "Zoe, you've lived years with challenges that have aged you in maturity that your peers wouldn't understand. You've learned for yourself that the world is made up of opposites. How else can we have gratitude for what's good if we don't experience what's bad?"

"That's fine for you and me, but can you really look at Abria and say that?" I ground out.

He looked at Abria. She flapped and giggled and he smiled. "Does she look unhappy to you?"

She was annoyingly happy, in fact. Totally free. "No. I don't want to talk about this anymore."

"All right."

I wanted to feel good when he was around. I had enough darkness clouding my life when he wasn't there. "Do you want more milk?" I asked hoping to lighten my mood and change the subject.

"I'm content, thank you."

Content. I hadn't heard anyone use the word very much, but it brought a sigh of certainty out of my chest. "You have your own…interesting vocabulary, Matthias."

"Our words are an expression of the times in which we've lived, I think."

My stomach whirled. *Lived?* "Yeah, of course. Which brings me to another question."

"Fire away." He clasped his hands together.

"Why do you speak so...formally?"

He laughed. "Is this a nice way of saying 'stiff'?"

"Just...formal. I'm not being rude. If I was, you'd know it."

"I'm sure I would. You're a very straightforward young woman."

"Like that—calling me a young woman."

His brows quirked. "What else would I call you? You're not a girl, and you're not a child."

"No, I like it. Guys today are so disrespectful. They call girls 'ho' and other names I wouldn't say because they're just nasty."

His eyes grew wide. "My..." his gaze wandered in thought. "I'd heard about the dissolution of society's language but I had no idea it had become so guttural."

I snickered. "It's guttural all right."

He let out a sigh. He shifted his attention to Abria and a slight smile lifted his lips. "Miss Abria will never have to worry about the whims of life, will she?"

No. And she is better off for it. I saw her in a different light now, and I was happy for her. "Kind of lucky, if you ask me," I murmured.

When I finally looked over at Matthias, he was studying me through undeviating eyes. "Yes."

I heard the front door shut and my heart jumped. Startled, I jerked around in that direction. Luke appeared, his mop of hair bouncing along with his easy-going stride. When I looked back at where Matthias had been sitting, my heart dropped. He was gone.

"Crap."

Luke snickered. "Good to see you, too."

"No, I didn't mean it like that." I looked under the table, then around the room on the off chance Matthias was perched in a cabinet or something.

"Looking for something?" Luke asked, noticing my curious scan.

"No…no."

Abria jumped off the seat and ran out of the room. She'd have her slimy banana hands all over everything in two seconds. I took off after her.

SEVEN

I cleaned Abria's hands and left her to wander the house in search of the toys and books she liked to stuff in bags and carry with her.

Luke sat at the kitchen counter, eating a bowl of Frosted Flakes.

Having never tried weed, I had no idea if Luke was still high some four hours after the fact. I grabbed a washcloth and wiped the counter down, stealing glimpses of his lowered face. I knew better than to approach the topic with anger in my blood and, strangely, I still carried some of Matthias's calm inside of me.

"So, what happened today?" I asked.

"What do you mean?"

"Saturday and today? How often do you use?"

His shoulders lifted, he took another bite.

"You don't know how much you use?" Familiar frustration simmered.

"Why do you care?"

Because you're my brother, you're ruining yourself, killing your brain cells and risking your future. "I don't want you to hurt Mom and Dad."

"They don't even know."

"What if you get busted? It's only a matter of time, Luke. You know that."

"It won't last that long."

"Oh, yeah, right. Because you can stop at any time?"

"Yup."

"Everything I learned about drug addiction in health class says it's not that easy."

"Well, I'm not like everybody else." He still had a half bowl of cereal left, but he stood and carried it to the sink. He dumped what was left down the garbage disposal, turned and burped.

"Do you have a plan?"

His face twisted. "I don't need a plan. When I want to quit, I'll quit." He strode as if he was heading upstairs and I left the washcloth on the counter and followed him.

"So what you're saying is you *want* to kill your brain off. You don't care about your lungs or your health?"

"Leave me alone."

"You can't keep abusing yourself and not expect to pay for it—"

He whirled around. "How is this any different than your drinking? Last I checked alcohol abuse was just as bad."

"I do not abuse alcohol." But the truth sent a quake of guilt through my bones. He strode into his bedroom—a den of rock posters, hanging beads, old boogie boards and faded incense.

I stopped in the doorway. "How are your grades?"

"Who are you, Mom?"

"'Cause that'll be Mom and Dad's first clue."

"My grades are fine."

"For now."

He crashed on his bed, closed his eyes. A picture of him flashed through my head of when we were little and our family had lived in a two-bedroom apartment. Luke and I had shared a bedroom then. At night, he'd lie in his bed, I'd lay in mine, and he'd stare at me with those big blue eyes, his cherubic face innocent and sweet. He'd beg me to tell him a story.

A sudden rush of tears filled my eyes and I blinked them back. My heart turned to mush. I took a step into his room. "I don't want this to get out of control, that's all."

"It won't."

78

"But it's an addictive substance."

He opened his eyes. "So is alcohol."

"This isn't a contest of who's more screwed up, Luke."

"Just stop casting stones, that's all I'm saying."

He was right. This wasn't about me getting my own, or Luke getting his. I was only worried about him messing up his life. I suppose he could have been worried about me messing up mine, but I found that idea doubtful. He was a guy. Guys don't think that deep at sixteen.

Matthias seemed deep. Had he always been that way? How old was he, anyway?

Thinking of Matthias caused me to search for calm, so I could pop the bubbles of anger percolating in my system and continue to talk to Luke without totally blowing apart. "Maybe it sounds like I'm casting stones. I don't mean it to. Just be careful."

He rammed his hands through his hair. "Look," he blew out a sigh. "I think you'd better leave now."

"I want to help."

"This isn't helping."

"What will?"

"I don't know. But talking about it won't."

"You can't ignore it. It won't go away on its own."

"Yeah, I know that, but I don't care."

"You really mean that?"

"Right now? Yeah."

"There are safer ways to relax, Luke."

"Here we go again. I could say the same thing to you."

"I don't drink to relax."

"Then why?" He sat up, glaring at me. "And don't tell me for social reasons. All your friends are already popular."

"I...to escape."

"Escape, relax, they're the same." He shrugged and fell back on the bed and closed his eyes again.

I wondered if we were both trying to escape the same things. I wished he'd open up to me and tell me how he felt, why he did what he did. I wanted him to trust me.

"How about we both stop?" I suggested. The idea was a long shot. I expected a sneer.

He covered his eyes with crossed forearms. "I'm not ready," he said.

I let out a quiet sigh. If he'd asked me to stop drinking, I wondered if I would. If I was ready. "You'll have to face the reasons why you use someday. Better to face it with someone's support than alone. But maybe that's just me."

"Yeah, that's just you."

Sarcasm had slithered into the conversation, so I went out the door before I threw one of his shoes at him.

How could he not see what was so obvious? He was traveling downhill in a runaway car. Why didn't he have the sense to open the door and jump out?

I needed to vent, so I headed to the office intent on losing my frustration by surfing the net. Halfway down the stairs, I realized how quiet it was. I stopped.

"Abria?"

Of course she didn't respond. But I thought at the very least I would hear her moving around somewhere. I didn't. I took the stairs back up to the second floor two at a time, racing to her bedroom. I threw open the door.

There, in the open window, Abria teetered.

Next to her, stood Matthias. He gently wrapped his arms around her and set her on her feet. He peered out the window then slid the glass closed. "You like heights, don't you little miss?" he said, then turned and saw me. "Zoe. Ducky seeing you again."

"H-how long has she been standing there?" I sputtered.

"A second, no more. She really does like to stand on high places, doesn't she?"

"You actually let her climb up there?" Heart still thrumming, I stepped into the room and shut the door.

"I interfere when it's dangerous, Zoe."

"And her opening a second story window, climbing up into the *unscreened* opening isn't dangerous?" I scooped Abria into my arms, holding her tight. The rangy scent of outdoors had latched onto her clothing and skin, and snuck into my senses.

He cocked his head back. "Are you telling me how to do my job?" he smirked.

"Um, last I checked, falls like this one usually mean certain death."

His lip lifted. "Sassy bearcat. I apologize if you thought my actions negligent."

"Not negligent," I said, taking a deep breath, at last calming. "I'm just protective, that's all."

"As am I."

"I know. Thank you…for being here."

He nodded. "My pleasure."

"So…you really don't have anything…better to do?"

"I'm here for her. That's the best thing I can do."

Abria squealed and wriggled, so I let her slip out of my arms and to the floor. She promptly climbed back up to the window and reached the latch, ready to slide it open. "No, no, Abria."

"She's a persistent little sheba, isn't she?" Matthias and I both reached for Abria at the same time, and he yanked his hands back, as if he'd been burned. For a moment, we stared at each other.

I gathered Abria against me. "No window," I said firmly, my gaze on Matthias.

He examined the latch. "This might have to be locked closed."

"But that's against the law. What if there was a fire?" He glanced over his shoulder at me and raised an eyebrow. "You mean to tell me you'll *always* be around?"

"For the time being, yes." He secured the latch, then faced me, wiping his hands back and forth. The idea that he was going to be here had thrill racing with my pulse.

"So, I could walk out this door right now, the house on fire, and you'd save Abria?" I taunted.

The left corner of his lip lifted in a grin. "Ab-so-lute-ly."

"Well, that's cool," I smiled. "The rest of us would burn to char, but Abria would be just fine. Hey, why don't we all have bodyguards like she does?"

"I'm not a bodyguard. Guardians come to each man, woman and child singularly or severally, as needed, provided the charge is open-hearted for angelic hosts—or, in Abria's case, is an innocent."

I looked around. "Seriously? Then where is mine?" And why hadn't I seen any around Luke. He was in just as much danger as Abria, to my way of thinking.

Matthias stuffed his hands in the front pockets of his soft slacks. "A person must be open hearted for heavenly assistance, or they won't respond. And guardians aren't always hanging around, Zoe…like some cricket on your shoulder."

"That's my conscience—at least according to Walt Disney."

He smiled. "I would respectfully suggest that, for Abria's sake and your peace of mind, you consider locking this window at least until she understands the danger."

I let out a snort. "As if that will ever happen."

"You don't believe Abria will ever understand danger?"

"Maybe in a thousand years."

"She's progressing, isn't she?"

"Of course she's progressing. But at the rate she's going, I'll be married and living in Zimbabwe before she gets it."

He studied me for a moment. "You have too little faith in her."

"I don't want to expect too much. I've done that. Believe me, it's highly overrated and excruciatingly disappointing. Besides, if she understood danger, that'd let you off the hook, wouldn't it?" I grinned.

His face broke in a glorious smile. "Your wit is dandy."

"Thanks."

"Who you talking to?"

The sound of Luke's voice made me whirl around. He stood in the doorway. My throat closed and I swallowed, trying to find the right words. I glanced at Matthias who hadn't moved. "What do you mean?"

"I've been standing here listening, Z. You're not talking to Abria. You've been carrying on a one-sided convo for the last five minutes."

My eyes widened. I looked back at Matthias. The issue of his invisibility again? What was wrong with everyone? He was standing right there—in his pale magnificence.

"Sounds to me like you've taken to 'shrooms," Luke snickered, before leaving.

Stunned, I couldn't move. My breath went still in my chest. I stared at the door through which Luke had just left. Matthias. Luke hadn't seen him. "This...can't be." I crossed to the door and shut it, pressing my back against the wood. "Why can't he see you? Why can't anyone see you?"

"Abria sees me."

I shook my head, put my hands over my ears. "No. You're playing some kind of trick on me. Maybe I'm still asleep. This is all a dream. I've had dreams like this that have gone on for days. I'm just not waking up. Wake up, wake up."

"Zoe, I thought you understood why I was here."

"Yes, yes, I thought I did. But....Luke is my brother. He was standing five feet away. He didn't see you. That has to mean you aren't really here."

"But I am."

"How can you be if he didn't see you?"

"I told you, visions come to souls particularly sensitive to things Divine."

"I...I'm not sensitive. I'm not special. I swear sometimes. I've cheated and lied. I—"

"No mortal is perfect. Your heart only has to be in the right place."

My heart rang like a bell, reverberating truth, warm and soothing through my system. I crossed the floor to him. Around me, the air seemed

83

to fill with the sound of a thousand beating hearts. I covered mine with the palms of my hands. Surging inside of my chest, waves of emotion rose and ebbed with each of my breaths. I closed my eyes, fighting tears. A delicious joy filled every space inside until all traces of doubt were satisfied, as if my hungry soul had at last eaten.

When I opened my eyes again, I looked into the clear blue of Matthias's.

"I believe you," I murmured. "I believe you. But...I still don't understand how I can see—"

"You have faith in me."

That same rush I'd just experienced surged again through my being. My knees buckled. I reached for the window ledge to steady myself and took deep breath. Abria played quietly on the floor at our feet, engrossed in spinning a top, and I watched her in awe of the simple miracle.

Matthias. Here. With me. The vein alongside his neck pulsed with life. And yet...I didn't try my brain with the logistics, too exhausted from the previous effort to intellectually understand and make sense of him.

My gaze traveled over the youthful skin on his cheeks in spite of the fact that a man his age should have stubble. The contours of his neck. The hollow at the base of his throat. His chest, what I saw peering through the opening of his pale pink shirt, was smooth and unblemished. My gaze continued traveling the well-toned body beneath smooth, caressing fabric draping over torso and legs.

At last my eyes met his. Something flashed in the depth of his irises. I blinked to make sure I wasn't imagining anything, and it was gone. All that remained was a teasing sparkle over his magnificent grin. "Are you finished?" he asked. "You're quite sure I'm real now, aren't you?"

Whatever he was didn't matter to me at that moment, overcome as I was with the desire to kiss him. I stepped closer. His eyes widened just enough to signal to me that if I'd had the guts to reach out and place my hand over his heart, I'd feel it pounding.

"I'm not sure." Slowly, I raised my arm to perform the test. My pulse quickened. His wide blue eyes locked on my hand as if I held a dagger. More than anything I wanted to touch him. Yet the sheer alarm on his face stopped my hand a mere inch from his rising and falling chest. The heat from his body pressed upwards against my palm, as if luring my flesh to his. Not once did he take his eyes from mine.

"Why can't I touch you?" I whispered.

Beneath my hand, his chest rose and fell erratically, taunting me. So easily I could press my hand there, so intensely I yearned to. I knew I should not follow through with my wish to touch him. Just as fleetingly luscious as the idea started, it ended in black confusion.

I withdrew my hand, fighting an inner demon that still wanted to satisfy my craving to feel him for myself. I had the sense come over me that I was very close to something off limits. Not unlike that whisper of warning I often had when I was close to danger or harm, only I knew Matthias meant me no harm and he was not associated with anything dangerous. The whispering was more about something beyond my knowledge that I couldn't understand, but was pertinent to who he was and why he was there, and my touching him might interfere with that.

I stepped back. A look of relief lit his eyes, replaced by concern. "You've done nothing wrong, Zoe."

"I don't feel that way."

"Yet you don't feel guilty. Do you?"

"How do you know what I feel?" I pressed my hand over my heart as if to shield it from him. "You seem to know everything."

"Spirits aren't confined to communicating with their lips."

"But you're human."

"In a manner of speaking."

"So you mean…you can read my thoughts?"

"In another manner of speaking, yes."

Holy crap. Just seconds ago I'd thought about kissing him. *No. Some thoughts had to be off limits, right?* "You mean…you've read every thought I have? Every one? I have no control over what you can hear and what you

85

can't?"

He laughed. "Actually, I can't read your thoughts, though that, I'm sure, would be most enlightening. I'm able to hear the thoughts of the person I am sent to watch over."

"Like Abria?"

He nodded. "Once someone is assigned to me, I am able to communicate with them in spirit. If the situation requires, I can also listen to the thoughts of those not under my care."

"For a minute there you had me freaking out."

His eyes narrowed in curiosity. "Freaking out? Now why would my peering into your thoughts cause you to...freak out?"

"No way am I explaining *that* to you. I want you to tell me what's going on in Abria's head. What does she think? Do you hear anything at all that makes sense?"

He chuckled. "Yes, I do hear her mortal thoughts. But her spirit, Zoe, is not handicapped."

How could he be sure? I stared into his calm blue gaze. He was certain. Convinced. I longed for that conviction. What a relief it would be. For the time being, I borrowed belief from the assurance in his countenance, pleased to hear what I'd hoped was true. At our feet Abria sat, content and flapping.

"Think of it as if she has two radio frequencies inside of her. I hear both. The first is a frequency the rest of the world hears when she communicates: her thoughts as they are in her mortal brain, a brain with imperfections. The second frequency is..." he paused, as if in prayer or reverence before continuing, "her second frequency is pure and clear."

Awed, I watched Abria with new respect. "Wow..." I crouched down and sat next to her. "What's she thinking? Right this very second?"

Matthias' concentration tightened on Abria, his body went still. "She's enjoying this moment. She's happy. Content. And she loves flapping, it's her way of expressing the excitement and joy she feels inside."

"Your explanation feels right," I told him. "Every other alternative seems too cruel to be real."

He sat down next to me, careful to ensure our crossed knees didn't come into contact. "Right manifests itself in the heart." He patted his. "Like truth. If more people listened to what was inside of them, things would be vastly different in the world."

"You're…" *amazing,* I thought but wouldn't say. Then I panicked, thinking he might hear it anyway. "You're absolutely sure you can't hear what I'm thinking?"

"I'm sure of it."

"But you seem to know…you even knew when I first met you, what I was thinking."

"Only because the circumstances and the look on your face made it fairly easy to figure out what was going on in your head. And I've always been good with females."

My eyes widened. Females? A little thread of jealousy tightened down inside of me. "That doesn't surprise me. You're…well, you're a hottie."

"A hottie?" He pressed his palms to his cheeks, then across his forehead, confusion on his face. "I don't feel hot."

I laughed. "You're good looking. Attractive. Handsome. Any of those words ring a bell?"

"Oh, oh, I see." The color of his cheeks bloomed into a lovely blush.

"I want to hear about you and females," I said. "Do you have a girlfriend?"

"My mission doesn't really allow me to associate romantically."

Too bad. But at least he wasn't taken. What was I thinking? If no one could see him but me and Abria, what was he exactly? "So…I don't mean to beat the issue down, but…you have skin and hair and I see blood in your veins. You're human but no one can see you except me and Abria. You're alive but…I still don't get it."

"Some guardians have bodies."

"So what I see is real, but how do you come and go so fast? Like earlier. You were in the kitchen, then when Luke came in, you weren't."

"With a thought I can be anywhere I wish."

"With just a thought?"

He nodded.

"Wow. Cool. How is that done?"

"The ability to move about at will is part of the job."

"Sounds powerful."

"It is. The gift is only bestowed when certain levels of progress are made."

"So not every guardian can do what you can do?"

"There are different levels of guardianship. Some merely assist in a spiritual form. As in when a whisper isn't enough and an extra umph is required. Others, like me, have bodies to enable them to fully do the work."

My gaze once again traveled the length of him, awe in my study. "Insane."

His brows crimped. "Pardon me?"

"Just an expression. You're not insane, obviously. But...what you can do...who you are...it's just so unbelievable." I let out a sigh of contentment. Feeling safe on such a deep level was not anything I'd ever experienced before, my closest experience perhaps in moments of profound gratitude when I'd chosen to ponder how blessed I really was.

Abria stood and, gaze locked on the window, once again relentlessly pursued her climb. I jumped up and grabbed her into my arms. "No, no silly girl." I squeezed her against me.

Matthias joined me at the window and I set her on her feet. I snatched her favorite spinning top and set it in motion on the window sill. She watched it spin for a few seconds and flapped. A huge grin spread on her face.

I wondered how many other people Matthias had helped. Who were they? Where were they now?

My cell phone vibrated in my pocket and I plucked it out. Matthias watched me with interest. A text from Britt.

wanna party 2 nite?

I smiled. Britt and I were back on. **yeah. where?**

brady's i'll drive incase you get wasted

lol k sounds good

9?

k

I was glad Britt was talking to me again. And I could always use a good time. I looked up from my phone and caught Matthias' keen blue eyes.

"What is that contraption?" he asked.

Everyone on earth knew what a cell phone was. Then a shocking thought occurred to me. "You've never seen a cell phone?"

"Cell phone? Is that some sort of derivative of the Alexander Graham Bell telephone?"

I stared at him. Why was his knowledge of worldly events so spotty? "So, you *have* heard of the telephone?"

"Of course. I even used one once or twice."

"Matthias, when did you use the phone?"

"In life."

"In...life...but you're alive *now*."

"When I was alive *then*."

"Then being?"

"In mortality."

My heart started the familiar, freaky pound I was getting used to feeling whenever Matthias dropped one of his shocking bombs of information. I took a deep breath. "But you *are* mortal."

"Yes, but not in the sense that *you* are mortal, Zoe. After my life ended, I passed on to the world of spirits where I—"

"Wait a second!" I held up a hand and steadied my wobbly knees by gripping the window ledge. "You...died?"

"Yes. I thought you understood that."

I closed my eyes, gripping the window sill with both hands. My head spun. "This only gets more bizarre."

"Zoe." He was closer to me, I could tell by the sound of his soft voice, now just over my shoulder. *Touch me*, I plead. *Touch me and show me you are really here so I can put this behind me once and for all and understand.*

"Trust the whisperings of your heart."

Eyes pinched tight, I listened to my rapid breath, the heavy pound of my heart against my ribs. Beside me, Matthias' warmth reached out in comforting assurance that what he was telling me was true.

Believe.

"Is that your voice?" I whispered. "Telling me to believe?"

"No." His warm breath on my neck sent a shudder down my spine. My fingers tensed on the sill. "That voice is your inner light. Listen to it."

I took in a deep breath, unable to do anything but stand statue still, my entire being searching dark corners, softening edges and deep recesses for the whisper. *Believe.* And then, with the release of breath, every cell inside bloomed, like flowers awakening to the sun's rays. I opened my eyes and looked out into the backyard, at the towering pines and bare aspen trees and the rising mountain peaks. How beautiful the starkness of winter was in its gray and ash, white and black with slivered evergreens reaching for Heaven.

I looked at Matthias, his clear blue eyes patient, kind and something more—caring. The same caring I'd seen for Abria was there for me. I was humbled. Pleased. And in a way disappointed, because the budding woman inside of me saw him as a man. A man I wanted but couldn't have.

"I understand now," I murmured.

His lips lifted in a faint smile. "I can see that."

Could he see that I was disappointed? Did he know why? I averted my gaze to the view out Abria's window. Sadness crept inside of me and tried to make itself comfortable, but I ignored it. Matthias was there. I may not have him the way I wanted to have him—though even how I wanted him was rather ambiguous to me at the moment. Boyfriend didn't feel right. No, he deserved something much more. *A love interest?* The word love sent silly flutterings through my body. *So soon?* How? *Could my feelings be real?* Definitely. He was in my life. An incredible person I was drawn to like no other.

I wanted to know everything about him. I had even more questions about his life, his death and where he'd been in the interim. I was bursting inside. And he was only in my life because of Abria. But I'd take that over nothing.

I turned so we were face-to-face. He seemed to notice our close proximity for the first time and took a step back.

I'd completely forgotten about Abria, and I tore my gaze from his long enough to see where she was: a few feet away on the floor, spinning the top over and over and over again, the hum fast then slow, fast then slow.

Glad she was occupied so I could continue to ask Matthias questions, I faced him again. "There's so much I want you to tell me. Can you tell me? Is it against the rules?"

"I'll share with you what I can."

The sound of the front door shutting in the distance nabbed my attention. I glanced at Abria's closed door. "My parents."

He nodded. "Yes."

"Are you leaving?"

"I'm not needed here now."

He was right. Abria would be under my family's watchful eye the rest of the evening. But the idea that he was going to go left me lonely and empty. His presence was so strong, full of light, comfort and certainty, I felt grounded when I was with him, even though the world around me was a teenage turmoil.

"When will I see you again?" I asked.

"When I'm needed."

"Anybody home?" Mom's voice snuck through the closed door. She was getting closer, and panic set in.

"I wish…" *you wouldn't go*, I wanted to say but the door opened and I whirled around. Mom smiled, and looked from me to Abria. My heart sunk. I knew Matthias was gone.

⋙ ✦ ⋘
91

EIGHT

"How was your day?" Mom came into the room, her long-day-weary eyes on Abria but the question was for me. She squatted down next to her, the faded scent of her perfume sneaking into the room.

"Fine. How about yours?"

Abria was still spinning the top and didn't notice that Mom had walked in. "Abria, Mommy's here. Abria, look at Mommy."

Abria finally looked at her. "Good girl for looking at Mommy." Mom stood, sighed. "Mine was pretty good. I got an offer on the Lambert house. It was a walk-in client, so kind of a surprise there. They saw the virtual tour and fell in love with it."

"Wow, that's great."

Mom reached out and played with some strands of my hair. "How about yours? You look…" She eyed me, smiled. "Happy."

"I do?" I touched both cheeks with my hands. Did Matthias' presence leave me looking like I felt—glowing?

"I'm glad to see it. Especially when you're with Abria."

"I'm always happy when I'm with Abria," I half joked.

Mom laughed. The sight was so pretty, I wanted to throw my arms around her in a big hug. She headed to the door. "Want to set the table for me? I brought home Little Caesars."

"Sure. Oh, I think we'd better put a lock on this window. When I came in here earlier, I caught her trying to climb out." I knew better than to tell

Mom Abria had actually been perched in the window frame. She'd go ballistic and take to sleeping in Abria's room to make sure she was safe.

Mom went to the window and examined the casing. She sighed. I didn't want her happy mood to change.

"I'll figure something out," I offered.

"The window has a safety latch." She fiddled with the mechanism, sliding the small lever I hadn't noticed before into place. Then she tested the window and it didn't open. "We'll see if that does it. But I wouldn't put it past her to figure out how to undo the safety latch," Mom said.

"She'll be okay."

Mom's face was tight with worry again. "I'd hate to have to put plywood up. Bars would look hideous. Nails would be so final."

I put my hand on Mom's shoulder. "I bet the security lock will do for now."

"You think so?"

I wished I could tell Mom about Matthias, but that was impossible. "She's smart," I said, "but not that smart. Yet." Abria, noticing our examination of the window, stood ready to climb up and into it again.

Mom scooped her into her arms and carried her out of the bedroom. "No window, Abria. No. *Dangerous.* Window is dangerous."

I followed Mom, a small smile on my face. As I went through the doorway, I turned back and took one last look into the room. *If you're anywhere nearby, Matthias, I'm glad you're here for Abria.*

※ ※ ※

Britt picked me up in her white mustang convertible and we headed over to Brady's house for the party. Brady was one of Weston's jock buds. On the hot level, he was about a nine. Weston was a twelve.

Matthias was off the charts.

⋙ ✳ ⋘

Britt was radiant in her cream short skirt and soft, fuzzy ivory sweater.

"You look like a snowball," I told her. "Or a bunny."

Britt laughed and threw back a chunk of her blonde hair. "Bunny, yeah, that works." She shot her wrist under my nose. "New perfume. You like?"

I sniffed. Strong, heavy, penetrating. "Yeah, what is it?"

"Miracle. It stays with me. That's why I like it. And it has licorice in it. Guys dig licorice, cause it makes them subconsciously think about food. Did you know that?"

"No. I want some."

"In my purse."

I dug through her pastel hobo and pulled out a magenta bottle, then sprayed some of the intoxicating scent at my pulse points.

"You're smiling a lot today, what's up?" Britt asked, glancing over. "Seriously, you look happier than I've seen you in a long time."

Matthias' face dangled in the back of my mind. I closed my eyes, wishing he was in the car with me, wishing it was him I was going somewhere with. Wishing he was alive and I could tell Britt about him.

"See?" Britt said, laughing. "You look like a girl with secrets. Juicy secrets."

"Maybe I am," I teased. I'd never tell her about Matthias. But I could imply. "I met the hottest guy."

Britt's eyes grew huge. "When? Tell me everything."

"I can't."

"No! Don't do that! That's just mean."

"I seriously can't. He's just this awesome, older guy."

"Older? Wow. Wait, he's not some freak from MySpace is he?"

"Ewww. Does that sound like me?"

"I figured you were smarter than that."

"I met him at Abria's school, actually."

"Yeah?" Britt's brows creased. "What is he, a special ed teacher?"

"More like an aide." I bit my lower lip to squelch a smile.

I could tell by Britt's unenthused nod she wasn't sure about whether or not that was cool. "Okay. Whatever works, I guess. So, is he into you too? Does this mean you'll be sidelining it tonight?"

"No way." I'd drop guy hunting altogether if Matthias was mine, but I needed an outlet tonight. "I'm gonna have some fun."

A handful of cars were parked out front of Brady's two-story brick house. Music rocked the neighborhood. It was cold outside, and I wrapped my long sweater around me when I stepped from the warm confines of Britt's car.

I looked up, saw stark, black clouds. No heavens. Maybe snow later. That'd make it cozy inside and slick on the streets. "Your car doesn't have four wheel drive does it?"

I asked after we got out. We headed toward the house.

Britt eyed her reflection in the compact mirror she'd pulled out of her purse. "Huh?"

"Forget it." I'd cross that bridge if I had to. Driving in dangerous conditions didn't bode well with my parents. But then they thought I was at Britt's house, a mere four blocks from home, enjoying a harmless evening of chick flicks.

Inside, Britt and I lit the place up like Whistling Pete's on the Fourth of July. Guys clamored to us. The attention was nice. How many had heard about her and Weston? Her unavailability rarely dissuaded guys, which amazed me because they were so anxious to take her any way they could get her. Too bad for them she was monogamous—at least until boredom set in. I didn't care that most of them saw me as second choice. I was there to satisfy a craving.

"I'm going to go find Weston," she said, her head craning for him.

"Okay." Her arm slipped from mine and she vanished. It'd only be a matter of minutes before the two of them slid quietly into a secluded room somewhere. I let out a sigh, envious. Yet, the craving I usually had inside at parties wasn't as acute tonight. I smiled at lingering gazes, flirted with a few followers, but mostly I wandered, listening to the music, sipping my beer and thinking of Matthias, wishing he was there.

Maybe I should have brought Abria.

He was her guardian, after all. For a flash, I almost wished I was

95

handicapped. Then I closed my eyes and took another sip, the bubbling bite scorching my throat on the way down. Abria didn't appreciate Matthias. She had no idea what a hottie was and she didn't care.

What a waste.

If Matthias was mine, I'd...I wasn't sure what I'd do, but I'd be wherever he was twenty-four-seven.

Wandering aimlessly through Brady's house, I allowed thoughts of Matthias to take me to a lofty high.

I bumped shoulders with a cute guy and smiled. My brain yearned for Matthias' brilliant grin and instead I got an ordinary smile from an ordinary guy. I kept looking.

A plush, fat chair sat unoccupied in the corner of the den where a fire danced in the fireplace. The wood-paneled walls, hunting pictures and golf trophies created a cozy feel to the small room where a couple I didn't know sat snuggling on a leather couch. I supposed they wanted the room to themselves, but I wanted that big, lush chair cornered in the window.

I plopped into it and closed my eyes, the cool bottle in my hand resting on my chest. Matthias. *Where are you? What do you do when you're not keeping watch over Abria? Float through the sky like Superman?* He'd be hot in that S suit. What did he look like underneath those silky clothes?

It didn't matter. He was too out of reach for me to really care what kind of body he had, though it was obvious he was perfect. He could have a club foot and I'd still be attracted to him. *Those eyes.* Penetrating, searching, knowing and yet without judgment. That, in itself was a miracle. I'd never looked at anyone and not seen judgment at some point in the relationship, no matter how insignificant the association.

"I bet two can fit in that chair." The voice was unfamiliar and aimed at me, so I opened my eyes. Brady. As guys went, Brady wasn't a slouch: dark blond hair and amber eyes. Nice teeth.

"How about we find out?" I scooted over, making room and he wedged himself next to me. He smelled of beer and faded cologne.

"Yeah. Nice fit." He tipped back his bottle and took a drink.

I almost rolled my eyes at our cheesy conversation. After talking with Matthias, this felt like a scene from a bad soap opera. But it was all part of the game and we both knew how to play. We both wanted to play, or we wouldn't be there.

I lifted my bottle signaling to him it was time for a toast. His eyes gleamed with delight. He raised his bottle and tapped mine.

"To those watching over us," I said.

He glanced around as if looking for 'those,' trying to hide confusion. "To the voyeur in all of us."

No. Wrong. Gag.

Clink.

He drank, and I pressed the bottle to my lips without taking another drop. Matthias. That someone clueless as Brady would infer something as raw and base as Matthias being a voyeur bugged me deep down. What Matthias did was so far from seedy, light years away from sexual, so far removed in fact that Brady repulsed me. That one comment killed any desire I'd had to make out with him.

He reached an arm around my shoulder and rested against me like we were lovers sitting on a bench overlooking a lovely sunset on the beach. The move was too much, too soon, and turned my stomach. I tried to ignore it, to tell myself how cute he was. He was here, next to me, willing and waiting.

This is why you came. Go for it.

I tried to find beauty in his amber eyes, gazing drunkenly into mine. Who cares if it's not Matthias? *He's a hot body and he knows what to do, so let him do it.*

I closed my eyes, tried to picture Matthias' clear, soulful gaze and the next thing I knew warm, wet, beer-lips were pressed against mine. My eyes flashed. His were closed. He sandwiched closer, his lips opened for more.

The female inside of me wriggled from dazed sleep like a drooping bud freshly watered. I heard him drop his bottle, it clunked to the floor. I dropped mine. His hands circled my waist with the ease of a well-practiced move. How many waists had Brady wrapped his arms around? Was I just another waist,

97

another pair of lips and legs?

My hands were free and I was just as practiced, so I slid mine around his neck and played in his hair. He groaned, moved closer.

His groan sent a shudder of revulsion through me. *Ignore it. Enjoy him. He's here, willing and he's yours.* I tried to block out the distaste, but it hung in the back of my throat like vomit in wait.

His lips broke free of mine, sending cool air against my mouth. His heavy-lidded eyes gazed into mine. "Wanna find a room?"

No you perv. "Ab-so-lute-ly."

He stood and held out his hand to me. I set my hand in his and he pulled me to my feet. Our bottles clinked when he stepped back, and we both looked down at them. His was empty. Mine spilled gold liquid onto the floor.

Since we were in his house, he knew where he was going. I trailed behind him, holding his hand. Eyes peered at us. Whispers followed. I knew what they were talking about: *They're going to hook up. Score.*

I felt like a game piece.

Matthias, where are you?

I closed my eyes. *Stop. Don't do this. It's wrong. You know it. But he wants me. He's here.*

I opened my eyes. I couldn't meet the curious gazes we passed, so I kept my head low, my eyes averted. Not my usual posture. *Shame.*

Forget shame, you deserve this. Your life sucks and this will make you feel better, it always does.

Brady nodded at his jock friends as we passed. *My next conquest, dudes. Check it out.*

Music pumped my blood into a swirling beat and I scanned his broad shoulders, his waist, and legs. He was a fine specimen. Fine. His kiss hadn't done anything for me, but I'd seen him in his glove-fitting football uniform. I could keep my eyes closed and focus on lean, hard muscles even if his kiss left me empty.

Upstairs, he opened the last door on the left. His room. Dark walls, dark shades, posters, trophies, jerseys hanging on the wall, baseball caps, the scent of body, boy and cologne reaching out from his closet, plaid bedding and the beige carpet under our feet.

"Here we are." He tugged me inside and closed the door.

"Nice room." At least Brady hung up his clothes. His backpack dangled from a peg sticking out of the wall. Coats and hoodies perched on a garment tree.

He put his hands on my shoulders and gently drew me to him, eyeing my mouth. *Look at me,* I thought, *like Matthias looks at me. Search. Pierce. Understand.*

His head dipped toward mine, his lips twitching, readying to take. Another wave of revulsion. *Please look at me. In the eyes. Do you see me?*

Angry, I pressed my hands against his chest. He stopped. *Yes, now you look you skeezball.* His amber eyes were so dazed he blinked as if to clear them. "What's my name?" I asked.

He blinked again, panic flashing, sobering his features. His mouth opened but nothing came out.

Snow fluttered down from dirty clouds overhead, a sour-milk veil I trudged through as I walked down Brady's front path toward the street. Pounding music from inside the house was muffled by the falling flakes. Chilled, getting wet, I clasped my arms around myself and eyed the slick pavement. I hadn't told Britt I was leaving, I'd just turned and walked out.

In hindsight, I should have insisted forgot-my-name Brady drive me home, but I was too annoyed with him and disappointed in myself to spend another second in his presence.

Now I was, walking.

I never took my purse to parties, too afraid I'd leave it behind or get ripped off if I became too drunk to notice, which meant my phone was also at home.

Silence forced me to face myself. I headed down the hill. My overriding thought: my life in since Matthias had come along. Being near him caused my whole being to lift to a place above the earth, as if I walked on a floating carpet that protected me from temporal influence.

Was that part of his gift? To make those around him feel better? Lift them higher?

Icy flakes fell and coated my clothes, seeping through to my skin. My teeth started to chatter and the first wedge of panic cut into me. I had a long walk ahead. I might freeze before I got home.

Home.

Abria was home, tucked in bed. I'd love to be there, too. Safe. It was doubtful Matthias was watching over her, but highly probable he was watching over someone else. Who was the lucky one?

I looked up into the black heavens, blinking fast to protect my eyes from the onslaught of falling flakes. *Matthias, where are you?*

More than being warm and dry, I wanted to know where he was. More than being safe at home, more than I wished I could take back the last hours at the party, I wished I knew where he was and what he was doing.

I let out a sigh, my breath pluming in front of my face. I should have driven myself. I wouldn't make that mistake again, especially not with Britt now Weston's new girlfriend. Three's a crowd. What I really should have done was stay home.

Why did I go to these parties? I knew what I was getting into, and the raunchiness of my actions, my weak willingness to run with the rest of the pack chilled me even more than the outside temperature. When someone like Matthias devoted every ounce of energy and all of his time to things that really mattered, my choice to party looked embarrassingly shallow.

Sure he was an angel, and maybe there wasn't that much to do in Heaven, but I didn't waste time with more rationalizing. Alone with my guilt, I couldn't deny my reasons for partying: escaping what I hated to face. And yet I never entirely escaped. I couldn't outrun blood.

I admired Matthias' strength, his conviction, so directed and unwavering. I couldn't imagine him ever giving into weakness.

Did immortals have weaknesses?

My mind spun with thoughts of Matthias and his life. I couldn't wait to see him again and find out everything I could about him. But that would mean waiting until Abria was in harm's way. I couldn't intentionally put her in harm's way just to satisfy my need to see him. A smirk chattered out. That'd get me struck by lightning for sure.

Had Matthias ever seen God?

My head reeled with questions, and the more I thought of Matthias, the greater the pressure inside me built to know more.

Body shaking, lips trembling, I hunched my shoulders and wrapped my arms around myself. I was soaked now, and any warmth pulsing through my veins was further from the surface of my skin.

Headlights coming from behind me shed an ivory glow onto the icy road and into the lacy snowflakes falling from the sky. I turned, contemplating waving down the driver to see if I could bum a ride, tossing aside all warnings I'd ever heard to never accept rides from strangers.

Luke's decrepit blue Suzuki rumbled toward me. Relief coursed my veins. He pulled alongside the curb and I opened the rickety door and got in The heater blasted in my face and at my feet, but I was shaking so bad, the warmth didn't help.

"What are you doing out here?" he asked.

I could barely sputter out the words, my lips were frozen. "Walking."

"In this weather? Were you at Brady's party?" After I shut the door, he pulled onto the road and we slowly drove through the snow building on the street.

"Y-yeah. What're you doing out?"

He shrugged. "Driving."

"Things bad at home?"

"No. I just needed to get out for a while."

I knew how purifying a solitary drive could be but I hated to think he'd been out smoking. "I can't believe you found me." My wet clothes clung, cold and icy, but the warmth from the heater finally silenced my chatters.

"Yeah. This weather's something, else, huh?"

"You know Brady?"

"I know his brother, Kevin."

I didn't ask for more. The days of him sharing truth with me were long gone. We both told each other what we wanted the other to know and nothing more.

At home, Luke pulled into the driveway and put the car in park. The engine idled. "You're not coming in?" I didn't want him driving in these rough conditions; the danger sent familiar panic-for-a-sibling through my system.

"I'm not ready to come in yet."

I held his gaze as long as I could and wondered where he would go, what he would do. He finally looked away, as if impatient or bored, I wasn't sure which.

I got out and leaned in the door frame. Begging was useless. "Be careful."

He nodded. "Yeah."

I shut the door and stood, shivering again, watching him back out the rattling car. The soft red gleam of his rear lights finally vanished in the white haze of snow.

Inside, the warmth of home sunk into my chilled flesh. The scent of our dinner, Little Caesars, still hung in the air. I shut the door. Lights were off, the house was quiet. At eleven o'clock, I figured everyone was in bed, so I crept upstairs anxious to peel off my wet clothing.

Mom and Dad's bedroom door was closed, no light underneath. I headed down the hall in the opposite direction to my room, passing a montage of family memories framed and hung on the walls. Like life passed before my eyes, the pictures brought to mind happy vacations, celebrated holidays, and treasured birthdays. Abria's door was closed and locked. I paused and didn't hear anything coming from the other side.

In my bedroom, my cell phone rang. I quickly plucked it from my purse, sitting on my bed. Britt.

"Where are you?" Britt asked.

"I came home."

"Something wrong?"

"Yeah. Brady and I were about to hook up and he didn't even know my name."

"What? No way. The skeeze."

"Yeah."

"How did you get home?"

"Luke."

"Oh, okay."

"You having fun?"

"Yeah, but I want you here."

Laughter and music blared in the background. I appreciated the thought, but knew it was just that: a thought. She was completely fine without me and we both knew it. "Go have fun. Tell me what happens tomorrow."

"K. I will. Bye."

I put the phone in my bag and heard a thump from Abria's room. Often, she awoke in the night. She'd climb and jump and make all kinds of noise, waking up the rest of us with her laughter and gibberish. I didn't want Mom to freak because she thought Abria was climbing out the window. Still damp and cold, I went to Abria's room in hopes of getting her back to sleep before she woke the whole house.

A line of white peered underneath her bedroom door. Yup, she was awake. Thrill rushed inside of me. What if Matthias was here?

I unlocked her door and opened it.

She stood at her window, but the window was still closed. No Matthias. Disappointed, I went in and shut the door so Mom and Dad wouldn't hear anything and wake up.

"What are you doing awake, Abria?"

She had her fingers on the lock and without caring that I was there, she went back to work, trying to figure out how to open it.

"So Mom's latch thing worked," I said, going to her. "See? You can't get out now, so why don't you just forget about this boring old window?"

"She sees the world out that window."

I whipped around. Matthias stood with his back against the far wall, hands in his pockets, a smile on his lips. I must have imagined the extra twinkle in his blue eyes. My heart started to pound. His gaze swept me from head to toe, and he came away from the wall. "You're soaking to the skin wet. Are you all right?" he asked.

I warmed at his question, loved that he was concerned about me. Could I fake being hurt or some other such ridiculous thing? Would he finally touch me? I couldn't lie to him, the pure honesty in his face and eyes pierced my conscience and wouldn't allow it.

"I'm fine. Just a little wet."

"A little? You look like a sewer rat."

I cocked back my head. "Thanks a lot."

"No." He held up a hand, apologetic. "I don't mean it like that. It's just you are so very…wet." His gaze traveled over me again, sending sparks just beneath my trembling skin. "You'll catch your death."

"Well, I guess if I was going to die, you'd be the one to tell me."

His face flushed. "There is no such thing as the grim reaper, Zoe. I'd have thought you were smart enough to have figured that out by now."

I was so happy to see him, I didn't care that I was soaking wet. I didn't even care what I looked like, which I imagined was pretty heinous. I didn't care if I was going to die. I couldn't take my eyes off of him, so relieved, so filled with contentment.

A long silence stretched between us. I wanted the keen look in his eye to be for me, though I was sure it was more due to genetics rather than desire. I had so many questions for him, but now my mind was annoyingly blank.

Behind me, I heard Abria at the window. Because Matthias' gaze was intense, almost unbearable, I turned and looked at her, a shiver racing down my spine. "Are you here because Abria was going to open the window?"

The warmth of his body came up behind me. He'd moved closer. I closed my eyes, aching to turn around and stand against him.

"Abria is safe." His tone was soothing.

Sure enough, Abria hadn't figured out how to open the window yet, though her small, deft fingers were working the latch. So, if he wasn't here for Abria…my mind let loose a flock of fantasies. *He's not mortal, you flamer. He's on a mission, a specific mission to help Abria so get your head out of your heart and stop thinking of yourself.*

"She's safe until she figures out this window," I rasped, then cleared my throat. The heat of his body and the overwhelming strength in his being radiated like the sun had dropped from the sky and was perched in Abria's bedroom, its fire pressing through my wet clothes to my shivering skin.

I turned and faced him, wanting to see how close he was. I caught the first scent of him—clouds in a bottle—wispy, fresh and clean. The front of his silky ivory shirt nearly came into contact with my sweater. For a long moment he stared deep into my eyes. I waited for him to take a step back but he didn't.

"If Abria is safe, then why did you come?"

"I think you know the answer to that already, Zoe."

I swallowed. *No, please tell me he's not reading my thoughts. Please.* "You were out for a casual late night check of the neighborhood?" I teased.

The sparkle in his eyes told me he was amused with my response. "That was it, yes. Flying around like Peter Pan, dropping pixie dust here and there."

"I'd like some of that pixie dust, if you have any left."

He lifted his hands and for an instant, I had the fantasy that he was going to set his hands on my shoulders, draw me to him and kiss me. Slowly he lifted his hands over my head and rubbed them back and forth, as if releasing invisible magic over me. I looked up and laughed. *So much for fantasies.*

"Now you're dusty," he said.

"Wet, cold *and* dusty. Nice." I shivered. A faint line formed between his brows.

He stepped back. "Perhaps you should change into something dry."

I didn't want to leave, in case he was gone when I got back. "That's okay. I'm drying, slowly but surely."

"Please. Get into something warm."

I passed him, my eyes glued to his, backing out the door like a star-struck groupie at a celebrity sighting. He smiled and nodded again, gesturing that it was okay for me to go, he'd be there when I got back.

I'd never undressed so fast. I tossed my wet clothes in a heap, grabbed dry underwear, my pink fluffy terrycloth robe and slippers and raced back to Abria's bedroom, tying the sash tight around my waist.

Matthias had Abria in his arms; both were peering out the window and into the dark night.

"You see the lights, Abria? They sparkle, don't they? Like the stars in Heaven."

Abria, silent, attentive, and calm, looked like any normal little girl discovering something for the first time. I leaned my shoulder in the jamb, let out a sigh. To have that kindly effect on people...that power, not for power's sake, but for the sake of comforting another.

"She's so good when you're here," I said.

He turned, gave my robe a once over, and his grip around Abria tightened. He looked at her and lightly skimmed her cheek with his finger. "I'm happy to help her."

I closed the door. "Why does it make you so happy? Not to sound harsh or stupid or anything. It's just that most people are pretty selfish."

"Few things bring satisfaction like being there for someone."

"Did you always feel this way? Or was this something that happened to you because you...after you...died?"

He chuckled. "Definitely after I died." He set Abria on her feet and she scrambled to the window.

I crossed his direction. "So you weren't always perfect."

His warm laugh filled the room. "I'm far from perfect, Zoe."

"No, seriously. Don't be modest. You have this way about you...it's...so real. Like there's nothing fake inside of you anywhere." Whoever he was, I understood that he was beyond special. "Are you Divine?"

"That's very flattering of you to ask. No, I'm not."

"Good, because then you'd have nothing to do with me."

"Why do you say that?"

"I'm a sinner," I smirked.

"Every mortal is."

"So, you don't sin anymore? Is that part of...being who you are now?"

"I can't be where evil is, Zoe."

I shiver chased down my spine. "Seriously? Wow."

He nodded. "Ironic because, in my life I was...let's just say I wasn't sin free by any stretch."

"I want to hear about your life." I moved to the foot of Abria's bed. Matthias, still standing next to the window where Abria stared up at the stars, leaned his back against the wall, crossed his arms and got comfortable.

"What would you like to know?"

"When were you born?"

"Nineteen oh seven."

The date slugged reality into my stomach. Slowly, I eased myself to the edge of Abria's mattress and sat. "That long ago?"

"What did you expect?"

"I don't know, I guess I kind of thought...by the looks of you...that, maybe...well...maybe you'd just died."

He laughed. "That I was a freshie? That's what we call them on the other side. Spirits who've just come through. No. I'm not a freshie. But compared to some of the chaps hanging around there, I guess I could technically pass."

"Nineteen oh seven," I murmured. "So, how old were you when you... sorry, it's kind of awkward to talk about it."

"I was twenty years old." His gaze shifted from Abria to me.

That was all? Gone so soon. "Oh..."

"It was a short life. And I'm sorry to say, not one I'm particularly proud of." He reached for a strand of Abria's hair, and the strand slipped through his fingertips. "But that's the miracle. It's not over."

Our eyes met. His sparkled, like looking through a mirror and into eternity. "I'm blown away by that," I said, marveling at him. "I guess, in my heart, I hoped there was more."

"You're a pondering woman."

I swallowed. *Woman.* "Why do you think that?"

"I never knew any women who thought beyond the moment. They were too distracted by, oh, I don't know, the latest fashions, which party to attend, the current scandal."

"Oh, I'm distracted by those things, too."

"Of course." A grin spread on his face. "But I can tell you ponder. That's a rare quality. It takes discipline to tune out so you can tune in."

"Nicely said. Were you a writer in your lifetime?"

He laughed. "I wish. No. Nothing that gallant."

"What did you do?"

He looked away a moment, and the corner of his jaw twitched. "I worked for my father."

"Oh, nice. Like a family business."

He snickered. "You could say that."

"Those were popular at the turn of the century. I love history. It's my favorite class in school. Wait, if you were born in nineteen oh seven, that would have put your right in the center of the roaring twenties. How cool is that!"

A curious smile played on his lips. "Cool. Another word from Zoe's vocabulary?"

I nodded. "It means awesome. Super nice. Really neat."

"I see. Cool."

"Yeah, it came into vogue around the nineteen seventies, went out of vogue and now it's back again."

"The world spins around and around. It only makes sense that its inhabitants and everything in it would as well, right?"

I laughed. "I guess so. Tell me about what it was like to live when everything was wild and carefree. Did you…" *Marry? Love anyone?* But I couldn't ask those questions. What if his past hurt to talk about?

"Ask. Don't be afraid."

"I'm not afraid. That's what I like about being around you. I just don't want to ask the wrong thing."

"Zoe, those kinds of social constraints are known only in mortality. Ask."

"Like that—what you just said about social constraints being only in mortality—are you saying everyone knows just what to say and how to say it and no one gets offended? Is Heaven like Stepford or something? That idea just blows me away."

"I don't know what Stepford is, but peace prevails in the next world. The argumentative nature no longer exists because death creates a certain, shall we say, equality. The question of continued existence is put to rest, eliminating wondering. With acceptance comes harmony. You see?"

I took a deep breath. Harmony. Peace. Ideals that sounded so foreign in today's world, I could hardly see them actually existing anywhere except maybe in another galaxy. "Were you married?"

The faintest of smiles lifted the corner of his lips. "No."

"Sad," I murmured.

"Marriage was the last thing I wanted. I was a hoodlum—young and selfish. I would have made a terrible husband."

Now I understood why he talked so cute. "I'm sure that's not true." *I think you'd make a perfect husband.* I knew there was no such thing, but a piece of my heart still held onto the fantasy that I would—in spite of, or maybe because of my challenging life—find the perfect guy for me someday.

"Ah, Zoe. Sometimes we can't see what's really valuable. Our vision is clouded by our, shall we say, blind ambition."

"So, was that you?" I said.

"That was very much me."

"What did you want?"

"To be rich and have fun. I wiled away my days in juice joints with any doll I could get my hands on."

"You sound like most of the guys I know. They don't want to do anything but live today and forget tomorrow." It was hard to believe that this beautiful, serene man had once been a player. Of course, he was gorgeous enough to be a player—but his countenance, his spirit, though upbeat and playful at times, was obviously tamer and mellow now, with a seriously deep core—the source of his light.

He shook his head. "Wasting even a moment of precious time is a mistake."

"You really believe that." The regret in his eyes was an echo, but there nonetheless. "But why was your life so short? I mean, you were only twenty. I know they didn't have the medicines and stuff back then that they have now. I'm sorry, this is probably a very personal question—how you died—but…I am curious."

"I didn't get sick, Zoe. I was bumped off in a knife fight." He lifted his shirt. "Fella sliced me from heart to guts. Then the blade caught me right here." He pointed to the scar above his eye.

My stomach knotted with the grisly news. All I saw was smooth skin and chiseled abs. "There's no scar…"

"Immortal bodies don't have imperfections." He smoothed his shirt back down and pointed to the light line over his brow. "I chose to keep this one." A sharp silence snapped the air. "A reminder of the price I paid." His face drew tight and he lowered his head a moment. When he looked up, the sober look in his eyes cut me to the core. "Some mortal reminders serve us best if we keep them."

I wanted to reach out somehow—to offer condolence—but was unable to move, so awed with what he was telling me. "We have gangs now, you know," I said, for lack of anything better to say. "There are a lot of people who get shot or stabbed."

He nodded. "Murder's nothing new."

"It's just so wild. I've never known anyone who was murdered before, but then, how would I? Generally, they aren't alive to talk about it."

"A rather unfortunate consequence, yes." He smiled. "People who pass from this world to the next, the first thing they ask each other is, 'So, how did you die?'"

"Cool. I guess I never thought of that."

"There's a lot of catching up that goes on. Think about it." Enthusiasm gleamed in his eyes. "You're greeted by those who've passed before you, and they're all there to meet you. It's a celebration."

"I never really thought of death as anything but sad."

"Because you've only seen it from this side. It's a nifty reunion."

"Kind of like when a baby is born."

"Now you're on the trolley. Except that people you don't know are there, too. Zoe, the family of Man is enormous."

"You mean…everyone is there?"

"Great, great, great, great grandparents, aunts and uncles. Fifth, sixth, tenth cousins and the likes, the line broken only by MIH's."

"MIH's?"

"Missing in Heaven. Those spirits not allowed to dwell with the good."

"Yikes."

He nodded. "Yikes is right."

My head swirled with thousands of fiery black images of hell. Did Matthias know anything about what happened to bad people when they died? "I have to admit I want to know where the others go, but…"

His jovial grin slowly vanished, replaced by a taut grief that stopped me mid-sentence. A feeling of heaviness filled the room. This was not a topic he cared to discuss, I could tell, and the thought occurred to me not to speak of it further. "What about the others?" I asked, ignoring the whisper of warning.

He studied me long and hard. I almost retracted by question. I was certain he expected me to. He expected me to have respect for a force I should respect without question. "What does your heart tell you?" His tone pierced my curiosity with caution.

"That I shouldn't ask you about them. But why? Why can you tell me about everything else but them?"

"I told you I can't be where evil is, Zoe. Even talking about evil is dangerous. It invites the dark spirit."

My heart thumped. "Okay."

"If people knew how wretched the endless the torment of evil consequence was, they would rather die than give an inch." His body turned stony and tense. He shook his head and closed his eyes. A chill rushed through me. Had he experienced evil for himself? Was that why he seemed tormented just now or did he know of someone who had?

"Is something wrong?" I reached out to lay my hand on his arm and he stepped back, his blue eyes flashing — alive and fiery.

"Nothing's wrong."

"Tell me why you don't want me to touch you."

"I told you, I can only touch whom I am called to serve."

I looked at Abria, standing in the window, on the sill, tapping her hands against the glass as she muttered and sang.

Matthias moved to Abria, scooping her into his arms with a smile that broke the tension. The heaviness in the room dissipated with her squeaking voice. "You're too close to that glass, little miss." Abria eyed his mouth as he spoke. When he let out a soft whistle she listened intently to the pretty tune. I marveled at his ability to keep her attention so riveted to him. She lifted a tiny finger, and, as he continued to whistle, her small finger slowly went to his lips until she finally plugged the small 'o' his mouth made, silencing him.

He threw back his head in a hearty laugh, then hugged her. "You don't like my whistling?" The sight sent warm floods of love through my body. I closed my eyes a moment, imagining what it would feel like to have a heavenly being wrap around me and comfort me.

Indescribable.

When I opened my eyes, he was looking at me, his eyes kind, lips curved in a soft smile. Heat flushed my cheeks. *Thank heavens he can't read my thoughts. He'd think I was a psycho.* "Why can you only touch who you watch over?" I asked.

"It's a law, Zoe. I don't ask why, I just obey."

"Don't you even want to know why? I could never do something just because someone told me to do it—never. I have to know the reasons."

His lips turned up in a teasing grin. "You *are* a bearcat. Your sister doesn't take any bunk from anyone, does she, Abria?"

"If you mean crap, yeah, that's me." His eyes widened, as if the word had shocked him. "Sorry, that's probably harsh," I said. "But you're right. I don't like bunk, never have never will."

"But I'm not giving you bunk, Zoe. Obedience isn't bunk, either. I know, I know, in the mortal state obedience is a foul word."

"Well, it's true. When I hear the word I have visions of belts and whips. And begging—something I will never, ever in my lifetime do."

Matthias' brows drew together over discerning eyes. "You really have an aversion to submission, don't you?"

"Yep, and proud of it."

He tilted his head and held me in a razor-sharp gaze for a moment. He set Abria down, and came toward me, slow. Easy. My heart jumped. He stopped close enough that his breath, warm and sweet with the scent of peppermint, tickled my face. His eyes held me still. "So, if I was to ask you to come with me this very second, no questions asked, you'd refuse?"

My knees shook, not from fear, but from being so close to him. I couldn't lie. Yes, I would go wherever he wanted me to go and do whatever he wanted me to do. The realization stunned me. I opened my mouth. No sound came.

His gaze dropped to my lips for a moment before he grinned. "Well?"

"I…uh…"

"You haven't answered my question."

"Your ques—well, maybe I would—for you. Because you do that thing…whatever it is you do when I'm around you."

"I don't *do* anything purposefully. You know that, don't you?"

"Yes, I know that," I said. "It's just who you are…*what*…you are."

"Mm, yes. So if you don't mind, tell me once again what I do?" His tone teased.

"You make me feel…good." I took a deep, content breath. Moments ticked by. Finally, his taunting expression shifted to something more serious and he stepped back as if the game we'd been silently playing was over.

"It's getting very late," he said, quietly.

I glanced at my watch. "It's three-thirty!" I looked around for Abria— she'd been so quiet, I hadn't noticed where she was—in bed, fast asleep. I kissed her goodnight and looked at Matthias.

He stood by the window, like Peter Pan ready to fly away. Please don't go, I thought. "You're leaving, aren't you?"

He nodded.

I'll go. Anywhere you ask. But I couldn't say that to him. Even if I felt like I could follow him to Mars, I wouldn't tell him. My will was the one thing I was not prepared to give anyone.

NINE

I couldn't wait to get to school the next day and talk to Chase. I dressed in jeans, a long-sleeved white tee and a red hoodie, pulled my hair back into a pony tail. I kissed Mom goodbye, got Abria on the bus and drove to school.

The parking lot was filling with student cars when I arrived. I found the closest spot I could, cut the engine and grabbed my backpack. I got out, locking the door with a click of remote. Winter was on the doorstep, its penetrating knock seeped through my clothes, bringing a shudder to my limbs.

I started toward the building, cell phone in hand. It vibrated. Britt.

hey where r u

in the lot u?

at my locker wanna do lunch

yeah. with weston?

yeah that ok?

im cool with it if he is

sure he is

he doesn't mind a third wheel?

U r not a 3rd wheel

lol k

It seemed like years since I'd talked to her even though it'd only been a day. When I thought about all that had happened with Matthias, it was like being on vacation in some far-off location, seeing and experiencing things no one else could relate to.

It was lame that I couldn't share what was happening with Britt. She was my closest confidant. There wasn't anything I didn't tell her. This was a first, and it challenged every female tendency I'd had since birth to whisper and share secrets.

Matthias, Matthias, Matthias. I needed school today; the distraction would get my mind off him. Yet, I couldn't help it: with every toffee-colored haired guy I passed I hoped to see his face.

What would it be like if he was here? What would he think of today's world? How much of today had he seen? Obviously, his exposure was limited because he didn't even know about cell phones.

He was so untainted. So pure. I was tired of jaded guys. Matthias was so far above jaded he floated in misty white clouds of purifying perfection, at least from my perspective. *Listen to you, you sound like a total psych case.* Thank heavens Matthias wasn't around to hear my blue genie thoughts.

"What's that smile all about?" Britt's voice tickled my ear. I'd been so out of it, I hadn't noticed I'd walked right by her locker.

"Oh, hey."

"Don't 'oh hey' me," Britt teased. "I know lust when I see it, and you've got it in your eyes, babe. I want to hear *all* about it."

I cocked my head, aghast. "Lust?" Decency and indecency collided in my brain. "This isn't lust."

"But there is someone."

"I told you there was."

"The special ed guy?"

"Yeah, that's him."

"I've never seen you so...taken." She eyed me, envy and curiosity flashing over her face. She leaned close. "Has he *taken* you yet?"

I was hit with another slug of disgust at her implication. Not too long ago I would have slathered all over the chance to share sordid details. But the friendship between Matthias and I wasn't raunchy, it was beautiful. "No, and he's not going to *take* me, either," I said, bite in my tone.

Britt stopped. Around her, bodies hurriedly filed to class. I stopped, turned and faced her, enjoying the white shock on her open-mouthed face.

"What?!" Britt asked.

I continued walking, smiling. Pleased. I felt like I'd just told her I'd won the lottery and chosen to give all the earnings to charity.

"He must not be hot, then," Britt decided. We stopped outside of her first period class.

"Oh, he's hot. Trust me."

"Then why won't you hook up with him?"

Because he's dead, I wanted to say with a laugh. But she'd just think it was a joke. And Matthias wasn't really dead. He had a wonderful body of flesh and bone. Pristine. Perfect. Beautiful.

I just couldn't touch it.

"He's what you might say *off limits*. It's a job-related thing." I started down the hall to class. "See you in Brinkerhoff's."

"Yeah." Her puzzled expression was priceless, and I carried it with me the rest of the morning.

The hours between first period and lunch dragged tortuously on. I took each class fifty minutes at a time, forcing myself to concentrate on what the teacher was saying.

I'd liked boys before, but that was nothing compared to the complete submersion of Matthias. Every door that opened caused my head to jerk upright, hoping it was him walking into the classroom, even though I knew he never would. Every toffee-colored head of hair caught my eye. I could have sworn I caught his breeze-in-the-clouds scent as I walked behind a group of guys on their way out of the building to lunch.

The obsession kept a grin on my face.

I met Britt at her car, where she and Weston were leaning against it, wrapped in a kissing session. His friends clustered around the back of her white convertible Mustang, trying to pretend they didn't see the lovey couple eating each other's faces. Normally, I'd let out a teasing whoop when I found her making out in public, earning myself a laugh from Britt. Today, her PDA looked so typically teenagerish, I rolled my eyes and greeted the guys standing at the back of her car, one of whom was forgot-my-name Brady. *Oh, brother.* I swallowed a lump of discomfort lodged in my throat.

"Maybe if we make enough noise, they'll come up for air," I told the guys with a good-natured snicker. They laughed. Brady smiled.

Britt must have heard my purposefully-loud comment, for she broke her sucker-fish kiss with Weston and looked over. "Okay, okay." They kissed one more time and then Weston opened the car door for her. She handed him her keys.

He's driving her car already? Britt usually insisted at least two months go by before she handed any guy her keys.

Weston came around the back of the car. "Meet us at McDonalds," he told the guys. They scattered to their vehicles. Weston sent me a glittering grin. "Hey, Zoe. You're riding with us, right?"

"Um, sure."

He opened the driver's side door and held back the front seat for me. I crawled in.

Britt's eyes sparkled, following Weston's every move. He got in, kissed her again, and started the engine.

Something wild poured out of the speakers. I'd never heard this CD before, and I looked at Britt, waiting for her to tell me who it was, but she only had eyes for Weston. She had hands and fingers for him too. She laced hers in his hair, twisting little waves of his curls around and around.

"That drives me crazy," Weston said, his low voice charged with what I knew was teenaged-boy lust.

"I know," Britt lulled, "that's why I do it."

I swallowed a snort. There was about as much love in their eyes as there was honesty. I cringed thinking about the countless times I'd talked to nameless guys that very same way.

"So, Britt tells me you've got a teacher you're trying to hook up with." Weston's gaze met mine through the rear view mirror. "Cool. You like older men?"

I fought rolling my eyes at him, and pasted a smile on my face. "Not older men, no." It wasn't any of his business who I liked. What was Britt doing sharing my personal life with Weston? Had she done that with every guy she'd liked all these years?

"You said he was a teacher," Britt said.

"He's not a teacher," I bit out. "He's…the closest thing I can describe him as is an aide. I told you that."

"I must have forgotten." Britt shrugged and she and Weston shared a look I only caught from the side but was clearly punched with 'whatever.'

I wanted to get out of the car but that was impossible. What made it worse was that I was stuck eating lunch with these actors and the scene was bound to get cheesier at McDonalds.

Finally, we pulled into the parking lot of the fast food restaurant. Weston's friends parked their cars next to us and we all piled out. I didn't have to let this annoy me. If Matthias had been here, I had the feeling he would make the best of it. I could try doing that.

Britt looked at me, gauging my mood. I smiled. The relief on her face made me feel better. Even if she was caught in this superficial play, I was still her friend and I cared about her. I'd played along countless times before. I could now.

She hooked her arm in Weston's and the two of them started toward the building, leaving the rest of us to trail behind. "Hey," I said to Brady walking next to me.

"Hey, Zoe."

"Ah, you know my name," I teased.

His face turned red. "Yeah, I try to learn from my mistakes."

"That's a good thing," I said, impressed with his honesty. Brady hung beside me as the group of us ordered and when we sat, he asked if he could sit next to me. McDonalds buzzed with chatter. Soon, Weston's friends were talking and joking. Weston and Britt nuzzled and fed each other fries while Brady struggled to carry on a conversation with me.

"We've never had a class together," he said.

"No, I don't think we have." I bit into my cheeseburger and hid the smile blooming on my face. He was trying so hard.

"I know your brother. Luke, right?"

A pit opened in my stomach. "Uh, yeah." When people told me they knew Luke I was never sure what to expect. "So how do you know him?"

"He was in metal shop with me last year."

Phew. At least it wasn't drug-related. "Oh. Cool. Yeah, he's pretty handy."

"Seems like it."

We both chewed for a moment.

"You're not really like him," Brady said after a while. "You party, I've seen you party, but he...well..."

My stomach rolled over. *Here it comes.* "He and I party differently," I said.

He nodded. "My brother, Kevin, parties like Luke. That's another reason I know him. I just didn't want to say, in case you didn't know."

"Oh, thanks, but I know."

His expression, a flash of sadness masked by a cool shrug told me he knew the depth of my worries and that he felt the same way for his brother.

"It's hard isn't it?" I said.

"Yeah."

"Do you ever feel helpless?"

"All the time."

"I wish I knew what I could do. I wish telling him to stop was enough."

"It's not that easy, though."

I scanned him in search of the meaning behind his comment. Had he been caught up in an addiction of his own?

Britt's laugh drew my attention. She and Weston were sharing sips of a shake. Weston's other buddies were trying not to watch her full lips wrap around the straw.

"Yeah, it's not that easy," I repeated, wondering if Brady would open up. One thing Luke's addiction had taught me was that I might feel helpless to do anything for my brother, but that didn't mean I couldn't do something for somebody else.

In the second it took him to tip back the last of his drink, his expression shifted from brotherly concern to a growing interest in me. His eyes lusted over a smile. "So, how about if I call you some time? Or do you have a boyfriend?"

"I wouldn't have been in your bedroom last weekend if I had a boyfriend, would I?"

He lifted his shoulders. "To some girls that wouldn't matter."

"Not this girl."

His brows drew together in confusion. "That surprises me, I guess."

"What, you heard I was a skank?" Shame flushed my skin and prickled my defenses.

"Well, kinda, yeah."

I set an elbow on the table. "Is that why you wanted to hook up the other night? I was an easy score?"

His wide eyes darted around the table to see if anyone was listening. I didn't bother checking to see whose attention we had, I couldn't care less.

"What?" I pressed. "Can't take the truth when it's broad daylight?"

"No, that's not it." His gaze averted just like it had the other night when he hadn't known my name.

Knowing my name hadn't really changed anything.

I stared him down until he wouldn't look at me anymore. *Forget what you might have heard about me, I'm no skank and I'm not somebody you can walk all over with your hot bod and it-guy charms.* "Look," I said matter-of-factly, "call me if you want to do something other than hook up."

His gaze brightened as if he'd just pulled his head out of an invisible barrel of social garbage. "Okay. Sure." He whipped out his cell phone and I recited my number while he entered it into his sim card.

"We good to go?" Weston asked, standing over me and Brady. I hadn't noticed he was there and wondered how long he'd been tuned into our conversation.

"Yeah, we are," I said.

After school, I pulled out of the parking lot and headed home. My cell phone vibrated on the passenger's seat of my car. Chase. I plucked up the phone and read his text:

how r u? any time you want 2 talk about…stuff…we can.

I texted back:

yeah starbucks at 7?

really? ok. cool.

My phone rang. Luke.

"Hi," I said.

"My piece of hud car won't start," Luke grumbled. "Can I get a ride?"

"Yeah, where are you?"

"Near Lambert Street."

He must have skipped his last class. Lambert Street was on the lower west side of town. Trailer parks, crumbling houses. Dead trees, scrungy cars and even scrungier people. I had to figure one of his drug pals lived there.

"I'll start walking to city center," he grumbled.

Because you don't want me to see where you are. "Fine, I'll see you in a few."

I headed west to the crusty part of town. Overhead, skies began to blacken with bulging clouds. I shuddered and cranked up the heater. Would seeing someone like Matthias do anything at all to Luke? If he knew there were guardians, that life continued after this life, would he be the same narrow-focused boy or would the knowledge broaden his mind? Change his choices?

When I finally saw him, head hanging as he walked shoulders hunched in his grey flannel coat, sympathy tugged at my heart. I put aside my frustration. At least he'd called me for a ride and hadn't bummed one from someone who could endanger his life driving under the influence.

I pulled over and he got in.

"Hey," I said.

"Hey."

The air he carried in to the car with him didn't smell like smoke, thank heavens.

"Are you going to have it towed?"

"Probably, yeah." He whipped out his cell phone, read text messages, answered them, then he dialed a number. I listened as he arranged for a tow. After the call, he stuffed his phone away in the pocket of his coat.

"Do you believe in guardian angels?"

"What the?" His face twisted.

"I'm just curious."

"How should I know? I've never thought about it."

"You've never once thought there might be guardians out there, watching over us?"

"Nope." He stared out the window, his face angled so I couldn't see it any longer.

"I have," I admitted, to see where it got me. He didn't respond. "I've thought about it for Abria. I mean, isn't it possible there's someone special watching over her so she's safe?"

"Yeah, *us*. Every hour of every day."

"I'm talking about heavenly beings."

"I guess."

"Haven't you wondered why we find her when she runs away?"

"Because we look?" A pinch of sarcasm lined his tone.

"Yeah, we look. But we *always* find her. And what about all the times she's put something in her mouth and never swallowed it? Or the times she stood on the stair railing and we found her just in time? How do you explain that?"

"Luck, I guess."

"I don't believe its luck. I think there's someone assigned to her."

"Assigned?" He looked at me for a minute, then out at the road ahead. "Then what about all those kids who get hit by a car? Or kidnapped and killed? Or the ones who drown? Who's watching them? I don't know, it sounds like a flawed idea."

"Maybe it was their time to go," I said, half irritated he wasn't at least giving my suggestion some credence.

"You're saying God is flawed then, that's what you're saying."

"No, I'm not I saying that." His answer made me realize he'd indeed given this some thought or he wouldn't have attached God to it. Nor would he have listed all those kids, the ones you hear about in the news and your heart tears when you read about them. I also realized I didn't have all the answers. "What do you think?"

He turned his face out the window again. I couldn't see him. "I don't know."

A thick pause filled the small space of the car. We were almost home. I wished we weren't. Even though we hadn't agreed, we'd talked, and I felt the broken overpass between us starting to come together.

I pulled into the driveway and parked. My eye caught Luke's bedroom window over the garage. It was closed, but standing inside the glassed frame was Abria, laughing. And in the shadows behind her stood Matthias. My heart jumped.

"Oh, no." I pointed to Abria. Luke froze. For a second, I wondered if he saw Matthias too.

We both got out. He whipped out his cell phone. "I'm calling Mom," he said, running past me and to the front door.

I smiled up at Matthias and sent him a tilt of my head. He grinned back.

By the time I got upstairs, Mom and Luke were in Luke's room. Mom clutched Abria to her chest like a newborn baby. Leaning against a far wall was Matthias. I tried to pretend he wasn't there, but that was like being in an elevator with the sun and not squinting from the light. His very presence sent my body into a fit of trembling warmth.

"She was in the window," Mom said, her voice shaky. She gave me a what-am-I-going-to-do look.

"Yeah, we saw her." I crossed to Mom and Abria with a smile on my face because Matthias was near and comfort swept through my system. My gaze was drawn to his like an artist to a Monet.

Mom noticed my giant grin and glanced over her shoulder. "What are you smiling about?"

"I'm just glad she's safe. Aren't you, Luke?"

"Yeah, of course." He seemed jumpy. Mom didn't catch his nervous glance around the bedroom, but I did.

Mom carried Abria out the door. "Can you help me set the table, Zoe?"

"Sure, be right down."

"Luke, I need you to keep an eye on Abria while I throw dinner together. Follow her. I don't want her climbing into any more windows."

"K. Be there in a sec."

Mom was gone, but I wasn't ready to leave, not yet. "Better go," I told him.

"After you," he said, clearly unwilling to leave me alone in his bedroom.

I tried to send Matthias a silent message to stay put by tilting my head when Luke wasn't looking, but Luke was more attentive than I'd seen him in months—suspiciously attentive in fact.

Leaving Matthias was hard, knowing that I might not see him again any time soon. I turned and left so Luke would also leave. He shut the bedroom door when we were both in the hall and went in search of Abria.

In the kitchen, I threw the tablecloth on the table, tossed silverware into place and Frisbeed paper plates in position. Mom looked over.

"Paper?"

"Thought I'd keep it simple tonight."

"You in a hurry?"

"Um, kinda, yeah." I plopped down green plastic cups that matched the flowered plates. "Be back in a sec." Then I raced upstairs. I stopped at Luke's door, listened for his voice and was pleased when I heard it coming from somewhere downstairs. He was talking to Abria. We weren't allowed in each others' rooms, but I couldn't *not* go in and see Matthias.

I opened the door, slid in and quietly shut it. Matthias had his back to me, his posture confident and sure as he stared out the window. He wore eggshell blue slacks in that soft fabric that draped alluringly down his long legs. His shirt was long-sleeved and off-white.

He turned and my heart leapt.

"Zoe." His smile filled the room and poured into my being like I'd just drunk a beam of sunlight. "I take it you were giving me a signal to stay?"

"Yes," I nodded, knees shaky, body quivering. I took a step his direction. "Thanks for being here, for watching over Abria again."

He nodded once, like royalty granting me a majestic confirmation.

"She's determined to get out these windows, isn't she?" I joined him and looked at the driveway below.

He raised a hand and gently ran his palm along the casing." It wasn't the window I was here about, actually." He faced me, expression sober.

"Oh?"

"There's something dangerous in your brother's room. Underneath his bed."

I crossed to the bed and dropped down, peering under the mattress. The sheer backing had been slit in one section and a small portion hung down, revealing the slats and springs of the box. I reached my hand up along the wood and felt a plastic bag and pulled it out. My stomach sunk. Three prescription bottles of Lortabs.

I swallowed and stood, holding them in my hand. "I guess I shouldn't be surprised."

"If Abria got into that, it could be fatal," he said.

"Yeah." I stuffed the containers into my jeans pocket. "How did you know they were there?"

"Anything that might harm Abria is brought to my attention."

"Good," I said, soothed by unspeakable relief. I thought about Luke's comment earlier when he'd asked me about kids who died. But I was too happy to see Matthias to get into a heavy discussion about life, death and fate at the moment. "That's good. I'd kill him if she ever got hurt because of something he did."

Matthias' demeanor went stony. "Please don't say that. You speak of serious matters when you threaten to kill."

"Well I would." Steaming, I paced the side of Luke's bed. "How could he be so stupid to hide drugs here at the house? No wonder he was nervous about her being in his room today. Did you see how anxious he was for me to leave?"

"Guilt has a tendency to wrack the bones."

"It'd more than wrack his bones if she ever got a hold of those Lortabs. He'd go to jail for about ninety years."

He studied me a moment, his head tilted. "In your heart of hearts you don't want to see that happen."

"No. But sometimes I wish he'd learn a lesson and shape up."

"Sometimes that's all it takes. But sometimes the road is much longer. Zoe, you have to be patient. Have faith."

"How can I have faith in him when he's not trying?"

"Do you know he's not trying?"

"He's not changing, is he?"

"Zoe." He stepped closer and though he didn't touch me, his nearness swiped away my anger. "Change isn't as easy as snapping your finger."

"It's easy if you just decide to do something. Come on Matthias, everybody's got their turning point, their rock bottom or whatever you want to call it."

"And for everyone it's different. If we all learned the lesson the first time around the track, there'd be no need for a stadium, for coaches, for cheerleaders, for those people who maintain the field so we can pick ourselves up and try again."

"Hey, that was pretty good," I grinned. "You sure you don't moonlight on the side as a writer?"

His cheeks flushed. "Very sure. But feel free to use anything I say in your work. Give Luke your faith, Zoe. Can you look into his heart?"

"No. Only you can do that, right?"

He smiled. "Everyone can look into another's heart. People just don't usually take the time to do it."

"Don't I have to have special vision or something?" I blew out, plopping on the foot of Luke's bed. Matthias sat at the head.

"No special vision needed," he chuckled, "just the pure desire for truth."

I took a deep breath. A thought struck me. "Then I should be able to look into your heart," I teased.

A grin spread his lips wide. "Yes. You can."

I brought my legs up on the bed and settled in. "This will be interesting," I said, wrapping my arms around my knees, locking my gaze on the clear depth of his blue eyes. He positioned himself a little closer, so he faced me straight on, close enough that I caught the scent of him—crisp, clean, with a bite of citrus.

As if a mere look could put me in a trance, my body and senses lulled into a relaxed, cozy state of total comfort, yet each nerve was alert and open, ready to be stimulated and nurtured.

"What do you see, Zoe?"

The most beautiful man ever. The kindest soul I've ever met. Real. Honest. True. "Your eyes…how do you do that?"

"I'm not doing anything but looking at you."

"But when you look at me, I…" I couldn't tell him that I wanted to put my arms around him and simply hold him. Feel him. The desire I had to touch him came from my heart, not from the female inside who'd wanted boys to scratch an itch. I wanted what he had, what he was: honest, real, full of love.

128

"There's so much love inside of you," I heard myself say. My eyes shot wide at the honest admission. I'd never spoken that frankly to a guy before for the risk of being too honest and facing rejection. But Matthias' aura lined the room with protection and safety.

He lowered his head a moment, as if humbled by what I'd said.

I continued, awed, "No games, no false humility for a swift pat on your own back. Just real."

He laughed. "You're the bees knees."

There was a compliment in that endearing phrase, I was sure of it. "You said you worked for your dad in a family business?"

"The term *family business* being very loosely applied here. My father ran a speakeasy in the basement of a church."

"In a church? Wow. That was…gutsy."

"Sacrilegious to say the least…" His blue eyes looked away, as if in painful thought. I was dying to know more. Had he seen his father since he'd died? Where was the man?

In spite of the old regret that flashed over him, he held serenity in his countenance, a feeling I yearned for but understood I couldn't have completely—not right now anyway. Whatever tranquility possessed him, possessed him because of who he now was. I had the fleeting wish that I was dead. Then I could really be at peace.

Another wish that would remain a wish from a fantasy genie who didn't exist.

Matthias rose and smiled down at me. "All is well here for the time being."

I shot to my feet, bringing our bodies close. "Don't go."

"When my work is done, I go on. That's the rule. Nothing is wasted. Especially not time."

"Am I a waste of time?"

"No, I didn't mean that. But I'm here for a certain purpose."

"And I'm not it, I get it." I looked away; afraid he'd see the disappointment I felt.

≥ ✦ ≤

"You're capable of understanding this, I know you are." His voice was tender. I met his caring gaze. Calm quietly crept in and settled around my yearning, soothing the bruised edges. "Until we meet again. Take care, Zoe."

This time, I would watch him go. My eyes locked on his. So tight, so intensely, the powerful vibe between us seemed to jerk my whole being into a fist. I refused to blink for fear he'd go and I'd not see him disappear. Gradually, light glowed from his every pore, shooting out in blinding, penetrating beams I felt like heat. The room filled with his radiance, so white and piercing I had to close my eyes, shield my face from the sheer power behind the force. My breath rang in and out. My heart sped. Then the light was gone.

I opened my eyes to an empty room.

Tears came. I blinked. My heart, still racing beneath my ribs, ached with longing. The void left behind by his absence was chilled by a deep silence that quickly moved into my vulnerable, exposed soul.

I lowered to the foot of Luke's bed and sat, staring at the empty place where just seconds before Matthias had stood. How long I sat there, I wasn't sure. My eyes remained fixed on empty air, undeviating, as if in a daze—dulled by the lack I now felt inside.

"What are you doing in here?" Luke's voice broke into my trance. I turned, saw him standing in the open door.

"I was thinking," I muttered.

"Well, think somewhere else." He stepped toward the bed, his suspicious gaze flicking to the bottom. "It's time for dinner, anyway," he said.

I stood, pulled the bag of Lortabs from my pocket and held it out in the palm of my hand. His eyes widened. "These can't be in here, Luke. Abria might find them."

"You searched my room?"

"Sort of. Not really."

He grabbed for the bag but I swiped my hand behind my back. His face flushed with fury. "Give me those."

"Like I'd really hand an addictive substance over to an addict," I snapped.

"They're mine!"

I stuffed the bag of bottles into the front pocket of my jeans.

He stepped back, and scraped his hands down his face, leaving red stripes. "You have to give me those."

"No way. And I don't want you bringing anything else into the house that could harm Abria. Use your head, Luke! She doesn't know the difference between candy and pills, food and marijuana! She just puts it in her mouth!"

"She would never have found that. How did you find it?"

"A little bird told me."

"One of my friends?"

I rolled my eyes. "Like I ever talk to any of your friends."

"I need to know who ratted me out."

"No one ratted on you, I just found them, okay?"

He crammed both hands into his hair. "I need those, Zoe. I can't sleep at night and those help."

"So you have your friends give you the leftovers of their parents' prescriptions? How much did you pay for these? Or are these friends of yours trading you Lortabs for weed? You're so deep into it it's scary. Take a good look at yourself and see where you really are."

He fell back against the wall, agitated, emotions bubbling near the surface. He'd been a zombie for so long, this display of feelings mesmerized me. "You don't understand," he wailed.

I shut the bedroom door so his voice wouldn't travel. "Listen to you. You sound like…" *an addict*, I thought. He *was* an addict. For the first time, I realized how desperate his situation really was. Frightening. Huge. A black hole ready to engulf him.

I debated giving him back the bag just to ease the taut anguish on his face, but something inside of me whispered I shouldn't give in. I needed to help him and helping him did not entail adding trees to an already out of control brush fire.

He was lost in his head, his cravings eating him from the inside out, scoring his face with torment. My heart ripped in two. *What should I do?*

Matthias? Can anyone help him?

"Just give me the bag," his voice scraped out.

A calming patience came over me. For a flash, I saw Luke as a little boy, blue eyes wide and happy, cherubic face shining in a contagious smile. Inside of that mixed up teenager, lived that little boy. I believed the child was calling out for help whether the teenager heard him, acknowledged him, or not.

"I can't," I said softly.

He let out a moan, scrubbing his face with his hands. "You know what, fine. Fine." He yanked open the bedroom door and stormed out.

"Where are you going?" I trailed him. We skipped like tattle-tails down the stairs.

In the kitchen, Mom glanced at Luke. He stormed by, snatching Mom's car keys on his way out the front door but with Abria to keep an eye on, Mom didn't follow us.

"I need your car," he called.

"Where's yours?" she asked. I glanced at her over my shoulder. She stood in the kitchen opening, confusion on her face.

Luke didn't answer just opened the front door.

"His car is being towed here," I told her, then took off after him. "Where are you going?" I stayed on his heels.

Luke jogged out into a thick blanket of falling snow. I hoped he wasn't going somewhere to get high, but in my heart of hearts, I figured that was reality.

He got in Mom's car and the mini van started up, sending a white plume into the air as he screeched out of the driveway.

My cell phone vibrated in my pocket. I closed the front door and reached in; hope in my heart it was Luke calling or texting me. Britt.

wanna hang?

where's weston?

busy. want 2?

Tempted as I was to ignore the pressing urgency building inside of me to go after Luke, I couldn't suppress the exigency to follow him. Not only that, but I was supposed to meet up with Chase at Starbucks later.

cant sorry

waaaahh pwease?

While Britt whined, Luke got farther away. I ran to my car. I started the engine and texted Britt back: **sorry** then tossed my cell phone into the passenger side seat.

Snow coated the roads, an inch of translucent sludge I drove through slowly, following the minivan tracks up the street that wound into the neighborhood East of our house. To my right, the screen of my cell phone lit up and vibrated, like a crying baby calling for attention. Britt's number flashed.

Far ahead, red tail lights from the mini van barely beamed through the veil of white coming down. *Where are you going?*

The van took a right. I didn't know the neighborhood he was driving into very well, so I sped up a little, afraid of losing him on another turn somewhere.

Luke pulled over in front of a dark brown house that looked like the cabin on the Log Cabin syrup bottle. Smoke from the brick chimney swirled into the black sky. I hung at the end of the block with my car lights off so Luke wouldn't see me. He didn't even look. He ran up to the door, knocked and waited. The door finally opened and he vanished inside.

Had I pushed him too far?

TEN

When I finally arrived at Starbucks, I was shocked to see the parking lot packed. What were all these people doing here? Hadn't they seen the weather? Driven on the roads?

I stomped from the car to the buzzing place, lit up like a lighthouse. Inside, the warm, heavenly-scent of coffee in the air eased my tense muscles. Low monotone chatter comforted. I let out a breath, shook off the snow and looked for Chase.

A frantic movement in the corner caught my attention. He jittered and waved like he had to pee. I quickly made my way over so he'd stop.

"Hey. I wasn't sure you'd make it."

"Me either." I reached to pull out a chair and he jumped over and did it for me. "Thanks." I sat.

He sat across from me. Four empty cups of what might have been hot chocolate sat in front of him. Maybe he *did* have to pee. "You been here long?" I asked.

"No. Not really." His cheeks turned the color of ripe apples. His gaze traveled my body. "No coat?"

"I'm one of those girls who don't believe in coats." I shrugged. "Or umbrellas. Or anything protective whatsoever." He, on the other hand, had on a thick sweater—a dark green cable knit cardigan he must have borrowed from his grandfather's closet because no guy in this millennium would be caught dead wearing a cable knit cardigan.

"Oh," he said.

I clasped my hands on the table. "So, here we are."

"Here we are," he chimed. He shifted in his chair as if needles were on the seat. "You want anything to drink?"

"Yeah, I'll take a sugar free caramel steamer. Thanks."

He blinked, stammered, "Oh. Yeah. Okay, I'll be right back."

I watched him go to the counter, then my gaze swept the room for anyone familiar. No one. The last thing I needed was another complication. Knowing we could talk without being seen by anyone from school relaxed me and I crossed my arms on the table, set my chin on them and closed my eyes, eager to savor the time away from my troubles.

Hearing movement some time later, I opened my eyes and was relieved to look into Chase's familiar puppy face. I bet he'd never done anything bad. He set down two steaming cups.

"Thanks." I reached for the drink he slid my direction. My cold hands circled around the warm cup.

"You're welcome." He sat, stared at me.

So he wasn't the most socially suave guy I'd ever met. Virtue had its price. I felt comfortable with him, that was nice.

"Tell me about your other sighting," I said before a sip.

He leaned forward. "Well, okay. Once when I was really young, I was camping with my family. I'm one of five kids, and my parents were pretty distracted, setting up camp and all that. My older brother and sister were fighting—as usual—arguing about who was going to get the red sleeping bag, because it was the fluffiest and smelled like cedar balls. My baby sister was screaming her head off, which killed my ears. I hated it when she cried. It sounded like a screeching train loose in my brain. So I walked a little ways away from camp. It was quieter in the trees, so I kept walking, looking at the flora and fauna on the ground. Pretty soon, I didn't hear anything. I looked around and all I saw was trees."

"Where you scared?"

"Oddly, no. The noise back at camp had been so loud, I was happy to

135

be alone."

"Did you know you were lost?"

He shook his head. "It didn't occur to me for a while. I kept walking, picking up bugs and rocks. The forest has the coolest ecosystem—" He stopped himself. "Anyway, when it started getting dark, that's when I got scared. I called for my parents but nothing happened. I cried. Then, out of nowhere, I heard my name."

A chill raced down my spine.

He leaned closer. " 'Chase,' the voice said. I turned around and there stood this pretty lady. Well, she wasn't really a lady, she was a girl. Older. But not too old. Just not young. Anyway, she was in a long, pink dress. She had blonde hair and the prettiest smile. Her hand was extended and she told me to come sit with her. She took my hand and led me to a rock and we sat."

"Wow," I murmured.

"Yeah," he nodded. "It's strange because I remember that she…" He glanced around, then leaned close. "She glowed. Like a pink candle. And her voice was so soothing…like being in a bathtub of warm water. When she touched me, I knew I'd be okay."

I nodded, knowing first hand how complete such comfort felt. "Did she say anything more?"

"She just told me my parents would come for me soon."

"And did they?"

"I don't know how much longer we sat there." He lifted his shoulders. "It didn't matter, because I was safe."

"Wow." I reached for my drink but was too enthralled by his story to sip. "Wow." I couldn't believe someone else on this huge planet had experienced what I'd experienced.

"I heard my mom crying. Then I heard Dad calling for me and— voila—there they were, running toward me. I remember looking at the puny flashlights they were carrying and thinking how tiny they were compared to the light around her."

"What happened then?"

"Mom squeezed me to death. At first Dad was relieved to see me, then he got all mad and started railing on me as we walked back to camp. I hate it when he does that—goes all bi-polar."

I sipped my drink. "I guess you've never lost anyone before. My sister has autism and she runs all the time. No one knows why kids with autism run, they just do. It's scary."

"Yeah, I've heard of that. That would be scary. So, is that how you saw your spirit?"

I nodded. "He's not my spirit, actually. He's Abria's."

"Tell me about him."

How do you describe a heavenly being? Of course I didn't have to; Chase had had his own experiences with them. As I explained my first interaction at the park, down to the last time I'd seen Matthias, Chase's attention remained riveted to me.

His eyes glittered. "You go your whole life thinking the idea of angels and Heaven is a fantasy and then, voila it's real."

"I always thought it was real."

"I guess I was more of a skeptic."

"So it took your aunt and the lady in the forest before you accepted that guardians are real?"

"I kept thinking what happened to me had to have been a product of fear, in the case of my aunt's death or fear and exposure the in case of the lady in the forest."

"It's a gift," I told him. "Matthias told me those with pure souls and open minds see spirits."

"He said that? Wow." He sat back. "You've had extensive visitations."

"It's safe to say I've moved from visitations to residency."

Chase's brows drew together in a flash of suspicion. "What do you mean?"

"I mean I've seen Matthias about four times now, and it doesn't look like his visits are over. He's Abria's guardian, and, lucky for me, that means he's hers forever."

He shook his head. "Not according to Sariah."

I bristled at the thought that Matthias was not going to be around indefinitely. I reached for my drink, squeezing the cup. "Who the *h* is Sariah?"

"A spirit I met last year when my nephew was in the hospital. The coolest lady. She lived around 100 BC."

I sat upright. "Serious? How did you find that out?"

"She told me. Really cool story, actually. She was one of like ten wives this old guy had. She lived in this ancient city…" He whacked himself on the side of the head. "I can't remember the name. This place sounded unbelievable. You know, houses built into the mountain sides, market places, sports arenas, parties that put Sodom and Gomorrah to shame."

"That was some conversation."

"I was getting smart." He tapped his temple. "By the time I met Sariah, I had too many questions to let her go without an inquisition."

"And she was okay with that?"

"She was totally okay with it."

"She said she'd been assigned to Nathan—that's my nephew and her zillionth great grand nephew—for the duration of his stay in the hospital. I asked her if she would always be his guardian, even after he was well, and she said no. Guardianship is transitory."

"Maybe in your nephew's case, but Abria has autism."

Chase blinked at my defensive tone. "I guess time will tell."

I chugged the rest of my drink, even though my stomach churned like a washing machine thinking that Matthias might be replaced—out of my life—Abria's life.

"Do you know anything else about Matthias?" He sat forward, eagerness spilling out like soda from a shaken bottle.

"He's not as…*old* as Sariah. Old being relative once you're dead. He lived during the nineteen twenties."

"He's a baby then."

"Matthias calls them 'freshies,'" I said, enjoying correcting him. He bristled. "This isn't about whose spirit is better," I pointed out.

"I know." Chase shrugged. "Still, you have to admit, Sariah's story beats the prohibition years hands down. I mean, we can read about all that stuff in our history books but to come face-to-face with someone who lived one hundred years BC. That's...that's..."

"Fascinating," I said, flatly annoyed he was trying to one-up our heavenly beings. "His father ran a speakeasy from the basement of a church."

"No kidding? And he still made it to Heaven?" Chase let out a whistle that turned heads. "He's obviously redeemed himself. That's why he's a guardian."

I was protective of Matthias, of his life and his death. In my mind I saw the scar on his face. From all intents and purposes, he'd died in the throes of an illegal business. How then *had* he become a guardian?

"Do you believe in God?" I asked Chase.

"I'm still undecided. I asked Sariah if she'd seen God."

The hair on my body stood erect. "What did she say?"

"She said, 'That's for you to discover for yourself, or the knowledge means nothing.'"

"Isn't it obvious?" I said. "I mean, forget the planet and how perfectly everything in the universe works. Why would we see these beings—as alive as you and me—and know that there is life after this, and doubt somebody bigger than us orchestrates everything?"

"You don't have to preach."

I grabbed my drink, letting out a breath. "So what if God is in charge. Obviously, everyone gets to live their lives. Look at my brother, screwing up like he is. Look at all the crap that goes on in the world."

"Some would argue if God is around, why does He let it happen?"

"Because He knows everything will work out in the end."

"A tidy statement. You can't nutshell the world. It's not possible."

"I don't mean to trivialize anything. One thing I've realized seeing Matthias is just how much I don't know."

"That's why we need to pump these guys for as much information as we can," Chase said.

"Excuse me, but that sounds opportunistic."

"Yeah, so?"

"So, what are you going to do, write a book?"

"Maybe."

"But how can you? What's happened to us is…special." I couldn't imagine cheapening my relationship with Matthias by making a profit off him. "I guess that's your choice." Suddenly, I was disappointed with Chase. I stood. "Best of luck on the road to redemption."

"Wait a second. You're leaving?"

"I've got to go." I looked out the windows. Snow had ceased falling, so I couldn't use that as an excuse.

"We were just getting started," he complained.

"Was this why you wanted to talk? To pump me for information you can use in some book or article?"

"No, of course not. Not really. I was curious."

I set my hands on the table and leaned over. "If you use anything I told you, I'll run over you with my car." I stood erect. "Then you can go hang with Sariah, if you get that far."

Chase's mouth opened but nothing came out. Satisfied I'd shocked him and shut him up, I turned and left.

How lame. I tread through slush to my bug. Here I'd thought Chase was with me on this. That the two of us and our connection was as unique as the experiences we'd had. All he wanted to do was snarf down as much intel as he could and write for the *National Enquirer.*

I got in the car and headed home. Coffee scented my clothes and hung with me for an instant, until the freezing air dashed the enticing aroma. Music blasted from my CD player, churning disappointment inside of me into a storm. I felt alone again and wished I could tell Britt about what was going on. Or Mom. Or Dad.

The thought reminded me that I'd probably be facing Luke when I got home.

ELEVEN

The house was eerily quiet. Snow blanketed the roof, walls and chimney and shut out any sound from the outside world. At nine o'clock, I knew Abria was in her bedroom. Whether or not she was asleep was a toss up. Mom usually went to bed early too, worn out from chasing Abria. Dad I could usually find reading in the family room.

I locked the front door and slipped off my snow-caked shoes, leaving them on a rug Mom set by the door for messy footwear.

Lights burned in the kitchen, but the room was empty. Not even the TV was on in the adjoining family room. An uneasy feeling itched inside me. I took the stairs up, heard voices mumbling from Luke's bedroom and crept to the door.

"How long?" Dad's tone was demanding, but also heavy with disappointment.

Silence.

"We can't help you if you don't talk to us," Dad said after a while.

My heart sunk. They'd found out about Luke. I closed my eyes. *Poor Mom and Dad.* This was the last thing they needed.

I couldn't interrupt something so pivotal. It wasn't my place to interject my feelings for Luke and his addiction, so I silently turned and headed to my bedroom.

I took off my clothes, set them on the bed and went into my bathroom for a hot soak. Part of me was relieved my parents finally knew the truth. In spite of the added burden this would place on their shoulders, at least now Luke might get some help. Hot water filled the tub, fragrant bubbly steam rising into the small space. I looked at my reflection in the mirror. Luke. I closed my eyes, a tear escaping even though I willed it still.

When I opened my eyes again, I had a flashing thought of Matthias. Surely he couldn't see me—naked. Eyes wide, I peered around the bathroom, my heart fluttering, skin warming at the thought. Thank heaven he wasn't one of those angels who couldn't be seen. Or was he?

The thought had me jumping into the suds. *Matthias.* I wouldn't be seeing him tonight, not with Abria quietly tucked into her bed. I could use his company. I longed to ask him all the questions my visit with Chase had stirred inside of me. I longed to simply sit with him and look into his eyes.

Time had the tendency to evaporate whenever my thoughts drifted to him. When the water was finally cool, I let it down, got out and dried off, still smiling when I wrapped the fluffy white towel around myself and opened the door to my bedroom.

My heart jumped. Mom and Dad stood by my bed. "You scared me." I held the towel tight. Their sober, pale faces told me Luke's news had devastated them. "What is it? Is Abria okay?"

Dad nodded. "She's fine. Can we talk to you for a moment?"

"Sure, yeah." They think I don't know anything, and are going to drop the bomb. "Let me get on my robe," I said. They agreed and I went back into the bathroom, chilled knowing their hearts were broken.

After I had the robe on, I went back out and stood with them, the three of us congregated around the foot of my bed. Mom's eyes were red, fresh tear tracks stained her cheeks. I reached out and touched her arm. More tears spilled from her eyes and she dabbed at them with a ragged tissue.

"Mom…"

"After everything we've been through with Abria," Dad's voice was quiet, like his heart had a blade through it. "How could you betray our trust?"

My eyes widened. "What?"

Dad held out the bag of Lortabs. "How long have you been using,

142

Zoe?"

My mouth fell open but my voice had vanished. I swallowed, stared at the bag of prescription bottles, then looked at Dad. It hadn't occurred to me that when I changed my clothes earlier, Luke might come into my room, seeking the bag out. "You think those are mine? They're Luke's."

Mom and Dad exchanged weary looks. Fury raced in savage flames through my veins. "Did he tell you those were mine? Oh, and I suppose it was him who told you they were in my jeans pocket? That is so ridiculous! I can't believe he'd lie like that. I'm not standing here and taking this." I turned to storm out of the room to go get Luke but Dad's hand wrapped around my bicep.

"Not now. We need to talk."

"And we will, once I get him and beat the truth out of him!" I paced away, so furious my body shook. "I found those earlier today, in *his* bedroom. I found them underneath *his* bed! You can check. There's a slit under the box spring. That's where he hides them."

"For you," Mom's voice was tired. "He told us everything, Zoe. I can't take the lying. Please, stop lying."

"I'm not the one lying. I went into his room earlier—remember when you found Abria in there? Remember how jumpy Luke was? After you sent him to keep an eye on Abria, I did some looking around. That's when I found the bag. I can't believe you don't believe me!" My heart thrummed in my throat.

"How long, Zoe?" Dad asked again, as if he hadn't heard a word I'd just said.

"I've never used prescription drugs. Ever. I'm telling you, those are Luke's. He's the druggie. He's the pot head. He's so baked all the time you don't even see it. That's not him in there anymore, that's a drug addict! Wake up and see what's going on!"

Mom's face drained of color. Her lips parted then froze. Dad's face blanched white. Mom's hand, with the tissue tucked inside her palm, slowly lifted to her trembling lips. She lowered to the foot of my bed, tears rushing from her eyes.

My insides ripped apart. I had hurled the truth at them with no mercy. No padding. Just the awful, horrid and tragic truth.

Dad shoved a hand into his graying hair. He lowered his head, shook it, covered his face with both hands and sunk down next to Mom.

The fury running wild inside of me drained at the sight of their distraught countenances. Tears filled my eyes. I dropped to the floor at their knees and looked into their faces, twisted with a fear I'd carried silently inside for so long.

"I'm so sorry," I whispered. Mom's shoulders buckled in a sob and she fell into Dad's embrace. "I should have told you a long time ago but I didn't want you to worry about him, not with Abria and all that. I didn't know how bad it was. I thought he would stop on his own. Lots of kids do. Maybe he will."

Dad shook his head, eyes glistening. His grip around Mom dug deep. Her sobs were silent, lost in his chest.

Then Mom pushed back from Dad, her red eyes swollen. She looked at me. "How long has this been going on?"

Telling them the truth would drive any spears I'd already hurled at their hearts deeper. But lying was out of the question. "About three years."

Their eyes widened. Mom gasped. "And you never told us? Did you know all this time?"

"Not all this time. Luke never told me, I just figured it out. I saw the signs."

"Why didn't we?" Mom looked from me to Dad.

I placed my hand on her knee. "This is Luke's problem, not yours. You can't blame yourself."

Tears spewed from Mom's eyes. "How can I not blame myself? I'm his mother and I didn't see this. What am I supposed to think? How could I have missed it? Why didn't I see?" She sobbed into Dad's arms again, her fingers gouging his sleeves.

The gravity of the news fell like a deafening bomb in the room. This wasn't going away now. Luke and his addiction was a part of our house, our lives, and our existence, just like Abria's autism.

I longed to melt into the floor and disappear. Rather than feeling relieved that they knew, the burden of Luke's addiction cast over my shoulders in another, weighty layer.

I needed a drink.

There was nothing I could say to comfort my parents. They told me that Luke denied everything. When they asked me what they should do, I felt the roles reverse. I didn't have the answers. I didn't have the power to do anything. My measly attempt to help Luke by taking his Lortabs and following him had only backfired.

"Call the cops," I finally said.

Mom's teary eyes looked into mine as I paced the floor. "We can't do that."

"Why not? He's broken the law."

"And you'd just love to see me put in jail, wouldn't you?" Luke's voice came from my open bedroom door. Mom and Dad looked over. Luke held himself in the jamb. His face was still pale, darker shadows circled his angry eyes.

Seeing him lit my brittle fuse. "Maybe that'd stop you, since you don't have the balls to stop yourself."

"You don't know what you're talking about," he shouted. "You have no idea how hard this is!" He wobbled into the room.

"You don't want to stop, that's your problem. Look at you, you're so wasted you can't even stand up straight. It's disgusting."

"Shut up bi—"

"Stop!" Dad shot to his feet. "Both of you stop now."

Tears streamed from Luke's eyes, aimed at me. "I hate you." He turned and went out the door.

"And I hate you, loser. Look what you've done to our family!"

"Zoe, please." Mom's pleading silenced me. She sat on the foot of the bed, her face so distorted with anguish I couldn't think about Luke anymore, I went to her, fell down to her lap, and put my arms around her. Tears streamed from my eyes, down my cheeks. I hated Luke. Hated what he'd done to us, what he was doing to himself.

"Please don't say that to him." Mom stroked my head.

"He's hurting you guys. I'm sick of it."

"I know you've carried this longer than we have," Dad's tone softened some. Mom's body rocked when he sat down next to her. I felt his hand on my arm. "I wish you'd told us. But I can't change that. We know now, and we have to pull together for Luke's sake."

I jerked my head up from Mom's lap. "Luke's sake? He's gotten himself into this crap. Let him dig himself out."

"Zoe, sometimes people get so buried they can't do anything more than reach, let alone summon the strength to climb out."

"He doesn't care if he stops, don't you get it? He only cares about his next bowl."

Mom's touch grew still. She closed her eyes, let out a long breath. All of this news was tearing her apart. Her face darkened with cavernous sorrow. Dad, too, looked like he'd just emerged from the front lines of a wretched battlefield.

I didn't say anything else.

I wanted to drown in a bottle of Vodka.

I stood. "I need to go to bed."

Mom stood, then Dad. The echo of our spoken words filled the silence, and no more could be said. Not now, anyway.

Dad reached out and stroked my arm. "It'll be all right."

It will? I doubted it, but I nodded. "Yeah." I needed that bottle, now. Sure, I drank, but my drinking was on a need-to-drink basis, not like Luke's addiction.

"I love you." Mom wrapped her arms around me, a fragile embrace from a beaten parent that had me hugging her as if she was a delicate flake of snow that might melt away any second.

"Love you."

Dad cradled Mom in his arms and they moved as one out the door of my bedroom.

I sniffed back my last tear.

After I was sure Mom and Dad were in their room for the night, I threw on my clothes and snuck out. After seeing the brutal truth hit my parents like an avalanche, I felt a moment's guilt for sneaking out. The moment passed. Raw anger surged through me again, once I was out in my car, driving. I couldn't believe Luke had twisted that scene around. Part of me was as frightened as I was furious. This meant he was far worse off than I'd known.

The weight of his life, my life, my parents' lives seemed to drag me downward. I needed a getaway, now.

Britt always had a stash of alcohol at her house, her parents pretty clueless, so I pulled out my cell phone. Eleven-thirty. She usually didn't go to sleep until midnight. I dialed.

"Hey honey," she said

"Sorry about tonight. You wouldn't believe the crap I've been through."

"Wanna tell me about it?"

"I'm coming over. Is that okay? I need a drink."

Her laugh was strung out. Apparently she'd been at the bottle herself. "Sure. I've got shhomething with your name on it."

"Be there in a sec." I clicked off the phone and took a deep breath. Relief was almost here.

Snow still fell in a thick veil and I drove the few miles to Britt's house with caution. I'd have to make it home in this thick slush, that thought hadn't escaped me. I'd never driven drunk before and knew I shouldn't. Then Matthias' face came into my mind. I was certain he wouldn't approve of me getting hammered, no matter the reason. I couldn't think about him now, too angry at Luke and way too uptight.

I was about a block away from Britt's when the snow fall thickened from a veil to a blanket, decreasing visibility to about two feet. I slowed, squinted, and tried to keep my eyes on what was road and what wasn't.

Out of nowhere, a snow-caked pedestrian dashed in front of my car. I slammed on the breaks, slid and swerved to a stop into the snow-banked curb. My heart pounded against my ribs. I searched for the person crazy enough to be out walking in weather like this. Hadn't they seen my lights?

"What an idiot," I gasped. After I'd caught my breath and my heart slowed, I tried to pull the car back onto the road, but my wheels only spun.

I banged my palm against the steering wheel. Where was that retard? I threw open my door and stood out in the falling snow, ready to tear the guy's head off. Surely the idiot saw me. No doubt he was too embarrassed that he'd almost caused an accident and was hiding now.

I took a few steps away from my car to assess the situation. My wheels were crammed in white ice. *Crap.* Again I looked around for the culprit who'd caused this mess and saw nothing but an empty street.

If I get my hands on you, buddy, you're dead. My gaze fell to the street. I'd follow his footsteps, bang on his door and tell him to come dig me out *the whack job.* Snow continued to drift to the ground, but the only footprints I saw were mine. No other footprints anywhere in sight. I was sure I'd seen him. Someone had darted into the road, someone had made me stop. Where had he gone?

Creeped, I got back in the car, shivering. My teeth chattered. I dialed Britt.

"I got stuck. Can you come get me?"

"Oh, maaaan."

Britt was already plastered, I heard it in her lazy tone. I didn't want her driving. "Forget it."

"No, no, no. I'll come get you. Where are you, anyways?"

"I'm not that far, I'll walk. See you in a minute, okay?"

"You sure? Cause I can come an' find you."

No way was I going to be responsible for her being on the road. "Just be waiting for me when I get there."

"I will. I yam." She laughed and the phone crashed off.

What had happened to her tonight? Though Britt had done her share of comfort drinking, she usually kept it to weekends. Had something happened with Weston? Last she'd told me, Weston had a game—that's why she wanted to hang out. I grabbed my bag and coat and locked the car. Then I trudged through the two-foot snowfall to Britt's.

Go home.

The walk home was twice as long as it was to Britt's. I'd die of frostbite. I kept walking, snow beginning to coat me from head to toe. I didn't want to go home. I hated home at the moment.

Drink. I need a drink.

Go home.

Forget it. I need this tonight. It'll do me some good to be *gone* for a while.

I kept trudging. Up ahead, I saw Britt's house and the dim glow from her upstairs bedroom window.

Go home.

"I'm not going home so just shut up." My angry voice cut through the silent air like a branch laden with too much snow, cracking. I cringed, and looked around, sure I'd upset nature's peaceful slumber. I wanted a little peace of my own. Could anyone deny that I didn't deserve it?

Nearing Britt's, the oddest sensation came over me. As if I wasn't inside myself anymore. I felt my legs moving, but I saw myself going there as if I was suspended above. Britt's house suddenly looked dark and ominous. The friendly place with wreaths and little yard characters poking out from the grass and bushes never bothered me before. Tonight, the elves and dwarves rose from the snow like creepy globs. Every window was dark except for Britt's, and that window had a scarlet glow coming from behind her wispy red sheers.

I stopped. I wasn't suspended above any longer, but saw Britt's house with my feet deep in cold, bitter snow.

Go home.

I closed my eyes. Why was this happening? I was over stressed. Too much had happened today. I needed a drink and the only place I could get one was in that house.

I sought shelter on the covered porch, dug into my bag, got out my cell phone and texted Britt. I waited. And waited. I couldn't knock, not at eleven-forty five. Her parents were clueless, but not altogether stupid. Bringing their attention to an inebriated Britt would cause Britt major problems. She'd never forgive me. She'd probably fallen asleep.

Great. Now what?

TWELVE

After texting Britt fifty times and not getting an answer, I figured she was comatose. I turned and headed toward my house. I wanted to feel anger at being stuck, alone and cold with the prospect of freezing to death, but a comforting warmth settled in. I found it odd that I wasn't stomping my way back through the snow, passing my abandoned car, cursing with every step. Rather, inexplicable relief coursed through me.

My cell phone vibrated. I plucked it out of my bag, my hands shaking so hard it was difficult to press the tiny buttons to see who was texting me.

Chase.

hey, i know u r probly asleep but i hope you get this. sorry about 2nite. can we still talk?

Shivering, I tapped out my reply.

i'm not asleep in fact im out walking my car got stuck I had the brief hope he was magically near enough to come rescue me. What a turn of events. But I had no idea where Chase lived. He could be miles away.

where? i'll give you a ride

im on lancaster dr. know where that is?

yeah be there in a sec

Shocked, I stared at the blank screen of my phone, the dim light softly glowing against the falling flakes in the air. I put the phone in my pocket and continued walking, so I'd keep warm. Most houses were dark with the exception of outside lanterns. How weird that Chase happened to be out driving.

Then my heart skipped. Maybe it was him who had darted out in front of my car. What if this whole thing had been planned, so he could get me alone and…?

Somehow, the idea didn't work, though parts of it made sense. If Britt hadn't fallen face down on me, I'd be at her house nice and toasty, getting blocked myself. Then Chase wouldn't have anything to do with tonight.

I couldn't worry about a simple thing like stalking. I was about to die of frostbite. To be found buried like a cipher in the snow, in one of the five foot snow plow banks that would thaw months later, leaving my body preserved in all of its eighteen-year-old glory.

A pair of headlights shone through the lacy snow ahead. The car was going so slow, it had to be Chase looking for me. I'd freaking be a statue before he got to me in time. My teeth rattled. I walked out into the middle of the road, waving my trembling hands.

He flashed his lights.

When I was finally inside his warm car, I laid back my head, closed my eyes and let out a sigh. My clothes were as if a wet, wool blanket covered me. The car smelled like coffee. Maybe he'd been at Starbucks all this time.

"How long have you been out here in this?"

"Just drive." I managed between chattering teeth. "I'm seriously frozen."

I heard him crank up the heat. My body shook.

"Maybe you should take off your clothes, you might warm up faster."

I opened one eye at him. "Yeah right."

"I didn't mean…that came out wrong."

"You stick your foot any deeper into your mouth and you're going to choke on it."

His laugh fumbled out. "So what are you doing here?"

"I was on my way to a friend's house and my car got stuck."

"Oh, that sucks."

"Yeah, all because some idiot ran out in front of me." I peered at him through cracked lashes and gauged his reaction, just to see if my stalker theory had any chance. He was too engrossed with driving safely. After smelling Starbucks on him, I threw the theory out the window.

"Someone was walking in this?" he cracked.

"Someone other than me, yes, hard to believe there are two stupid people out tonight isn't it?"

"I didn't mean to... I didn't mean for it to sound—"

"Forget it," I clucked, smiled. Wait, I was mad at him for being an opportunist. "So I live on Silver Tree Drive. Do you know where that is?"

"I know where all the streets are in town."

"Why doesn't that surprise me?"

He looked over, as if to see if I was playing with him. "No, really," he said. "I have a memory for maps and numbers."

"And money?" I raised a brow.

His blank expression was clueless. "I'm pretty good with money," he admitted.

"I mean, greedy. Like what you said tonight about writing a book. Blood money."

"But there is no blood, the guardians are dead."

He was a literal sucker. I stared ahead at the snow. At the speed he drove, it was no wonder he was still out this time of night. "You always drive this slow?" I asked.

"In this weather, I do." Both of his hands gripped the wheel and he sat like a ruler propped in the seat. "I'm not an opportunist, Zoe. I just think people would be interested in knowing about the existence of spirits."

"Do you think they'll believe you?"

"They will if I can find more people like you and me to share their stories."

"But some may not want their stories told. It gets back to that special thing. We're special because of what's happened to us. I don't know about you, but that makes me feel responsible to protect them."

"Guardians don't need our protection. They can disappear at will."

"Do you really think they'll let you see them if your intentions are to expose them?"

"Not expose, I want to bring hope to people who might not have it. That's why I have to find others."

"And how are you going to do that? Put an ad online? You'll sound like a lunatic."

His expression paled, as though that was exactly what he had planned. "You don't think anyone will respond?"

"You're serious?" I sat up, hating that I was soaked to the skin soggy. "You run an ad anywhere looking for people who have seen spirits and every creepy worm will crawl out of the wood to talk to you. You won't know who's telling the truth and whose blowing smoke."

He let out a sigh. "It's just a thought. That's all."

I pointed out my house and he pulled up in front and stopped.

"Nice house."

"Thanks." I didn't believe for one second his dream of writing for the tabloids was just a thought. "Forget about it, Chase. Leave the stories of heavenly visitations to the Bible."

Chase studied the house. "You've seen Matthias here," he murmured.

"Lots of times." I opened the door and got out.

"You're lucky your sister is handicapped," he said. "It pretty much guarantees you'll be seeing them all your life. Maybe it won't always be Matthias, but you'll see them."

Did he really just say that? I thought about slamming the car door, but the naivety on his face wouldn't allow for that reaction. I glanced up at Luke's bedroom window where I'd last seen Matthias and imagined seeing his face there.

Cancer moved into the house. Mom's countenance was quiet, morbid, hopeless. Dad was clipped, irritated and edgy. I tiptoed on fragile eggshells, offering a smile and a hug to Mom every now and then. My heart ached for her. Throw Abria into the funeral-like mood and it was like having a sparrow loose in a tomb.

Luke sulked from room to room. One minute he was plopped in front of the TV. The next he was wandering aimlessly. I guess Mom and Dad grounded him, because he hadn't been around this much since he was ten.

He glared at me when our eyes met. I glared back. At one point, we bumped into each other in the hall.

"This is your fault," he mumbled.

"Excuse me," I snapped. "This is your pit, Luke. You dug it all by yourself."

He sneered, cursed and passed me, continuing to mumble under his breath until he vanished into his bedroom with the slam of the door.

He was restricted from his car. It sat abandoned at the side of the house, snow collecting on the peeling blue body like a stained headstone in a graveyard. I was assigned to take him to and from school, something both Luke and I hated. I complied to ease my parents' suffering but Luke and I ignored each other during the short trips.

Whether or not he stayed at school once we got there, I don't know. I wasn't his babysitter. I found solace in being away from home. Midterms were approaching, so I stayed after class in the library in an effort to study, but my mind was pulled a thousand different directions. Between home, Mom and Dad and Luke, not to mention Abria—who was actually behaving miraculously well lately— I hadn't seen Matthias in weeks. I could hardly focus long enough to internalize whatever I was studying.

Britt and Weston were on the outs. That's why she'd been wasted the night my car got stuck. She'd leeched onto me in the days after, crying one minute, moaning about him the next, though she'd been vague about what had happened. All she'd said was that Weston had found her phone number in Brady's cell phone.

I sat in the library one day, determined to get through my history notes when she plunked down next to me, reeking of alcohol.

She crossed her arms on the table and dropped her head down, eyes closed. "I feel like crap."

"What are you doing drinking during the day?" I whispered. "Are you nuts?"

"He won't take my calls. He ignores my texts."

"Because he found your phone number in Brady's cell. What did you expect?"

"What kind of guy checks his friend's cell phone?" she mumbled.

"A suspicious guy. A jealous guy."

"Nothing happened." Britt lifted her head and it bobbed like a newborn baby's. Her eyes opened, her lids hung halfway over her irises. "He just had my number, that's all."

I shut my history book. "You shouldn't have given Brady your number to begin with. What did you think he was going to do with it? Stare at it? Sell it?"

"I dunno. Brady's nice. He's just nice. That's all."

I rolled my eyes and put an arm around her shoulders, hugged her. "And you're smashed. You can't drive home like this. I'll take you."

"I want him back," she said against my chest.

"I know."

"You don't know what it's like to lose someone you love."

I took a deep breath. I hadn't seen Matthias in what felt like forever. I missed him. Missed him so much I sang stupid songs to keep my brain filled so his face didn't sneak in and distract me. But he was like a catchy tune I couldn't get out of my head.

"Let's talk about how we can get Weston back," she mumbled.

Mrs. Deuterhaus, the spindly librarian was headed our direction, her black eyes sharp behind her silver-rimmed glasses.

"Let's talk later though, I think Mrs. Deuterhaus is getting mad."

"I don't care about that witch," Britt's shrill voice carried with the pitch of breaking glass. "I have to figure this out. I love him, don't you get it?"

"Shh. Yes, I get it." I held Britt close, hoping she'd bawl in my sleeve or something—anything to shut her up.

Mrs. Deuterhaus stopped at our table. "She's drunk. Get her out of here before I call security."

"Um. Sure."

"So what if I'm drunk," Britt spat. "How would you know what lost love is like? You're old and ugly and—"

"That's it!" Mrs. Deuterhaus whirled around and marched back to the desk.

I jumped to my feet, gathered my books and nudged Britt. "Come on, we have to get out of here before you get nailed."

Dragging Britt from the serene library was like yanking a wet cat out of a bathtub.

"You're old and you don't know anything," Britt hissed at Mrs. Deuterhaus, now behind the counter and on the phone, her eyes blazing.

"Stop talking," I told Britt. I ignored the curious faces we passed on our way out the door. A whoosh of book-scented air and we gusted out of the library. I broke into a run. "Hurry!"

Britt stumbled along behind me, laughing, tripping, making a fool out of herself. I'd never seen her drunk in daylight. She usually reserved this Britt for nighttime.

We finally made it to my car and I opened her door. She collapsed inside, laughing hysterically. There was no way security would find us, not if we booked it right out of there.

But I was supposed to bring Luke home.

I got in, shut the door and whipped out my cell phone, then texted him.

where r u? i'm leaving

No answer. I re-sent the text, started the car and backed out, my heart pumping. I kept my eye out for grey-uniformed security guards but didn't see any. I wasn't sure if our escape was enough to protect Britt from the consequences of her actions in the library. Mrs. Deuterhaus could ID her. Surely the school administration had better things to do than pad the librarian's bruised ego by stalking a student and punishing them.

157

I drove out of the parking lot, searching for Luke. Still no response. Where was he?

"So," Britt finally stopped laughing. "You gonna help me get Weston?" She sniffed.

I looked over. Her face was puffy, her eyes red. A tear streamed down one cheek. I was amazed that she felt so strongly for a guy she hadn't known very long. This was not her usual disposable MO.

"I'll do what I can. Right now, I have to find Luke."

"Brady said he's been hanging with his brother the last few days."

My head whipped around to face her. "When did you hear this?"

Britt lay against the seat, eyes closed, face taut. She shrugged. "Don't remember."

"Why didn't you tell me? Why didn't Brady say something?"

"No one wants to say stuff like that, Zoe, you know that. That's like being the grim reaper."

I'd thought Brady and I had a connection—our brothers being users—and that meant we'd look out for them. If it had been me who'd found out Luke and Kevin were hanging together, I'd have told him.

I circled the school, but didn't find Luke.

"I'm going to Brady's," I said.

"Oh no," her voice cracked. She covered her face with her hands, and cried again.

"What?"

She shook her head.

Panic flushed through me. "Is it about Luke?"

Sobbing now, Britt shook her head again.

"Oh," my heart slowed a little. "Then what is it? Britt talk to me."

"Nothing." Her face was crimson when she took her hands away, wiping them across her eyes and nose, smearing mascara into snot.

I reached over, opened my glove box and handed her a napkin I'd stuffed in there when I'd taken Abria out for fries. Haphazardly, she dragged it across her face. "I screwed up is all. Screwed up." Her deathly silence spoke volumes: she'd done more than give Brady her phone number.

"What happened? Tell me."

Tears streamed from her eyes. She turned her gaze out the window. "We ran into each other that night. The night you wanted to come over? Remember how I wanted to meet you at Starbucks? Weston was doing something. Since you couldn't make it, I called Brady and asked him if he wanted to, you know, hang out."

"Britt!"

"I know, I know. But I was lonely."

"You couldn't wait a couple of hours for Weston?"

She shook her head, sobbed. "I'm so weak. It's pathetic."

I agreed, but didn't say anything. *The flesh of man is weak.* I heard Matthias' voice clear as stream water in my head. He was right. Now, Britt had lost everything because of one weak moment.

"So what happened? Weston see you guys?"

"No. We went to the gas station and got a drink. Then Brady asked if I wanted to go back to his house and watch a movie or something. I said, sure. We drove separately to his house," she added emphatically but it didn't help— she was defending a dead horse.

"Everything was fine. We talked, watched the movie. We even talked about you. That's when I found out about Luke and Kevin."

"What else happened between you two?"

"He kissed me."

"You…let him?"

She nodded, turned away. Sobbed.

"Britt. Why did you let him?" I couldn't understand when a heart loved another heart, how something like a kiss could happen. For a second, I imagined Matthias. I wouldn't let another guy anywhere near my heart if it belonged to him.

"He was so sweet and cute and he wanted me."

"You don't do that when you care about somebody else, though."

She bawled into the soggy napkin. "I know, I know. I couldn't stop myself."

I let out a sigh. "So how did Weston find out?"

"Brady leaked it. I couldn't believe he told him!"

"You were a trophy kiss to Brady, that's all. In some twisted way, he wanted Weston to know that though Weston is Mr. Hotshot he couldn't hold onto you."

"Why would he do that?"

"Guys have huge egos." I pulled onto Brady's street, ready to storm up to his door and rip his eyes out. "Did you really think he'd keep it to himself? You're Britt. Every guy wants a crack at you and if they can take one, they will."

She whipped her head at me. Her face was streaked black from mascara and purple and pink from eye shadow. Red blush mottled her cheeks. "You think I'm a slut?"

"I didn't say that. Besides, it's not what I think, it's what the guys think." She had been around, that was truth. But so had I. I wasn't about to cast the first stone, no matter how tempting it was to show her how wrong her behavior really was.

"You're such a hypocrite," she shrieked. "You don't know half of what they say about you!"

The blood in my veins simmered. I yanked the car over in front of Brady's house and slammed on the brakes. Britt flew forward, banging into the dashboard. "This isn't about me. I'm not the one who couldn't wait two hours for my boyfriend I supposedly love, and hooked up with his best friend!"

"We didn't hook up!"

"What's the difference? Infidelity is infidelity."

She slapped me.

Our breaths were heavy, fast and angry. The windows of the car started to fog. I glared at her. The slap didn't have much punch; she was weak in more than just commitment.

"Get out," I said.

"Fine." She pushed open the door.

"Ask Brady to give you a ride. Oh, wait, you already did that, didn't you?" I snapped.

Hurt flushed over her face. Instantly, I hated myself for saying something so ugly. I wanted to apologize but couldn't. The sight of her standing there, her beauty smeared like war paint, her demeanor miserable and lost—I didn't want to think I'd ever looked like that, much less *been* like that. I never wanted to be like that again.

Rather than go to Brady's door, she turned and started down the street, stumbling in her heels.

I got out, slammed my door and fumed. *I should go after her.* She'd probably take a ride from Jack the Ripper she was so upset. It was a long walk to her house. Maybe she'd text somebody else for a pick up; she had a million guys in her cell phone. I looked at Brady's house, anger firing up and stomped through the snow to the door.

I pounded.

Brady's brother, Kevin, opened the door. He had black, shaggy hair and wore the uniform all skaters and druggies wore: pants past the butt and huge tee shirts. His eyes grew to the size of dinner plates. "Uh."

"Is Brady here?"

"Uh…" He glanced behind him, then looked at me. "No, he's not."

"Do you know where he is?" I demanded.

"Zoe?" Luke peered out from behind Kevin. "How did you find me?"

Anger turned to twisted pleasure. I grinned. "I know everything. Get your butt in my car."

THIRTEEN

"Why didn't you answer my text?" I shifted gears as we headed down the street.

"I just wanted some chill time, you know?"

"Except your definition of chill includes pot."

"Not today. Look, I'm not breaking the rules. I'm here. So don't say anything to Mom and Dad, k?"

I took a right and headed into our neighborhood. "I'll consider it."

"We weren't doing anything."

He didn't look high and he only stunk of cigarette smoke. Maybe he was telling the truth. "Okay. How about chilling at home, like you're supposed to?"

"I can't be there anymore. It's too depressing."

"Of course it's depressing." *And you're the cause of it.* "Why do you think Mom and Dad are so down?"

He turned his face away, stared out the window, and shrugged.

He had to know. He just didn't want to admit he was the reason for the gloom that resided in our house now.

When Luke and I got home, Mom and Dad were seated at the dinner table with Abria. Garlic and spices scented the air and tickled my stomach. For a second, the two of us stood together at the table. I had hopes of Luke eating with us, knowing the gesture would soothe Mom and Dad.

"Luke, I'm glad you're here," Mom said. "I planned dinner early, hoping to catch you."

"How was school?" Dad asked, his expression as eager as Mom's.

"Good." Luke stuffed his hands in his front pockets, lowered his head.

"Sure smells great." I pulled out a chair but didn't sit, anxious to see what Luke was going to do.

"I'm not hungry." Luke started toward the stairs.

Mom's expression sagged like an apron with cut strings. She looked at Dad.

Dad took his cue from Mom. "You sure?"

Luke was already out of sight. "Yeah," he called.

Mom closed her eyes.

Appetite gone, I wanted to run away from the depressing mood we'd brought into the house. "At least he came home," I offered. Abria was crawling on the kitchen counter like a hungry cat.

Mom picked up her fork and resumed eating. "But I want more than that."

"We all want more than that," I said. "But he's here and he's clean. That's worth celebrating."

From the counter, Abria clapped her hands and made chirping noises, her gaze flipping around the room. She broke out in a long stream of laughter. The day's events had worn me to tissue. I was ready to rip. I had a sudden craving for a drink, and hated that I did. I tried to finish my dinner but the craving gnawed at my bones until I thought I'd scream.

Mom and Dad went back and forth discussing Luke but I didn't tune in. I was eaten alive with the urge to drink.

I put my fork down. "I'm done." I stood, picked up my plate. "Thanks. Dinner was really good. I think I'll take Abria on a drive now if that's okay with you?"

"Okay," Mom said. "She'll love that."

I took my plate to the sink like a robot, my mind spinning with only one thought: drink. I closed my eyes, tried to force the obsessive thought out, but its roots spread fast and deep. Already, I was planning. Drive to Britt's.

Knock on the door.

Grabbing my head, I vainly squeezed. Maybe pressure would rid me of the urge. Nothing. I let out a deep breath. I had to get out of there. That would help.

Abria now laid on the counter, flapping and staring up at the canned lights in the ceiling. "Come on." I picked her up, hoisting her at my hip like a sack of potatoes and headed toward the front door.

"Be careful," Mom called.

I drove aimlessly through town, my mind crowded with the obsession to drown pressure with a bottle of vodka. In the backseat, Abria sat strapped in, looking wide-eyed out the window. Abria's angelic chatter made me sigh. How could I go to Britt's? Not that Britt cared if I brought Abria over. She liked Abria. Drinking then driving us home was the problem. But the gnaw inside of me intensified.

If I gave into this craving, I'd be no better off than Luke.

A strong presence filled the car—as if a magnet the size of the moon had been dropped in the back seat. My gaze whipped up to the rearview mirror.

Matthias.

Happiness flooded me. "What are you doing here?"

"Nice to see you again, Zoe." His radiant face was so captivating I couldn't take my eyes away from him. With a nod he gestured to the road. I looked at the street and swerved to keep from hitting an oncoming car.

"Phew," I couldn't very well tell him he was so gorgeous I couldn't stop staring like an idiot. "Is that why you're here? That almost-accident?"

The right corner of his lip lifted. "No, Zoe." His stream-blue eyes held mine for a long moment before I blinked and focused on the road. I was thrilled he was in the car—no matter the reason. We were safe with him there, and the urge to go to Britt's house vanished.

He looked heavenly in his morning-sky blue silky shirt and beach-sand toned pants. He turned to Abria and took her hand. "Hello, Miss Abria. Are you enjoying the ride?"

Abria stared at him too, her saucer blue eyes unblinking as she studied him.

"I can't believe how quiet and subdued she is around you," I observed.

"I tend to have that affect on people," he said.

"Hey, can you tell me why Luke's guardian hasn't made an appearance?"

"Sassy," he murmured, sending a tingle of warmth down my body. "I told you, guardians only come to those open to Divine help, or those who are innocent, like our Miss Abria here."

"You mean God thinks Luke can help himself out of this mess?"

"I never presume to know what God thinks. However, if you'd like to take the issue up with Him, I'm sure He'd be happy to hear you out." His blue eyes twinkled.

I snorted. "No thanks. Think I'll leave destiny and fate up to Him."

"Wise choice." Matthias took Abria by the hand and looked at her. "It's a cloudy day, isn't it?" His gentle voice wove in the air like floating cotton streams. "That means another storm is on the way. Don't be afraid of storms, Abria."

"Is she afraid of storms?" I asked. I had no idea.

"A little," he murmured.

How I wished it was me he was talking to with that soothing voice. "Is there weather where you come from?"

"Not in the traditional sense."

"In what sense then?" I laughed.

"There is light and warmth all the time."

"Now that would be perfect."

His eyes glittered. "It is."

"No cold, no snow, no blistering heat you die in the minute you step outside because it feels like somebody left a zillion oven doors open."

He laughed, his head tilting back for a moment. *Beautiful.* I swerved.

"Your sense of humor is the berries, Zoe. I like it."

"So what brings you here this evening? Abria's safe. She's with me."

"Of course she's safe with you." His tone was strong but with an edge that troubled me. "You wouldn't do anything to put her in harm's way, would you?" His gaze pinned mine.

I shifted. "Of course not." Britt's house flashed into my mind. I tore my eyes from his piercing gaze and focused on the road. Outside, night was falling, throwing grey and black shadows across the streets, behind buildings and in city crevasses.

When I chanced a peek at him again through the mirror, he was still watching me. "What?" I asked. Surely he didn't know that I'd been on my way to Britt's to get hammered.

"I'm glad we're on this drive together," he said, then his gaze swept the inside of the car. "Automobiles certainly have changed since I last drove one. They're so small. I can barely stretch out my legs back here."

A grin broke on my lips. I watched him try to get comfortable in the compact space of my backseat. His height didn't fold well. "Cars have gotten smaller because smaller is more practical, Matthias. They don't eat up as much gas. You know, gas costs a million bucks a gallon now."

His eyes popped. "My-oh-my. Gas was fifteen cents a gallon when I drove my Roadster."

"I'm exaggerating. I can see you in a Roadster."

"She was a stunning beast. Thirty-five horsepower and light weight. Sleek, sharp and built for impressing. The inside was magnificent with polished wood and leather seats." His hands skimmed the seats he sat on. "What *is* this material, anyway?"

I stifled a laugh. "Some kind of poly blend. Leather's for rich people or those not conscious of being 'green.' Too many animals have to die for a coat or a couch, you know?"

His brows lifted. "Is there a shortage of cattle?"

I chuckled. "No. It's just leather seats in a car are not necessary."

"Well, this Polly person has created a decent substitute, I suppose." He looked around. "Tell me, Zoe, do you not have a trash receptacle?"

I cringed. My backseat *was* the trash receptacle. "Um. Sorry. I know it's a mess. But I wasn't planning on having any visitors."

"Cups, napkins, paper bags, books…"

"I know, I know. I bet your car was perfect, wasn't it?"

"I had a receptacle for trash, so, yes, it was clean."

"Do you hate me now?"

His eyes widened meeting mine in the rearview mirror. "Of course I don't hate you. I'm only suggesting—"

"Suggestion noted. Jeez. Embarrass me why don't you."

I saw him bend over. And bend over. Again. And Again. Sweat broke on my skin. "Please don't clean my car," I shrieked. This couldn't be more humiliating.

A gas station was coming up on the right so I pulled into the lot and stopped near the trash containers. "I can do it. Please don't." I turned around. Matthias had stuffed every last bit of trash into an old McDonalds bag, now splitting down one side.

He held it out with a smile. "Done."

"You didn't have to clean my mess. I feel terrible."

"It's the least I can do for you escorting Abria and I on this enchanting drive."

I took the bag. Overstuffed and brittle, it started to rip. Matthias grabbed for it at the same time I did and our fingers met. A bolt of energy shot through my system, knocking my back into the steering wheel. Every cell burst open, like flowers reaching for the sun, pulsing with a force that stole my breath. Power whirled through my veins like a tornado. Our eyes locked. For the first time, I felt his flesh. Real. *Warm.* Connected with mine. I gasped, breathed. What did this mean? Would he vanish? Would the heavens quake and roar? Had he broken some divine law and would he be eternally punished now? Horrified, I opened my mouth to say something but nothing came.

A hard swallow shifted in his throat. Slowly, he eased his hands away from the bag—his fingers disconnecting with mine—stealing the rush of pulsing electricity out of my body in a sucking vortex that left me drained. I slumped, blinked, and searched for strength. I looked at the lopsided bag again in my hands.

"I'm so sorry." My voice cracked on a whisper. Maybe no one had noticed.

He sat with his back pressed against the seat, his crystal eyes piercing me to the core. Surely he didn't think I had touched him on purpose. "I—that was an accident. I would never—"

He held up both hands and closed his eyes as if in deep thought.

"Matthias I am so sorry. I…"

He took a deep breath. His jaw locked. Was he praying?

What had I done? I wanted to shrink. I sat back, clutching the trash-filled bag to my breast, panicked. If he went away because of me, I would never forgive myself. Anticipating the loss gouged a hole so vast and deep inside of me I wanted to crumble into nothingness.

Next to him, strapped in her car seat, Abria stared at Matthias intently. Had she noticed that Heaven had reached down and touched me? How could she not have felt that?

Awed, I stared at Matthias, at this being in my presence. Subtle. Powerful. Miraculous. *God, please don't take him from us. Please.* I closed my eyes and whispered the plea over and over in my head—begging.

When I opened my eyes again, Matthias' gaze held me in calming blue comfort. His chest rose and fell in a soft rhythm. I let out a sigh. Peace surrounded me. I knew—with no uncertainty—everything was going to be all right.

"Are you all right?" his voice was a tender whisper.

I nodded. His touch had connected us. I felt his every move, every breath as though his movements echoed through the valleys and mountains of my soul. His heartbeat thrummed faintly in my ears. The sensation was both odd and natural as if our souls were now one.

"I feel you," I whispered. "I—feel—you."

His eyes were alive, vibrant. He nodded. "Yes."

"What does it mean?"

"I'm your guardian now, Zoe."

My heart leapt to my throat. I blinked back a sudden rush of tears swarming my eyes. "You mean you aren't...damned?"

His lips lifted slightly. "No."

I turned and fell back against my seat, overjoyed. "I don't know what to say." Matthias. *My guardian.* I closed my eyes. Tears streamed out and ran down the sides of my face. I felt ready to burst.

He was silent, and the lack of sound caused a thread of worry to wind through me. I turned around, faced him. A sober expression covered his face.

"Are you okay?" I asked.

He blinked slowly, as if he was tired, then focused on me. "Dandy."

"Did we *do* something when we touched? Ruin something? Change the course of time or the future or something?"

A weary smile broke the soberness on his face. "No."

But I had the feeling he wasn't telling me everything. In some dark corner, deep inside of me, I felt his concern for something. The feeling didn't leave, but was as if a door had been opened wherein I couldn't see clearly.

Then I had a sinking thought. "Does this mean you can't watch over Abria anymore?" Had my stupidity robbed Abria of the protection she needed? I shrunk at the thought.

He shook his head. "Guardians often watch over more than one person."

"Oh." Why did that open door gape like a nightmare waiting for me to fall asleep so it could suck me in? "Why do you look like you're not happy to be my guardian?"

He ran his hands down his face, blinked, then smiled. "I'm very pleased to...protect you. I just wasn't expecting it to happen this way."

"So this—you being my guardian—is a result of an accident?"

"It doesn't matter now, Zoe. What's done is done."

"It matters to me. All this time I got the feeling you were terrified of touching me because...well, I don't know why. Then when you did, I find out

I forced you to be my guardian?"

"You're worrying about something you needn't worry about."

"I'm not sure I like feeling like an accident."

"You're not an accident." He sat forward and laid his hand on my shoulder. I fell back against the seat as if sucked by an unseen power that, if possible, would draw me through the very fibers of the seat and into Matthias. His warm, soothing aura flowed through my body in a comforting swirl, as though his arms wrapped around me. I closed my eyes, took a breath. My worries vanished.

Then his hand was gone.

"Will it always be like that when…you touch me?" My eyes fluttered open and my gaze met his through the mirror. His penetrating gaze dove through every barrier that separated us.

"Yes."

I closed my eyes again, enjoying the luscious residual tingling left by his touch. Like nothing I had ever experienced before. Every cell completely satiated with love. No wonder Abria was calm.

I opened my eyes, a content smile on my face. My eyes magnetically went to his, drawn as I was to the way he made me feel. He dipped his head. I had the distinct feeling his power humbled him.

"What's it like?" my voice was barely a whisper. He lifted his gaze to me. "Having that effect on people?"

"It's a gift of the calling. I won't take credit for a divine endowment."

Speechless, lost in total awe, I merely stared into his unblinking eyes. He was amazing. Didn't he know that?

I stared straight ahead, at the gas station buzzing with people filling up their cars, coming out of the store with Big Gulps even though it was freezing outside. A miracle had happened in my car, and life—tedious, unimportant—went on around us without noticing the phenomenon. It didn't seem right. Because we'd been sitting a few minutes in the idling car, the air started to chill. I turned on the heat and scrubbed my arms.

"It's cold." I looked at Matthias in his Easter egg colored clothing.

"Are you cold?"

He shook his head.

"You're not dressed very warmly. I mean, you look like you might be visiting from the tropics."

"My body doesn't feel temperature the way yours does anymore. A result of the refining process. I feel heat and I feel cold, but neither affects me negatively."

"Cool." So much about him pricked my interest. Would his being my guardian allow me unlimited access to the answers I sought?

"I guess I should head home now." I put my hands on the wheel and drove out of the parking lot. The trip to Britt's had been worth this, if it meant I had Matthias as a guardian, even for a day.

"Where were you going tonight, Zoe?"

Purposefully, I kept my eyes on the road. "Oh...just out for a drive."

"A house," he said. I gulped. "Brick, two-story, lawn laden with jolly creatures of the night?"

"How do you know that?"

He leaned forward, the motion sending a wave of energy surging my direction. My body absorbed the movement, a powerful thrust that made my breath skip, my heart flutter. "When we touched, I connected with your spirit. It happens when a guardian takes on a charge."

Uh-oh. "What does that mean, *exactly?*"

His lips lifted in a light grin. "It means I have a direct line inside of your head."

I was in trouble. "You're joking, right? Because that would be a major breech of privacy. Major."

He nodded. "Nevertheless, that's how it works."

My throat clutched. Surely, this connection didn't allow him a front row seat to my thoughts. I would never be free to think what I wanted again. "I'm sorry, but that's just wrong."

Matthias looked too pleased. He sat back like a king who'd just made a decree, and took Abria's flapping hand in his, his touch stilling her on contact.

"Like it or not, I know what you are thinking, don't I, Miss Abria?"

Abria broke out in a long string of giggles. Her effervescence annoyed me. "That's fine with someone like Abria who can't communicate. But I can talk just fine. It's not fair for you to jump into my head. This could be... embarrassing."

"You think you're the only one to think something rude or nasty?"

"Oh, man. I'm going to have to do some heavy editing."

His hearty laugh filled the car.

"Are most of the people who are watched over children?" I thought of Chase's experience with the lady in the forest.

"A good percentage." He took Abria by the hand, placed her palm across his and tickled the back of her hand in light fluttering strokes that caused her eyes to widen and her body to go still. "There is nothing more precious than a child, and nothing more heinous than those who hurt them."

"How long have you been Abria's guardian?"

"I stepped in when your Mother's aunt Janis moved onto another assignment."

I nearly slammed my foot on the breaks. "Aunt..." I was speechless for a moment. I'd never met Mom's aunt, but Mom had adored her. She'd passed away before I was born. "Aunt Janis was Abria's guardian?"

Matthias nodded

"Why didn't I see her before?"

"You weren't ready, Zoe."

No doubt. I probably would have freaked. "Still, Aunt Janis...cool."

"Family members, if they have been refined, receive first priority to watch over their loved ones. After that, those closest to the family line are called in."

"That is...wow. That's so awesome." Aunt Janis was a relative, so it made sense to me that she would be in the position of guardian. "You said those closest to the family." I eyed him. "Where do you fit in?"

His lips lifted. "Nifty question." His gaze fastened to mine, and flickered with sapphire light, sending a beam of excitement shooting through my veins as if I stood on precipice, my hand in his hand. "Zoe, you and I…"

What? What? Are friends? Distantly related—please, I hope that's not it. Meant to be together? Don't leave me hanging. He smiled, as if he'd heard me, and my face prickled with heat.

"That's one question I'm not able to answer yet."

"Grr. Of course not."

He laughed and held up both hands. "But I promise, in time, you'll understand."

Sweet peace tingled in my blood. Someday, I'd know what Matthias and my connection was. I couldn't wait. In the meantime…I let out a smiling sigh. In the meantime—*deal with it Zoe.*

"So, where was Aunt Janis assigned? Or can I know?"

He smiled. "You can know. She's helping out in Transition."

"Transition?"

"When spirits first come into the afterlife, they've a lot to deal with. Many are surprised to find that life goes on. In Transition, other spirits help them adjust."

"That blows me away. Do you know her—my aunt?"

"She's a dandy woman."

I could hardly believe this was happening to me. I was the luckiest girl in the world—I was certain of it, for possessing this gift. "I have a friend, Chase, who has seen spirits. You told me that someone has to be spiritually sensitive and open, but…" Did he know Chase had ulterior motives?

"Your friend possesses the gift as long as his heart is pure." Matthias' eyes met mine in the dark reflection of the mirror and something flashed in his that sent an uncertain shiver through my body.

"So…he won't have the gift any more?"

"As long as his heart is pure."

When Matthias spoke of a truth, my bones quaked. Power and conviction was in his every word.

I took the road that wound up the hill to our house. Snow started to fall. White dusty air came at us like millions of falling stars reflecting against my headlights.

What had started out as a drive to self-indulgence had turned into an uplifting night with the hottest guy on the planet—when he was *on* the planet. The evening was over. Abria and I were safe at home. Matthias would go.

I let out a sigh and lifted my foot off the gas pedal so the car inched along. I snuck a glance at Matthias to see if he noticed my obvious change of speed. He was watching Abria, whose head was starting to loll, eyes starting to droop in sleepiness.

"Looks like our Miss Abria is ready for her dreams." The warm-milk tonic of his voice nearly put me into a state of total relaxation, too. I yawned. "It doesn't feel like this automobile has the horsepower of my roadster." His face lit in a teasing expression that snapped me out of sleepy comfort.

I sat erect, and gave the gas pedal a press. "Okay, so you knew I was trying to slow down."

He nodded, smiled. "Yes, that much I heard."

Yikes. I'd have to watch my thoughts when I was around him, or I'd implicate myself in all sorts of potentially humiliating scenarios.

At home, I pulled into the driveway and cut the engine. I turned in my seat. Abria was out like a light so I looked at Matthias, coveting each precious second. "We're here. Mission accomplished."

"Yes." He patted the backseat with both hands, as if readying to launch himself into oblivion. "For now."

"Okay, I admit I was going to a friend's house. But I would never put Abria in danger, you have to believe me."

His gaze softened. "You know, Pop used to tell me, when impulse is driven by desire, it can be perilous."

Kind of funny coming from a man who ran an illegal drinking establishment. "I'd like to know more about your pop. He sounds interesting."

He lowered his head without responding. My heart pounded hard and heavy as if trying to beat not just for me, but for him. My mind swirled with images I'd never seen before, nor could I see them clearly now, the speed with which they spun like the wheel of a racing car. Matthias' memories? Smiles. Laughter. Faces. Soft dresses. Men in suits. Drinking. Dark hallways. Darker alleys. Money fluttering through the air like snowflakes.

In a blink the images were gone. No sound. No pictures. My mind was blank.

Matthias lifted his head and his clear blue eyes met mine. "Pop was a man who enjoyed his life." Regret lined his tone. Had his dad been a *good* man? Where was he now?

"I saw your memory."

He nodded. "Connections can be that way sometimes. I must go now."

"Matthias—" How could I express the depth of my gratitude? "Thanks."

"You're welcome."

"I'd better get Abria inside. It's getting cold out here. I know you can't feel it, Mr. Tropic, but for those of us here on earth, freezing temps are nothing to play around with." I got out my car, jogged around to Abria's door and opened it. She slept soundly in her car seat. Matthias was gone.

✤ FOURTEEN

Matthias didn't leave me.

I wasn't sure if it was the direct line he talked about or what, but in my heart and soul, I felt a definite change—a presence. Not in a way that he hung over my shoulders, watching me twenty-four-seven, but as though the love inside of me had opened its arms and embraced him into my being.

As if a missing piece had been found. And fit.

At school the next day, Chase kept a wary eye on me from his desk. After Matthias told me Chase would only be able to continue seeing spirits if his heart remained pure, I was tempted to share that bit of fact with him. Maybe then he'd drop the opportunistic idea about exploiting guardians.

I shocked Chase when I smiled and waved him over. He looked around, wide-eyed behind his glasses, then stood and joined me at my desk. "You're not mad anymore?"

I pulled over the chair from the empty desk next to mine. "Of course not. Sit down."

He did. "That's good. I was worried about it."

"Chase." I patted his shoulder, and his gaze locked on where my hand made contact with his shirt. "You're worrying about something you needn't worry about."

Chase swallowed. "You've been touched."

My hand froze on his shoulder. Slowly, I drew it back. "How did you know?"

"I felt it. Just now."

"But...how?"

He leaned close. "I've been touched, too, remember the lady in the forest? I know what it feels like. It just happened, right?" Chase pressed.

"Last night. And now, he's my guardian."

"What?! That might explain why you didn't feel anything different when I...uh...touched you. You didn't, right?"

"No, I didn't."

Chase tapped his chin. "Must have something to do with how long ago my experience with the lady in the forest was. Anyway, tell me." When I hesitated, he looked like a cricket had jumped down his underwear. "I won't say anything to anyone, I promise."

"It's what you'd *write* that worries me."

"I put my pens away." He flashed a grin.

I tried to gauge whether or not he was really telling me the truth. His big puppy-dog eyes seemed sincere behind his glasses. "I doubt God would allow one person to foul things up. Look what happened to Lucifer."

Chase's eyes grew huge. He swallowed. Without thinking, I patted him again, this time on his knee. His eyes shot to my hand.

"Did you feel it again?" I asked.

"Yeah." He nodded. "This just reaffirms what I thought before."

"What?"

"People who have been touched by guardians are interconnected. Like Kevin Bacon and actors."

I doubted his theory had any merit. In my mind, the connection might feel like an invisible cable, but it was the spirit residing within me that was different now because of Matthias. The bond was internal.

"This deserves further discussion," he whispered, stood when he noticed our teacher, Mrs. Brewer glancing over. "Starbucks. Seven. Tonight."

He walked away before I could answer him. I held back a chuckle. He sat at his desk like James Bond—cocky, with a flair of drama—then sent me a solemn nod. I nodded back, then turned so he wouldn't see the smile on my face.

※ ※ ※

After Journalism, I headed to US history. I had a few butterflies lodged in my stomach anticipating seeing Britt. I walked in, greeted a few friends, then sat at my desk. Hers was empty.

Where was she? Having not heard from her in over twenty-four hours, I started worrying that she'd done something stupid—she was so distraught about Weston.

Covertly, I slid out my cell phone and texted her.

where r u?

Ten minutes into Mr. Brinkerhoff's lecture and still no word from Britt. I decided I'd go by her house after school just to make sure she was okay.

We were still studying the 1920's, so I listened, even more curious now about the time period. Mr. Brinkerhoff, rotund in his brown suit and pasted hair, looked like an English beetle. When he got passionate about a subject—which was most of the year because he loved any and all history—spit coagulated at the corners of his mouth into stretchy balls so distracting, it was hard to listen to what he was saying.

Today, the stringy white stuff held the class glued—those of us observant enough to pay attention in the first place—to his every word. "You have to understand that most of the population was conventional," Mr. Brinkerhoff began. "Working jobs, farming. There was only a small percentage of avant-garde who enjoyed themselves, indulging in the lifestyle associated with the roaring twenties."

"The speakeasies were a manifestation of the disillusionment that followed WWI."

I opened my history book and browsed the chapter we were studying as he rambled. Photos fascinated me, and were reminiscent of the flamboyant celebrities and parties of today: girls in dresses dripping with fringe and satin sashes. Pearls and beads dangling around their necks. Men in suits accentuating shoulders and lean hips, their shoes shiny and polished, hair slick and flat, parted with a straight line. The posh crowd looked like nifty designer dolls. This was how Matthias had dressed. This was his world. My fingers traced the photos with longing. I wished I'd lived then. Known him.

"Life was the cat's meow for some—a popular term then. But it was a hazardous time for others," Mr. Brinkerhoff said. "If you ran a juice-joint or speakeasy, you watched your back, your front—as in the door—and your sides—as in any entrance to the place. Double crossing was a danger. When you had something that people wanted, like money and booze, there were always those who'd bump you off just to prove a point. Owners often paid for protection and when they didn't, wham."

I looked up. Mr. Brinkerhoff made a gesture of having his throat cut. I shuddered.

"All for alcohol?" somebody asked.

"That's so tame compared to today's violent outbreaks," someone else put in.

"People die over alcohol every day," another girl said. "They get drunk, get on the road, and kill some innocent person and maybe themselves."

Murmurs followed. I shrunk in my seat remembering last night. That could have been me.

A plain-faced girl in a molly denim jumper sat across from me. Her comments through the semester spoke volumes about how she hated partiers and socialites. "Serves them right," she said.

Outrage broke out in a verbal fight. I was shocked Miss Molly—I didn't know her real name— had spoken out. She must have known it was going to cost her. But socially, she was a nobody anyway—which sucked for her.

Her face blanched red and she looked down at the desk, at her hands clasped so tight her knuckles whitened. I almost jumped into the fight but I saw her lower lip tremble. A pang of anguish rippled through me. Poor girl.

Mr. Brinkerhoff quieted everyone with a loud fingers-in-the-mouth whistle.

"Psycho," a guy mumbled.

The girl lowered her head. Her whole body looked like it had turned to steel. I had the urge to reach over and pat her arm, but didn't.

When class was over, everyone filed out, still spouting off disagreements with the molly chick who timidly hung back so as to not go with the flow. That's when I noticed him. An older man dressed in soft shades, and similar to the clothing Matthias wore. He stayed close to her side as she wove through the desks toward the door.

My heart tapped against my ribs. I followed her down the hall, staying a safe distance behind. The man's white hair was slicked back, baring a kind face with gentle angles and a ready smile. He was completely attentive to her, watching her every move, not one second wasted on where he was going because he flowed through the crowds like an unseen current.

She went to the end of the long hall and took the stairs up to the second floor. It was Friday. School was out for the week, so I imagined she was going to her locker to get books to take home.

I followed.

Sure enough, she went to her locker which was at the very end of the hall, on the bottom corner. Robotically, she kneeled down, twirled the dial, opened the locker and neatly stacked her books. Then she shut the door. Odd. Most kids took home their books for further study over the weekend and I figured a brain like her would do the same.

Her guardian stood over her shoulder, watching intently. The hall started to empty out, and I realized it would be very obvious that I was there without a reason, so I picked out a locker nearby and pretended to fiddle with it, throwing occasional glances down the hall.

She shut the locker, rose to her feet, smoothed her denim jumper and stood in the hall for a moment. Keeping my face toward the locker door, I tried to sneak peeks at her without her noticing. Her eyes shot straight ahead, her posture was erect as a post.

She started in my direction and I played with the locker dial. They drew closer. My heart thumped. I looked at the man, waiting for his eyes to meet mine. But his attention never left hers and as they passed, I couldn't stop myself.

"I see you," I blurted.

They both turned. Both stared at me.

"You," I nodded at him. "I see you."

Her eyes widened. "Me?"

"Yes, you." I walked over, my gaze shifting from her—she was shocked that I was talking to her—to the man standing at her side. He looked mildly surprised, but his smile was genuine.

I tried my best to communicate with him without her noticing, but I couldn't take my eyes off him. He had the same soft radiance Matthias had. A magnetic field surrounded him. His eyes were kind, his smile calming and gentle. I wished Miss Molly could see him. Matthias said seeing heavenly beings was a gift. I was certain she could handle whatever was troubling her if she knew she wasn't alone.

"Where are you going?" I asked her.

She seemed stunned that I'd ask, let alone care. "Home."

I verified her answer with a look at the gentleman. His smile faltered some.

"That's not where she's really going," he said. His voice was laden with tenderness. He must be a grandfather, some relative of hers. Thrill shot from my toes to my heart. I smiled at him, then at her. He was there to protect her, to make sure she didn't do something to hurt herself, the unspoken message was clear.

"Where do you live?" I asked her.

"Why do you care?"

"Um."

She started walking, throwing annoyed, fearful glances at me. Her guardian kept steady pace at her side. I tagged along. "You don't have homework?"

Her brows went up. "Why do you want to know?"

"You left your books." I gestured with a nod in the direction of her locker. "Most of us have to study at night, but, obviously you don't have to. That's lucky for you."

She stopped, glared. "Look, you don't know me, I don't know you and this attempt at being my friend is about as transparent as glass."

"You're right," I said. "You want to know why I'm talking to you?"

She shifted. "I guess."

"Because you looked so upset in class. I followed you because I thought you might hurt yourself."

Her face twisted. She took a step back. The gentleman's lips curved up slightly and he gave me a nod of approval.

"That's ridiculous," she stammered, walking on. I stayed at her other shoulder.

"Leave me alone, okay?"

"How about we go to Starbucks and get a drink? My treat. We can talk and—"

"Like that's going to happen." She smirked. "Don't you have some jock you want to go sleep with?"

My mouth fell open. The guardian's face flashed with frustration and embarrassment. "She's out of sorts. I apologize."

"Don't worry about it," I said. "I understand."

"I'm not worrying about it," she spat and took a left down the stairs.

"What can I do?" I asked the guardian. I felt like water was evaporating before my eyes. "I should do something. What? Tell me." I stopped on the stairs.

The girl continued, taking the stairs at a half-skip. He remained at her side, but looked over his shoulder at me, his appreciative gaze holding mine a moment. "You've done enough. Thank you."

A burst of calm filled me. I walked in a euphoric glow to my car. I'd seen another guardian. Outside of seeing Matthias, nothing more thrilling had ever happened to me. I couldn't stop smiling. Would I see more?

In the parking lot, I glanced around—then felt silly. Few students remained at school so of course I wouldn't see any guardians here, not now anyway. Interesting that I hadn't seen any others at school earlier. But then I'd been so locked on Miss Molly and her guardian, I wouldn't have noticed.

I unlocked my car and got in.

Luke.

I texted him and waited, mulling over the kind gentleman assigned to Miss Molly. Who was he? I itched to know. But if Heaven was filled with Earth's former residents, that meant zillions of people lived there. That meant the chances of Matthias knowing that girl's guardian were slim to none.

So what. I'd seen another angel, that was the miracle. That was enough.

My cell phone vibrated and I clicked it on.

im busy

doing what?

He didn't answer. Could this be more frustrating? Strangely, my blood didn't boil like it usually did when Luke broke the rules.

The girl's face came into my mind. I'd seen her around since freshman year. She'd been in some of my classes. She started high school wearing a pony tail and still wore her hair that way. Who wore denim jumpers? Pregnant women. I was pretty sure she wasn't pregnant, just fashion-challenged.

I shouldn't think of her like that, she was a lonely girl who probably didn't have a lot of friends. But she probably had family who cared about her. I'd looked into that gentleman's eyes and saw deep caring, the kind a grandparent has for a grandchild. *He* cared.

For a moment I wished I knew where she lived. I would go there and see how she was. Make sure she was okay. I was unspeakably glad that I'd seen her guardian with her. Whatever happened next was out of my control, but the assurity that she wasn't alone enabled me to let go of my concerns.

I started my car, and texted Luke: **so u'll tell mom and dad why you didn't come home with me?**

No answer.

I pulled up to Britt's and parked. Her white mustang sat out front, so I figured she was home. Both her parents were still at work since their cars

183

weren't in the driveway. It was only four o'clock.

I knocked. Waited. Knocked again.

I took out my cell phone and texted her.

hey

After a few minutes of waiting, I gave up and went back to my car just as I heard the revved growl of an engine barreling down the street. Weston's silver truck was speeding toward me. He had Brady in the car with him. Both guys looked surprised to see me. The truck jerked to a stop and the boys jumped out and ran toward Britt's door.

"What?" I jogged after them.

Weston's fists banged on the wood door in heavy thuds. "Britt!"

"What is it?"

"She's crazy." Weston pounded again.

"What do you mean?"

"Britt!" He gave one last bang on the door then started around the side of the house, Brady and me at his heels.

"What happened?" I asked Brady as we followed Weston.

"She told him he was going to be sorry." Brady shrugged. "Psycho if you ask me."

"But not too psycho for you to hook up with, right?"

Brady shot me a fiery glance before we met up with Weston at Britt's backdoor, his fingers skimming the top of the door frame for Britt's extra house key. He found it and jammed it into the lock, then thrust open the door. Brady and I stayed close to Weston's heels as he raced through the kitchen, up the stairs, and straight to Britt's bedroom.

"Britt!" He threw open the door and we all tumbled in to Britt's bright pink and red bedroom. Britt lay with her eyes closed, sprawled on the bed in her sheer black bra and panties, her hair a scraggly mess, empty vodka bottles littering the floor around her bed.

Weston and Brady both came to a screeching halt. Weston crammed his hands into his dark hair. Brady's face turned crimson. He covered his gaping mouth with a hand.

I broke between the two of them, embarrassed for Britt that she was practically naked but more than that, I hoped she was still breathing. I darted to the bed, sat next to her and pressed my fingers to the vein in her neck. A pulse beat hard.

I let out a breath. "She's alive." I patted her cheeks with my hands. "Britt? Britt?" When she moaned and moved, my racing heart started to slow. I got up and pulled the bedspread up and over as much of her as I could, but she was laying on half of it.

"Get over here and help me," I demanded.

Weston and Brady came to my aid, Weston glaring at Brady. "This is your fault."

"She's your ho."

"Shut up both of you! Weston, take her upper body. Brady, grab her legs."

"I don't want him touching her," Weston bit out.

"Get over it."

Brady lifted her legs, his eyes trying not to gravitate up the rest of her.

"Just do it," I said. They raised her and I pulled back the covers. "Lay her down."

After they did, I arranged the bedspread around her. Weston and Brady stood back, watching. Thick, mucky silence hung in an invisible triangle. Britt groaned again. Her eyes fluttered open.

"Wes?"

"Hey." He kneeled down next to the side of the bed. "What are you doing? You scared the hell out of me."

"I did?" She blinked. Her voice sounded tiny, pathetic. I cringed. Did she really want him to save her? Did she think that was what a healthy relationship was all about—manipulation? She looked like a weakling. I'd never find myself like that. Ever.

I saw concern in his eyes but also fear—like he was wondering if Brady's "psycho" comment was justified. I had the troubling thought that Britt's efforts to reel in and hook Weston might catch her in the snare.

"You came," she muttered, dreamy-eyed to Weston.

Weston glanced at me and Brady—as if he was trapped in a terrible version of some white trash movie.

"I knew you'd come." She rolled closer to him, and her backside was exposed.

Weston nodded and appeared at a loss for words. Brady fidgeted next to me. I walked around the side of the bed, next to Weston, so Britt could see me. Her dazed eyes shifted from Weston to me. "What are you doing here?"

"I came to check on you when you weren't at school today. I ran into Weston out front."

"I don't need your help, he's here." Britt warbled out, and reached for Weston's neck to hug him. When he didn't lean close, she settled for clinging to his sweater sleeves.

"Yeah, he's here. So is Brady." *You've got your whole fan club.*

Britt jerked around, saw Brady, and her eyes widened. It was then she seemed to realize that she was in her underwear, and she pulled the blanket up around and over her body. "You two talking again?" she asked but since she was looking at Brady, it wasn't clear which guy she was addressing.

Brady's gaze fell to his shuffling feet. Weston cleared his throat and stood, the distance he created between himself and Britt an obvious message. "You sent us both the text."

Uh-oh. "She probably hit Brady's name in her address book by accident," I put in, hoping the suggestion might help somehow. Weston's tilted head told me he doubted it. Brady didn't meet my gaze, his eyes still on the floor.

Britt sat up, the bedspread falling around her waist. Just a second ago, she appeared to care whether or not any of us saw her. "My head is throbbing," she muttered, holding her skull with both hands. "Wes?"

Weston's eyes flicked from Britt's chest to Brady. He jerked his head in the direction of the door in a silent gesture of *get lost*. I took the cue and crossed to Brady, tugging his sleeve. "Let's leave them alone."

Brady followed me out and I shut the door. I leaned against one wall,

Brady against another. "How did you end up in Weston's car coming here?"

Brady shrugged. "The two of us settled this. It's no biggie, you know?"

"No biggie," I said. "That's why he asked you to leave."

"You asked me to leave."

"So, what, are you going to make a play for Britt? Share her? I don't get it."

"You don't have to get it. It's none of your business."

Just a few weeks ago, Brady had spoken to me civilly. I didn't know what had changed, but I figured Britt had probably poisoned him because she was mad at me. "You're right. None of this is my business."

I headed down the hall. Let Britt solve her own problems. I'd come to make sure Britt was okay and gotten myself chastised for the effort. The unfairness rubbed me raw.

In the kitchen, I bumped into Britt's dad, tall, suited and sophisticated. My heart skipped. "Oh, hey, Mr. Walker."

"Hi Zoe." He loosened his tie and smiled at me. I thought of the triangle upstairs, of the trouble Britt would get in because she was drunk, had missed school, and had two guys in her bedroom when she was in her underwear. My first instinct was to distract her dad. She'd do the same for me.

Or would have.

"Where's Brittany?" he asked.

"Upstairs." I headed for the back door, opened it. "She's not feeling very well."

Mr. Walker's dark brows drew together. "Oh? I'll go and see what I can do. Nice to see you again. Don't make yourself so scarce." He winked and walked out of the kitchen.

The door shut behind me and I headed to my car. I got in, started the engine and drove toward home. I'd been friends with Britt through all of high school. We were each other's constant. Losing her hurt. What would happen to our friendship now?

I pulled out my cell phone to check for texts. None from Luke. Five from Chase. I opened one.

c u 2 nite

Sent five times. I smiled. The guy was a geek. Likeable, but definitely a geek.

Where was Luke? I drove, my gaze searching the streets of town. Of course I wouldn't see him—I was in a nice neighborhood, with sturdy houses and tidy fenced yards. His world was in neglected, broken down places.

I texted him. ***where r u?***

I set my phone on the empty seat next to me and continued to glance at it as I drove home.

Nothing.

I was anxious to meet Chase. Maybe my excitement to see him was due in part to the fact that Britt and I weren't speaking to each other, as much as the fact that Chase and I shared an unusual kinship. Would I tell him I'd seen that girl's guardian?

The towering pines and aspens surrounding home shimmied and shook, causing a soft roar from the wind. A shiver ran through me. I darted into the house and was overcome with warmth and the scent of garlic and tomatoes. Pizza. Mom would be disappointed that Luke wasn't with me, and my heart took a hit.

"Mom?" I dropped my purse and keys on the coat rack seat and headed toward the source of the aromatic scent.

"In here."

Abria ran past me, giggling. I doubled back to the front door and bolted it, noting that she locked her gaze on my fingers, turning the bolt. *Uh-oh.* I'd seen that intense look before: she was going to make a break for it.

I scooped her up in my arms and wagged my finger at the door. "No unlocking the door. No running away."

Then again, if she happened to get out, at least Matthias would be with her. I grinned.

I carried her back to the kitchen and set her at the table. The act did little to dissuade her: as if an invisible magnet drew her to the front door, and her eyes stared in that direction.

Mom's face was remarkably radiant. I didn't have the heart to tell her Luke wasn't with me.

"Hey," I said. The table was already set. "Who set the table?"

Mom opened the oven with two-mitted hands. "Luke. He did a great job, didn't he?"

"He's here? Who brought him? I texted him and he didn't answer me."

"He said he got a ride from a friend because his phone died and he couldn't reach you."

Mom set the pizza in the middle of the table. The steaming aroma reached up and took hold of my senses. My stomach growled. I sat down and dished up some leafy greens for Abria, then for myself. At least Luke was home. I wasn't sure if his story about the phone was real or not, but clearly Mom had bought it. Maybe it was true.

"Where's Dad?" I reached for a piece of pizza, noticing that Dad's place was set.

"Up changing his clothes. Isn't it great we're going to get to eat together?"

Mom's joy was so sweet, I smiled. I liked being at the house when it was home—like now. Mom yelled for Luke and Dad and then she sat down next to Abria and gave her a piece of pizza.

"It feels good to be out of those work clothes." Dad came in wearing jeans and a green knit shirt. His face radiated like Mom's, no doubt because Luke was home. I hoped Luke took a good look at their faces.

Dad pulled out a chair and sat. "I thought Luke was here?" Dad craned around, looking.

I waved my hand. *I'm here.* But Dad missed my wave. He held out his plate to me, indicating he wanted a slice of pizza. Since I was closest to the platter, I cut him a piece and plopped it on his plate.

"Luke!" Mom called before sitting.

Abria dug into her pizza, peeling off the pepperoni and sticking the red quarter-sized pieces into her mouth.

Luke ambled in, jerking his hair off his face. I swear he kept his eyes covered so no one could see them. He plunked down in a chair and grabbed three pieces of pizza. Mom grinned. Dad eyed Luke with a hesitant, curious expression that told me he was wary of jumping on the Luke's-here-so-he-must-not-be-high band wagon.

"So your phone died?" I asked.

Luke's mouth wrapped around the tip of a pizza slice.

"Who'd you ride home with?"

He chewed, staring at his slices. In our family, a full mouth exempted you from conversation. His rotating mouth slowed.

"How's the pizza?" Mom interjected, as if she was trying to buy him time. I couldn't believe she didn't want to know the truth.

"Who?" I pressed.

"He said it was a friend of his, Zoe." Mom looked at me with that please be quiet look. I ignored it, and turned my attention back to Luke who swallowed his bite.

"Kevin?"

Luke lifted the slice to his mouth, eyeing it.

"Who gave you a ride?" I asked.

"Zoe, is it really necessary?" Dad's glare told me to zip my lips.

"I thought you'd want to know. I mean, he's supposed to ride home with me and only me. If I was his parent, and I had a son who'd just gotten caught with a bag of Lortabs in his room, I'd want to know who he was spending his time with."

"Shut the hell up!" Luke threw down his pizza slice and pounded his fists on the table. Everyone jumped.

Abria laughed.

"That's enough," Dad boomed.

Abria always laughed when tension sung in the air, as if she heard the pitch and her only way of responding was to mock it in the face.

Luke leapt to his feet. "I am so sick of you always condemning me! What about you coming home so late Mom and Dad don't see the five bottles of vodka you drank? What about that? Screw this!" He stormed from the table, heading right for the front door.

Both Mom and Dad stood. Mom ran after him.

"Luke. Luke don't go!"

"Debbie." Dad followed her.

I shook from head to toes. Of course Luke knew about my partying, and I shouldn't be surprised that he threw it in my face. I had it coming. I just didn't think he had the nerve to do it.

Rather than face the questioning and yelling I knew was coming, I got up, took my plate to the sink and headed for the backdoor.

"Zoe!" Dad. I froze.

Mom returned to the table, face twisted in a sniffling mess of tears. She collapsed into her chair. Resentment bubbled inside of me that Luke could illicit such a reaction.

I crossed my arms over my chest, waiting for Dad to chew me out. When the anger on his face melted into hurt, my own anger withered. Mom's weeping mixed with Abria's giggles.

"I know you feel angry about Luke and what he's done, but I don't think it helps for you to attack him like that," Dad's voice was quiet.

In my heart I knew he was right, but it was hard for me not to protect them. "I'm sorry," I whispered. My condemnation of Luke had hurt them miles more than it had offended Luke.

I crossed to Dad. "I'm really sorry. I didn't mean to say those things and hurt you guys. I'd never do that."

"Abria, please…" Mom's plea for Abria to stop laughing went ignored by my sister who simply stood on her chair and continued in hyena mode. The sound grated on my nerves.

"Abria, stop!" I shouted.

"Zoe." Dad's anguished eyes looked into mine. "Is this true? About you and the drinking?"

A knot formed in my throat. If I lied to protect their hearts, that would be okay, wouldn't it? They'd taken too many hits lately. I could tell them the truth later. Abria stood on her chair at the end of the table and flapped like a bird. If only I could take flight, I'd fly far away from this pain and never disappoint them again.

If I lied, I'd be no better than Luke.

"It's true."

Mom let out a soft cry. I couldn't look at her.

"How long?" Dad's voice was quiet and deadly as a torpedo.

"I haven't done it in a long time."

Mom stood, shaking her head. She gathered her full plate, fork and glass. "Unreal. I can't believe not one child but both of you. Both of you." She went to the kitchen, dropping the plates into the sink in a clattering of breaking glass. "And you have the gall to criticize Luke!" The veins along the sides of her neck lifted. "You both sicken me."

"I had a few drinks, so what? I told you, I don't do that anymore."

"And you expect us to believe you? Like you expected us to believe that Luke lied to us about the Lortabs?"

"Don't go blaming those on me!" Fury burst in my heart. "Those were Luke's!"

Mom jerked out a nod. "Unfortunately, Zoe, I don't know who to believe when both of my children lie to me. Abria, stop it!"

Abria was running back and forth across the table. None of us had noticed. I wanted to yank her down to the floor. Dad stomped over and grabbed her, holding her tight against his body. She whined and writhed. Dad's stare locked back on mine.

"So you two have had this secret pact, is that it? Did you think you could keep something like that from us forever?" Abria screamed and tried to bite Dad. He wrapped her arms around her chest and held tight. She let out a yowl.

"Of course they were hiding it," Mom spit out. "It was too much to expect us to believe in their trust."

"Why are you taking this out on me? Luke is just as guilty as I am and where is he? Of course he's gone. He always splits when the fire turns up."

Mom cleared the table in military fury, dropping her dishes into the sink as if they were paper. The breaking glass didn't stop her. And it didn't stop Dad.

"You're right. Luke is a part of this. But he's not here right now."

"Well, I'm not going to take his share *and* mine just because he left." I headed for the front door, my heart thrumming. I always took it all—the stress, the tears, the frustration. I grabbed my keys, purse and yanked open the front door.

"Zoe?" Dad's voice—as if he couldn't believe I would leave him. Tears rushed into my blinking eyes. The sting in my heart went deeper.

FIFTEEN

I had an hour before I was supposed to meet Chase. I was so frustrated, I wasn't sure I'd be able to sit down, let alone speak civilly to anyone. I wanted to crawl into a corner and sob. At the same time I wanted to rip someone apart.

Tears ran down my cheeks. I crossed through crunchy snow toward my car. Luke's was gone—another rule broken—no doubt he'd driven off in a fit. Like me. I got in my car, cranked the engine and pressed the gas pedal to the floor and screeched out of the driveway and into the street. Gray skies loomed, threatening more snow, and the roads were already wet. Ice would sheathe the streets soon. I didn't care.

This was Luke's fault—if he hadn't broken our unspoken trust and blurted out about my drinking none of this would have happened. I'd never said a word to Mom and Dad about him—not until he started this whole mess with his lie about the Lortabs. I headed in the direction of the log cabin, ready to lay into him.

My phone vibrated and I dug it out of my purse. Britt. Just what I needed. I was curious about what had happened at her house after I left, but at the same time knew there was a strong possibility she was calling to yell at me. I was angry enough to take whatever she dished out.

"What?"

"Thanks." Her tone was hard.

"For what?"

"Don't play stupid, Zoe. My dad went ballistic when he came upstairs."

"He asked where you were, I said upstairs."

Click.

I threw the phone down on the empty seat next to me. "Whatever. You had it coming."

"Most people do."

Matthias' voice had me screeching to a halt in the middle of the road. He sat in the center of the backseat, arms extended along the back of the bench, long legs cramped. The expression on his face was matter-of-fact. My heart soared at seeing him. But, soon after, it took a dive back into the angry pool of frustration churning in my gut.

I pressed on the gas again. "I'm fine, Matthias. You don't need to be here. In fact, I highly recommend that you leave. I'm really furious right now. *Really furious.*"

"Nice to see you too, Zoe. And this sounds like the perfect time for me to be here."

"Look, I'm angry but I wouldn't hurt myself, okay?"

"Like I said, most people have it coming—whatever it is they get." He continued, ignoring my protests. "Of course, that's how they learn. Like with me, for instance. I knew I shouldn't be in the business of distributing illegal alcohol. I knew it was dangerous. I'd seen what happens when debts aren't paid. But did that stop me? I thought I'd be the lucky one, the odd one out, if you will. But not so." He gestured with a swipe to the long cut he'd once had on his abdomen underneath his robin's egg blue shirt. "Old Mack the Knife bumped me off anyway."

"Mack the Knife?" I snickered. "There was really a guy named Mack the Knife?"

Matthias nodded. "More than one—the name was a symbol of death and bravery. Each mob family had their own Mack. The Cracciola family had Junior. Junior was the chap who bumped me off."

"You talk about it like you're talking about neighbors or some dude down the street or something. Not like you're talking about the guy who killed

195

you."

"I don't dwell on the act anymore, Zoe. What's the point?" His gaze was intense with layered meaning, and he tilted his head in taunt that said, 'And neither should you—dwell on things' I had to look away. I wasn't ready to stop dwelling on Luke and his lies. "Like I said, people get what's coming to them. Mack sure did," he said.

"What happened to him?"

"His body was distributed unequally between New Jersey and New York."

"Yikes."

The road was starting to ice under my wheels and I took my foot off the gas a little.

"A pretty doll like you shouldn't waste her time being angry."

A sigh fluttered from my lungs. "You keep saying stuff like that and I'll find ways to be riled just to hear you talk."

He smiled.

"Still," I took a left. "I need to find Luke and chew him out."

"Whoa. Let's back up a bit, shall we?" He sat forward, his energy like an unseen wave crashing through me. I gripped the wheel. My breath held in my chest. Would I ever get used to the way he moved through me? "What good is going to come of you talking to Luke at this moment?"

"I'll feel a hell—excuse me—*heck* of a lot better."

"Better than you feel now?"

Nothing could top the way I felt after his infusion of peace, but how easily the dark tentacles of frustration reached back in. "Those are your feelings, not mine."

"I can share them with you."

A long silence tied us together. When I tore my eyes from his, I found myself idling in the street in front of the log cabin. Luke's blue Samurai was parked out front, along with an old red Camero and a yellow and black truck that looked like a giant wasp.

I pulled next to the curb and turned off the engine, staring at the dark house. It was six. Didn't these people believe in electricity?

I wanted to go in there and yell at Luke, sure, but the sight of the place sent a shudder through me. This was probably a drug dealer's house, not a friendly neighbor's place where my little brother was playing.

"Think about what you want to accomplish here." Matthias said. "Luke is learning valuable lessons from his own actions. Your interference may jeopardize the outcome."

I opened the door, got out, and took a deep breath.

I felt a presence beside me, turned and jumped. Matthias. I glanced at the car, then eyed him. "How did you—I didn't hear the door...."

He rocked back on his heels, his hands in the front pockets of his slacks. His grin flashed. I headed up the path and Matthias stayed at my shoulder. Just having him with me infused me with power, even if the power wasn't mine. Still, I felt like I could do anything now: take these creeps and get my brother to safety.

Matthias stopped on the stoop and looked down into my eyes. "Don't take any wooden nickels."

"Wooden nickels haven't been used since, well, I don't know but it's been tons of years."

"I mean don't do anything stupid, Zoe. These guys are pikers through and through."

I knocked. "I can take care of myself. And if these *pikers* get out of hand, you'll be here, right?" I smiled.

He shook his head. "I can't go inside."

A knot formed in my throat. I realized then how awful this place really was. My heart banged.

"You don't have to go in either."

"I have to get my brother." I faced the door, my palms sweaty. I knocked.

The door ripped open and I looked into the face of a towering Paul Bunyan in ragged jeans and a red plaid, flannel shirt. His eyes narrowed over his scruffy beard. He stood more erect, his bulk blocking the door. "What?"

I rose to my tip-toes, searched over his shoulder. "Luke! I need to talk to you!"

"There's no Luke here," his tone scraped out.

"Nice try. His car's out front. Luke!" I ignored the big man's planted his feet and crossed arms. I glanced back at Matthias.

My heart stopped.

His jaw was knotted, his gaze stony and locked on the stranger in the doorway. His lean body was poised like a panther ready to attack. I took a breath, hoping the soft sound would break his determined concentration but Matthias remained statue still.

"Matthias," I whispered. His eyes didn't deviate from the big man. They shot like a sniper's red beam aimed for a kill. A ribbon of fear wove through me. I'd never seen Matthias like this: so intense, as though his look alone could cause this man to disintegrate into nothing.

When I heard movement, I turned. Paul Bunyan backed into the darkness of the house. I took a step. "Luke!"

The door slammed in my face.

Around me, an unseen current vibrant and electric burned and bounced off the walls of the house, door, and surrounding shrubs like a thousand firecrackers gone haywire. The hair on my body shot up.

I faced Matthias. His hardened gaze was still locked on the door. I panicked, thinking something had happened to him, but I was so charged with this electric element I was afraid to move, sure the very act would cause me to burst into flames.

I opened my mouth to say something. No sound came. Suddenly, he closed his eyes and let out a long, slow breath. His bunched muscles eased and smoothed beneath the soft fabric of his shirt and slacks as he stood erect. As his breath poured out, and the current in the air—the current swarming inside of me—ebbed, as if vacating my body at his silent command.

I crumpled to the stoop in an exhausted heap, breathless, sweaty and faint.

Matthias crouched down in front of me. He reached out and took my hands in his, gave them a warm squeeze, and then laid his palms on my head. "Zoe." The mere utterance of my name from his lips infused me with renewed strength, carried by the sound of his voice to my every cell.

I reached up and wrapped my fingers around his wrists. The blue in his eyes deepened, a kaleidoscope of midnight, moon and mystery that stole my breath and hypnotized my soul.

His hands gently eased from the top of my head to my cheeks. How I wanted him to hold me. Whatever had just happened had left my body quaking like an earthquake. I had strength in my limbs, but I wasn't sure I could call upon it to hold myself up.

Tenderly, he lifted me to my feet, his hands still at my cheeks. Then his hands slipped to my shoulders. "Are you all right?"

I nodded. I was sure my voice was gone after that experience. Somehow that electric vibe had wiped it away, the power so intense the residual jangling of my cells left me jumpy and so alert, my eyes were wide and open and I couldn't blink.

"What happened?" The sound of my voice was small and insignificant, like a distant echo in a cave.

I felt his palms on my shoulders, warm, potent, protective, the power gushing into my body like water from a shattered dam. His gaze left mine for the first time since the door had slammed shut, and focused on the house. "This is not a place for you."

"No kidding."

His sharp gaze penetrated to my core. The pressure of his hands on my shoulders sunk deep into my body as if he was making his point perfectly clear. "Never come here again."

Fear rushed up my throat, brought tears to my eyes. *Luke.* As if he read my thoughts, he nodded, spoke, "He'll come to know for himself that this place will only bring him misery. You mustn't endanger yourself again. Understand?"

I nodded. *Please don't let go. Take me away from here.* The protection of Matthias' touch slid from my shoulders, down my arms until his hands took mine. He stepped back, urging me along with a resolute tug. Comforted by his presence, mesmerized by his countenance, I followed in step with him until we were at the car.

In a blink, I was inside with Matthias next to me in the passenger seat. How did I get there?

"There seems to be more leg room up here." He glanced around, shifting like a cat settling into a comfortable position. "Do you mind if I ride up front?"

We drove in silence for a few moments. My mind spun. The energy whirling inside of me nearly burst my body into a million pieces. I was sure I'd evaporate, or levitate out of the car and into the night sky. The contented smile wouldn't leave my lips. I couldn't stop looking at Matthias.

Each moment he spent with me built on the last, creating a mountain of awe and respect so vast the thoughts in my head swirled and vanished trying to coherently understand themselves. Whatever had happened at that house, he'd taken complete control of the situation—not surprising, but utterly convincing. "Is that why you came tonight?" I asked.

"Your intentions are excellent. But I know you, Zoe. You're impulsive. Impulsive can be dangerous. Believe me, no one knows better than I."

"I can't imagine you reckless."

"A characteristic I possessed while mortal. Consequence was not a word in my vocabulary."

"What did you do? Come on, it couldn't have been that bad."

A half-smile tipped his lips up. "I don't need to fill your ear with my hoodlum ways."

I laughed. "I most definitely want to hear about your hoodlum ways. Hey, you know all about me."

He settled in the seat with a grin. "All right. What do you want to know?"

Were you close to your family? Did you have any brothers and sisters? What about your mom? And why do you always look sad when you mention your dad? I had dozens of questions, none of which I was brave enough to ask. His past seemed to pain him, and the last thing I wanted to do was hurt him.

"Yes. No. Mom left when I was four, and my father is not in a good spot right now. I suppose that's why I get a little melancholy when I speak of him."

"You heard me?"

He nodded.

"Lame that your mom left. I'm sorry." Pain needled my heart. *Was the pain his?*

"Pop did the best he could, raising me." *But times were hard and he was easily distracted, Zoe. Like Luke.*

An old sorrow in his eyes reached out to me. My heart banged in an agonizing ache, an ache I realized that even Heaven and its peace couldn't fully erase. Not when love was involved.

Pulsing into my mind came a flash of foreign images: startling blue eyes smiling down into mine as if I was a child, peering up. The brown shade of a ragged pair of wool slacks my fists clung to—for dear life. Bodies flowing around the two us. The sound of a train. Steam from bulky engines filling cold air. Voices. A conductor shouting, "All aboard!" Fear of the unknown.

I gazed up the pant leg, following the line of tattered coat with elbow patches, on up to chestnut hair beneath a rimmed hat. My body craved a look—*please look at me Pop. Don't let me get lost.*

Matthias' memory.

I blinked and the image vanished. *I want them back, let me see them again. Please.* My eyes met Matthias', his shadowed with an old sorrow.

"I saw another memory," I murmured. He nodded. "You still love him, don't you? Where is he?"

"Whatever you felt of me just now is the hope that my father and I can someday be together again."

Questions flew like a flock of birds in my head. "What does that mean?"

"There's not enough time for that discussion."

"Time! Crap, what time is it?" I looked at the clock in my dashboard. I had ten minutes until I was supposed to be at Starbucks. The evening was beyond my dreams, and the last thing I wanted to do was cut it short just to go sit and talk with Chase. Maybe if I drove aimlessly, the night would never end. Maybe I could keep Matthias with me.

I glanced at him. My heart swelled.

Thoughts of him reaching over and touching my face with his gentle hands, kissing me with his beautiful mouth…His eyes, fastened to mine, glittered with midnight stars. *Oh no!* I faced forward, a flush racing under my skin. *Had he heard me? No. No.*

I turned onto State Street and headed in the direction of Starbucks. *Supercalifragilisticexpialidocious.*

Supercalifragilisticexpialidocious.

Supercalifragilisticexpialidocious.

Anything to get those thoughts out of my head. Nothing worked. He was so close, his aura so strong. My mind weakened, and drifted back to the image of him reaching out and touching me.

He cleared his throat. I didn't dare look at him. "So, what do you think of…" My mind scrambled. "Of the leg room up front?"

His low chuckle teased me. "I like it much better up here."

Drawn to the sound of his voice, I looked at him. A smile danced on his lips. "This isn't fair."

"Would you like me to go?"

I shot him a smirk. "Didn't you just hear my thoughts?"

"I got some sort of abstract picture, yes. But I couldn't make out exactly what you were thinking. Perhaps if you put it into words—"

"*As if.* I'm almost at Starbucks. You want to come in? You could… hang…with Chase and me."

He craned a look around. "Starbucks. Isn't that a coffee joint?"

I nodded. "You've heard about it… in Heaven?"

"People are always talking about how much they miss their Starbucks. Is it really that outstanding?" He eyed the building as I pulled the car into the packed parking lot.

"It's a billion dollar corporation. I guess it is to some people."

"I was never much of a coffee drinker."

I was disappointed to think the evening was coming to an end. "They have other drinks, too. Lattes, frapps, steamers, stuff like that. You should try it."

"Not tonight, thank you."

I killed the engine and our eyes met. Time drifted. The sound of laughter tickled the air when the door to Starbucks opened. Would I ever know about his connection to me?

I opened my mouth to ask, and was startled by a light tapping on my window. I turned. Chase stood smiling behind his round glasses. He shot me a quick wave and then he smiled at Matthias. I whipped my head around, looked at Matthias who returned the wave back.

"He sees you," I croaked.

"Yes." Matthias nodded, still smiling at Chase. "Is this your friend you spoke of earlier? The one who's seen guardians?"

"Yes."

"A chipper fellow, isn't he? Perhaps you should open the door."

I rolled down the window. "Hi."

"Hey, you coming in?" Chase's curious gaze flicked from me to Matthias.

"In a minute. Did you just get here?"

"I've been waiting inside. I saw you pull up."

Chase couldn't take his eyes off Matthias. The vibe between them bounced and jumped like the current of a tazer gun. "I'll be right in. Can you get us a table?"

"You're Matthias, aren't you?"

Uh-oh. Was there some divine law we were breaking by having a conversation with Chase? Matthias appeared his usual calm self, so I assumed none of us was going to turn into dust for the interaction. Still, it freaked me out a little that Chase could see my guardian. An odd possessiveness flushed through me.

Matthias nodded at Chase. "I am."

Chase blew out an excited breath and nearly jumped up and down. "I knew it! I knew it! This is beyond cool." Chase's smile was huge. "You know, when I saw you pull up, I had a feeling that was him." Chase slapped the top of my car with his hand. "Wow. This is really awesome." He shifted feet with the enthusiasm of a two year old on his birthday. "So what are you guys doing? Was Zoe in danger?" He popped his head up over the car, looked around. "Is something going to happen? *Did* something happen?"

I'd had enough. I turned to Matthias. I didn't want him to go, but Chase made continuing our talk impossible. "I'm going inside now."

"Very good."

I don't want to. I really don't want you to leave. Can't you stay?

Matthias's eyes remained with mine, as if he was listening to my silent plea. A look of understanding passed over his face and the thought came to me that he would see me again, not to worry.

Matthias leaned so he could say goodbye to Chase and his energy whooshed through me like a strong breath. Every muscle drew tight and locked into place, my fingers tightened around the steering wheel.

"Grand meeting you, Chase."

"Oh, it was very grand meeting you, Matthias. And don't you worry. I'll take good care of our girl. She's safe with me."

When Matthias moved back so he was sitting against the door, my body eased, my heart steadied, and my breath whispered out. *You almost knocked me out. Do you do that on purpose?* I looked at him. His brow barely lifted over a teasing smirk.

I shot a twisted grin at Chase. "Our girl?" I got out of the car and he took a step back, his eyes wide.

"It was just a figure of speech," he sputtered.

"Mm-hm." Satisfied I'd made my point, I leaned down into the open door to say goodbye to Matthias. The car was empty.

Sixteen

"You're in love him," Chase said, his voice quiet.

My heart pounded. I stared at him across the small table we shared inside Starbucks. Between my palms, my hot chocolate seemed to boil.

"It would be easy to do, fall in love with your guardian," he murmured.

"Don't interpret my silence as admittance."

"Kind of a Stockholm Syndrome," he observed.

"Nothing like Stockholm Syndrome," I retorted, sipping from my hot chocolate.

"You have this… *being* who looks out for you…like a bodyguard only totally amped. It's bound to happen."

"Nothing has happened. Did anything happen to you?"

"I was a child when I saw the lady in the forest. You…you're a woman."

A strain of butterflies danced through my stomach. A woman. I was flattered that he used the term. Is that how Matthias saw me?

Chase's face was taut with underlying frustration I couldn't decipher. "So I'm a woman."

"He's a man."

I leaned across the table. "He's also a *dead* man."

"Not dead. You've touched him."

I swallowed a knot.

Chase fell back in his chair, scraped his fingers down his face.

"What? So? You touched your guardians."

"I know, but...don't you see? You can't help it. You were bound to have feelings for him. First, he's this knight in shining armor protecting your handicapped sister—an innocent. You look at him and see this perfect protector. Then you find out he's your guardian, too?" He sat forward, urgency building in his tone. "He touches you and bam! That thing happens. That thing that fills up your soul and blows you into another stratosphere. You can't stop thinking about him because he's there, he cares about you, would do anything to protect you—*does* anything to protect you. There's no one else on earth who can do that for you. How can you not love him?"

He was right. I stared at him, stunned that the words were in the air. Truth. Not just a thought in my head that I'd pondered in secret moments. Words. Real words.

"You've thought a lot about this, Chase."

"Like you, I can't stop thinking about guardians. But unlike you, I don't have a relationship with one."

I squirmed. "We don't have a relationship. He's an angel!" I glanced around to make sure my voice hadn't carried. "I'm a mortal with a life to live. He's dead."

"Well, we both know how insignificant that is, don't we." He blew out a breath. "He's got flesh and bone just like you and I. He's a man—with feelings."

"Are you suggesting Matthias has feelings *for me?*" The tilt of his head told me that was exactly what he was suggesting. My heart fluttered. *No. Never. Not happening. Impossible.* Not only impossible but so wrong. Big time sin. I shook my head. "No way. You're wrong, Chase. Wrong, wrong, wrong." My hand shook when I lifted the cup to my lips.

"Then why is your face red?" He leaned across the table. "Why are your hands shaking?"

I gulped more of my drink and kept the cup near my lips. The thought of Matthias and I as anything more than what we were—protector and protected—sent a jumble of dice through my nerves. Uncertainty. Wonder. Risk. Where would the dice stop? *No.* I closed my eyes but that didn't serve to keep Matthias' angelic image out of my head. His smile drifted tauntingly, his laugh echoed through my system and his touch…I shuddered. *No. I won't allow myself to think like this.*

I plunked down my cup, opened my eyes. "You're making me think things that aren't true."

"I'm only pointing out reality."

"What reality?" I hissed, crushing the cup between my hands. "He's not even *in* reality." I stood, jittery as a caged cat. "I better go."

Chase jumped to his feet. "But we were just getting somewhere."

"We're not getting anywhere. I'm getting…this is wrong to talk about him like this. I can't do it. I won't."

"Okay, I'm sorry." He touched my elbow. I looked at where his fingers connected to me. Nothing. No buzz, no whoosh of energy. Just a human touch.

My eyes lifted to his. "Look, Chase, I'm sorry. Maybe tonight's just not a good night. I've had a ton happen today and I'm tired. Give me some time to catch up. It's the weekend, right? So, hey, maybe we can meet up later."

"Oh." His hand slipped to his side. "Sure. No problem."

"So, I'll see ya."

"Okay. See ya."

I headed to the door, the dice rolling.

My cell phone vibrated during the drive home. Brady. *Brady?*

partee at westons 2morrow nite come?

Why was Brady inviting me to a party? Was Britt going to be there? She was mad at me. I doubted she wanted me at Weston's. On the other hand, maybe this was a sign that all things were back in place. Maybe Britt was too proud to invite me herself, but wanted an even playing field—in her book that meant a party— so we could make up.

I texted him back: ***maybe*** then tossed my phone on the seat next to me. Matthias had sat there. A smile filled my lips, followed by a warm rush underneath my skin—a rush I got whenever I thought of him.

Which reminded me of Chase. I frowned. Chase was trying to make me feel guilty for liking Matthias. What was I supposed to do, resent him? Hate him? *Impossible.* My feelings for Matthias were close to my heart, I could admit that. But Chase said I was in love. I took a deep breath. *In love.*

In my heart's heart, that was true. The love seed had been planted back when Matthias had looked me in the eye and told me he and I were connected…and then conveniently not finished the sentence! I was glad Matthias wasn't there when Chase and I had talked. If he'd heard those thoughts—I would rather dissolve into nothingness. But how stupid and irrational was I falling for a guy who didn't exist? *Of course he exists, he's just not alive. He's alive, but he's not mortal. Not real. Not available.*

I blew out a sigh. Snow fell in light, transparent flakes sticking to the icy road, thickening the pavement to a white sheet. I inched along busy streets with other evening travelers. Obviously, I wasn't in any danger or Matthias would be here. Would I question my safety every time he was with me? Yet I was sure he wouldn't be with me just to hang out.

I snickered. "I wish."

Matthias had told me that nothing is wasted in Heaven. That made sense. When I thought of God, running a place like Heaven—and even having a hand in Earth—I didn't see Him chilling. That idea collided with common sense. God and everyone associated with Him would be cognizant of time—or whatever measuring stick they lived by.

I pictured Heaven as a serene place in the clouds. The frothy image came from years of sermons at church and my own childhood imagination. Matthias had said Heaven was a lot like here, only supremely better. Peace from worries, rest from cares. What a relief that would be.

Yet, unmistakable old sorrow had held in his gaze earlier when he'd told me about his father. Love is a permanent resident in the heart. If I died suddenly, I wouldn't stop thinking about and loving the people in my life.

Driving up the hill toward home brought my thoughts to Luke. I hoped he'd left that place and was at home now.

The higher altitude meant a thicker snow fall and slicker roads. The back end of my car fish tailed as I accelerated. My fingers gripped the steering wheel. A pair of headlights was coming toward me. Hopefully that driver was being as careful as I was.

Sweat burst under my arms as the other car neared. I was almost at my street and would have to turn. If I stopped in the road, I wouldn't get enough traction behind my wheels to start again. I had to keep going or I'd get stuck. I slowed so the other driver would hopefully pass by before I got to the turn.

The bright yellow and black truck—the wasp from the log cabin—flew by, sending a splash of snow and slush onto my windshield and door, temporarily blinding me. I couldn't believe anyone would drive that fast in these treacherous conditions. *What an idiot.*

With a fast press on the gas pedal, I was able to turn onto my street. I let out a sigh, seeing home. Luke's car was out front, and the sweat under my arms started to cool. Even with our earlier argument, I was always relieved to find him home. I parked in the driveway, got out and made a dash for the door.

Inside, the house was quiet, except for the TV—news—coming from the family room. I'd left in a huff, forgetting that my parents now knew about my drinking. I owed them something—an apology at least—for walking out like I did.

Mom's voice came from upstairs, where I heard water running in her bathroom. She must be bathing Abria. I headed upstairs and passed Luke's open bedroom door on my way to Mom's. He sat cross-legged on his bed, strumming his acoustic guitar. My movement in the hall caught his attention and he looked over.

"Zoe," he jerked his head, indicating he wanted me to come in. I stood in his doorway. He jerked his head again, his shaggy hair flopping.

I walked in and stood next to the bed. "Yeah?"

He set aside the guitar. "Something happened tonight," he said.

"What?"

"How did you find out about the log house?"

I shrugged, unapologetic for my actions. "I followed you."

Luke studied me, as if trying to decide if I was telling the truth. "Weird, but, whatever. That's not what this is about, anyway. When you came by, something happened."

"So you were there?"

He nodded.

"What happened? Did you get high?"

He looked at me, trying to decipher if I was going to pass judgment. An innocent, childlike look that speared through the wall of anger I erected whenever I was around him and went straight to my heart.

"No. I went there, fully intending to, but…"

"I really am glad that you didn't," I said. I was overjoyed. Relieved. Matthias was right, Luke was learning.

"Yeah, well, I wanted to. After dinner and all, I wanted to."

I let out a chuckle. "Mom's pizza not as good as it used to be?"

His lips barely curved up. I hadn't seen him smile in so long, my heart warmed. "No, seriously," he said. "Something happened at the house. I thought you could tell me what it was."

"All I did was knock on the door and the big giant, answered. He told me you weren't there. Not surprising from a drug lord."

Luke snorted. "That's Hank. He's not a drug lord."

"Dealer, lord—whatever. They're all the same."

"No, they're not. So you didn't do anything else? You didn't say anything?"

"Just what I told you. Why?"

"He was so freaked. I've never seen him that freaked before. He was white and shaking and could hardly talk after he shut the door."

My heart banged. "Seriously?"

Luke nodded. "I thought maybe you'd pulled out a gun or something."

"Where would I get a gun?" A zillion chills raced along my skin.

Matthias.

Luke shrugged. "I don't know."

"Honestly, I didn't do anything to Hank."

Luke scratched the sandy stubble on his chin. "Well, he kicked me out. Told me to never come back again." Luke's blue gaze locked on mine. I saw both relief and frustration pass over his face. He'd just broken one big link in the chain he carried. I was thrilled.

I kept my expression even. "I can't say I'm sorry about that. How do you feel about it?" I asked.

He lifted a shoulder, crossed back to the bed, looked at his guitar. "I've been hanging at that place for too long anyway. Those people are so out of it. They don't care about anybody but themselves. Hank's the worst. He won't give you anything free. Not one eighth. If you don't have something he wants, you don't get anything. Period."

"The Lortabs?"

He looked over, nodded. "I get them from other guys and use them to exchange for weed."

What a web. I was shocked but not surprised at the lengths he'd gone for a hit.

"So, in a way do you think it's a good thing?"

"I can get whatever I want somewhere else, if I want to. Hank just had the best price." He shrugged. He picked up his guitar, brought it against his body. Engaged in the song he was playing, Luke then sat on his bed, continuing to strum the guitar. I took that as a cue to leave and did.

Abria raced past me, naked and giggling. Mom was on her tail, towel in her hands, stress on her face. I scooped Abria into my arms, and her damp body squirmed against mine.

"You little stinker," I said, giving Mom a smile. "Want me to get her ready for bed?"

Mom's expression was wary, remnant shadows of our earlier argument still in her eyes. She followed me into Abria's bedroom. "Were you and Luke talking?" she asked.

"Yeah." I set Abria on her bed and she started jumping. I reached for the towel and Mom handed it to me. Questions flashed in her eyes. "Things are better. Don't worry about it."

"I'm glad to hear you two made up."

"No jumping, Abria." I started toweling off her wiggling body. Luke and I hadn't exactly apologized, but we'd talked. "Yeah. Good girl." After she was dry, I gave Mom the towel and went to Abria's dresser where Mom had laid out one of my tees. "Zoe's tee shirt?"

Abria started jumping again—as if she was on a trampoline—with no idea that she could miss and launch off the bed. Mom stood close, arms out and ready to catch her if necessary.

I took the diaper and pajamas and crossed to the bed. "Let me take care of this. You go relax," I told Mom.

She took a deep breath, let out a sigh and rubbed the wrinkle of stress away from her forehead. "Okay." She turned and headed to the door.

I caught Abria mid-jump and held her, meeting Mom's gaze. Mom's lips curved into a quiet smile, then she left. I dressed Abria amid her bouts of flapping. Followed by bouts of giggling. "All done! Good job!" I applauded and she joined me, laughing.

"Gu jo," she parroted.

"Time for sleep." I gathered her into my arms and pulled back the covers with my free hand. Abria leaned toward the pillow and I laid her down in bed, smoothing the covers around her.

She flapped and the whole bed shimmied. Her eyes were round and vibrant as the sun. "You're not tired, are you?" I sat on the side of the mattress. Reading to her was an exercise of patience. She rarely looked at a page longer than four seconds, so distracted by her own need to self-stimulate. Still, Mom was exhausted. Dad needed his down time. I needed to talk to Dad, but putting it off was okay by me. I had to do something to relax Abria.

Books lay all over the floor. Toys she carried around for a week then discarded from lack of interest also littered the room. My gaze wound around the walls covered in crayon and permanent ink from her scribbling. White gashes scarred the paint. The carpet was stained from food and drink she spilled. When she tantrumed, she often threw something, unaware that the consequence would break or ruin something else.

I let out a sigh. It was hard for Mom to watch the room fall apart. My gaze fell on Abria, tucked in, flapping, rambling nonsensical phrases and words in a tune with no melody. If I allowed myself, I could fall into the whirlpool of she'll never do this, never experience that, never have this, never know love—that was more than I could bear. I remembered what Matthias had said to me. "Does she look unhappy to you?"

Contrarily, Abria was happy—in fact she seemed to exist in a never-ending state of joy. A carefree existence I envied.

"Zoe's going to tell you a story," I began. "Once there was this special princess named Abria." Abria flapped her hands. "She was so beautiful that the king cast a protective spell on her. No one could ever hurt her, or say mean things or treat her meanly. Little Princess Abria grew up in a castle, surrounded by people who loved her, people the king could trust. She liked Playdough and crayons and little Matchbox cars she could drive around the wood floor. She liked to eat everything and she liked to jump on everything, too." Abria's eyes opened wide, so did her mouth, as if she was cheering, except no sound came. She flapped again.

"Little Abria's favorite place to go was the zoo to look at all the animals. She especially loved the monkeys—probably because she liked to climb like a monkey. When nighttime came, Princess Abria didn't always like to go to sleep. Sometimes, she stood in her window and looked out, which scared the king and queen. So, the king found the bravest knight in the land." I grinned. "His name was Matthias. *Ma-tthi-as.*" Her eyes met mine, held for a second longer than usual. Her lips formed the syllables 'Ma-thi-as.' "That's right, Abria. Matthias. He was strong and powerful, and very handsome." I leaned over her and tickled her under the arms. She didn't burst out in laughter, she turned stiff as though she was trying to figure out if she liked the sensation. "Matthias watched over Princess Abria day and night, to make sure she was safe. He was the coolest knight in the kingdom. All the maidens thought so."

Again, Abria's lips formed the word *Ma-thi-as* but no sound came. "Princess Abria, are you sleepy yet?" She flapped, her eyes bright. I let out a sigh. *I could be in here all night.* With Abria, nothing ever tied up neatly. Even bedtime was uncertain.

I leaned across and kissed her goodnight, then stood and went to the door, taking one more look at her. She lay staring up at the ceiling, tickling the palm of her hand, her eyes wide.

SEVENTEEN

I locked Abria's door and went in search of Dad. Nerves crimped my stomach, thinking about apologizing. Anticipating the act was like swallowing a cup of vinegar.

Luke's door was closed. Through the pipes, water hissed. Mom was taking her bath. I went downstairs, the sound of the TV indicating Dad was still unwinding. I took a deep breath and quietly rounded the couch. The minute he saw me, uncertainty crossed his face.

I sat on the opposite side of the couch. "Hey."

"How are you?" He faced me, tuning the rumble of news to low with the remote.

"Good. You?"

"Better. Luke came home about an hour and a half ago."

"Yeah, I noticed. That's good. I talked to him, by the way. We're cool now."

Dad stretched out his right arm along the back of the couch. "Glad you two talked. He seemed better when he came in. In fact, he apologized for what happened at dinner."

"He did?" The news surprised me. Luke wasn't much of an apologizer. "That's good."

"And he didn't look high. But then what do I know." Dad let out a sigh. "When I was your age, I knew a few kids who used drugs. My close friends weren't users, so I couldn't spot someone who was high. Here my own son is addicted and living right under my nose and I didn't see it." He shook his head.

"Dad, everybody has to make their own choices. Luke is no different. Neither am I. I admit I liked drinking. *Liked.* I haven't done it in a long time so I don't want you guys worrying about me, okay? I don't plan on doing it again, either. I've kind of had my eyes opened. All that stuff is so stupid. I mean, at first it's fun—or you think it's fun because everyone else is doing it. But when you see how it disables people, how it turns them into weaklings, it's pathetic." In my mind I saw Britt clinging to Weston's sleeves.

Dad nodded. "I think the hardest part of this whole thing for Mom and I is that we trusted you two. It would have never occurred to us that either of you would indulge in that stuff. And we've talked about how bad smoking and drinking can be."

I shrugged. "I can't answer that question for Luke, but for me it doesn't matter what else is going on. I drank to drown my problems. Facing problems is much harder."

A line creased between his brows. He gave a thoughtful nod. "Do you want to talk about the problems?"

I took a deep breath. "It's hard sometimes. Seeing you guys so...focused on Abria. Again, I don't know about Luke, but..." I swallowed. "Sometimes I feel...ignored."

Dad blinked and his green eyes glistened. Pain surrounded my heart. The last thing I wanted to do was hurt him. But I felt amazing relief having told him my real feelings.

"I'm sorry, Zoe." I opened my mouth to say, 'It's okay', but he held up a hand. "And don't say it's okay. You're right. Your mother and I have been completely focused on Abria and you have every right to as much of our attention as she does. I'm sorry. Everyone wants to be noticed in a family." He let out a sigh. "I'm just sorry I wasn't on top of this a long time ago."

"I know, so don't stress, please."

"Is there anything I can do?"

I shook my head. Though he was offering me his shoulders to carry my burdens, I was determined to carry my own. "I'm taking care of myself. Don't worry, Dad."

"So what opened your eyes?"

Dad was a religious man, he might even believe me, but he might also think I'd joined some cult or something. Since our relationship was tenuous, I decided against telling him about Matthias. "Lots of things. Mostly seeing Luke...I couldn't keep drinking, not when my own brother has a serious problem with addiction."

"Do you think you're addicted?"

"Dad, I drank for social reasons. I'm not going to lie—if I hadn't stopped, who knows where it would have ended. But—it just doesn't appeal to me anymore." My lack of interest in drinking really was a miracle. I wasn't even sure why I felt like I was done with it. Just a few days earlier I'd been intent on going to Britt's and downing some of her stash. Now, after seeing her desperate and pathetic, after knocking at the front door of Luke's addiction, the idea of drinking both repulsed and scared me.

Relief passed over Dad's taut features, softening the lines and creases in his face. "You know Mom and I would do anything to help you."

"I'm okay." Matthias' influence had also helped me, given me something to reach for, a place to elevate myself to.

"Zoe, I want to know where you're going and who you're with from here on out. Can you do that for me?"

It'd be nice having them care enough to want to know where I was. The feeling of security wrapped me in agreement and I nodded.

"And, is it unrealistic of me to ask you to try to come to me next time?" he asked. "Before you feel like drinking?" The earnest love in his eyes penetrated my heart. I shook my head, blinking back tears.

"Dad, I'm so sorry about tonight." I leaned over and hugged him. His embrace took me back to childhood: comfort, complete protection, and unconditional love. "I'm going to keep my mouth shut," I mumbled against his shoulder. "I'm too hard on Luke."

"You care about him."

I nodded and eased back. "Yeah. I care about you guys, too."

"We all need to give each other a little more credit."

I swiped away tears and nodded. For the first time in months I felt the tight seam that held my soul closed, open just a little.

I woke Saturday to the aromatic scent of pancakes. My stomach grumbled. Out of habit, I rolled onto my side and reached for the cell phone on the nightstand. No texts. The vacancy left me lonely. I had the sharp prick of panic that Britt had started some lame rumor, one that had turned every person I knew against me.

I let out a sigh. If she chose to do something vicious like that, I'd live.

I rolled onto my back. Matthias's face brightened my mind. I smiled.

Where are you this beautiful Saturday morning?

I didn't expect an answer. All was well in our house. I lay staring up at my smooth ceiling imagining him somewhere surrounded by other beings such as himself, talking, laughing, spreading that serenity he carried with just one look, or touch.

Did he have friends in Heaven?

Who did he hang with?

I laughed, turned and buried the laugh in my pillow. "You are hopeless. Hopeless!" I kicked off my covers and leapt to my feet, so energized by the mere thought of Matthias that my body surged with the rush his aura swept into me as if he was with me. I stood in front of the full-length mirror on the back of my closet door. Beneath my pink sleep shirt, my skin flushed with a vibrant rosy hue. Though my dark hair was mussed from sleep, my green eyes were bright and alive, my lips in a constant grin.

You're in love with him.

Chase's words popped my exuberant balloon. I stared at myself. How can you be in love with someone you can never have? But Matthias had said he and I were connected…oh, why didn't I know the rest of his thought? Why didn't I understand the grand plan? *Because the only grand plan is the one you're creating in your lovesick head, Zoe.* My smile faded, along with the brightness in my eyes.

I lowered myself to the bed, my gaze still on my reflection. *You can't let your heart go places it's not supposed to go.* In theory, this was true. But when I thought of Matthias, my body, mind and soul had an instantaneous reaction—like hunger after starvation. Need and want reaching out for satisfaction.

This isn't as simple as hunger. Matthias is from another world. Another existence. A place you won't be for years and years. By the time you get there you'll be old and wrinkly and decrepit. What would a beautiful, vibrant man like him want with an aged crone?

The scenario was depressing.

I let out another sigh and fell back on my bed.

"Pancakes!" Mom's shout slipped under my closed bedroom door. I didn't feel like eating now. *Come on, Zoe. You've never let a guy get to you before.* But Matthias wasn't just any guy. He was…irreplaceable.

There was too much I didn't know. How long was he going to be my guardian? Would I see him when I died? How big was Heaven? Did people run into people they knew or did everyone wander aimlessly through misty clouds?

What a joke. Matthias had already told me Heaven was a lot like here. *Supremely better,* he'd said. Trying to envision a world supremely better than this was impossible. Could people really exist together in complete peace? How could opinion, pride and ego not interfere? Not to mention the diverse ocean of wants.

How had a beautiful Saturday morning suddenly turned murky? I sat up, determined to enjoy the weekend and not think about the impossible.

At least not for the next five minutes.

I had a lot to be grateful for: I'd apologized to Dad last night. That felt good. Luke and I were talking. A step in the right direction. I had yet to apologize to Mom, but I could do that this morning.

I walked downstairs to the kitchen. Mom was dressed in her raspberry-colored robe, her dark hair in a claw at the back of her head, her morning face free of makeup. She smiled at me over the mixing bowl. Abria stood on a chair at the table, flapping, singing words that had no rhyme or reason. Dad was halfway through a plate of pancakes. He wore flannel pj's on the bottom with a soft old shirt. His salt and pepper hair stuck up like a hedge of dead weeds.

He smiled at me. "Morning, Zoe."

I kissed his stubbly cheek and the gloom I'd carried slipped away. "Hey." I sat at my usual spot. "The pancakes look great." My appetite crawled back. I looked across the table at Luke's empty place setting.

"What have you got on tap today?" Dad asked.

"Not much. Probably a party tonight." Dad's green eyes flickered with concern. "You wanted me to tell you. Don't worry, I'll be okay." I glanced at Mom, pouring batter onto the griddle. Her smile had vanished. "By the way, I'm sorry about yesterday, Mom." I forced myself to look at her—I owed her that much. She finished pouring the vanilla-colored batter and met my gaze with a smile of relief.

"We were all upset."

The last heavy layer of the previous night peeled back. My soul was free to take a deep breath. "I shouldn't have run out of here."

Mom took the spatula in hand. "I know how it feels to want to run, Zoe." Her eyes stayed with mine speaking unspoken words we all carried in our hearts about life with Abria. But Mom never ran. She stayed, stuck it out.

She flipped the pancakes, then smiled at me—a smile I recognized after living with her for so many years: *it's all right.*

Apologizing cleansed me.

I picked up my plate and went to the cooking island where she stood. Mom slid four pancakes onto my plate, then she put down the spatula. I was ready to turn and head back to the table but she reached out and put her hands on my shoulders. Her blue eyes filled with tears.

My heart swooped in my chest.

"I love you," she whispered.

My throat clogged with a surge of emotion. I wanted to say I loved her, too. But I was certain any words at that moment would trigger a waterfall of tears and I didn't want the morning to be hard for them—recalling last night. I smiled. "I know you do."

She released me and wiped her eyes with the hem of a nearby dishtowel, then she picked up the batter bowl and resumed pouring.

I sat at the table. Dad had witnessed the moment between Mom and I, his eyes were rimmed in red and glistening. I loved that Dad wore his emotions like a well used accessory—without pride or vanity—over his heart.

I wanted a man like that someday.

Luke came in on a yawn. His scruffy gray sweats hung a lazy inch below plaid boxers. Blond hair on his chest feathered down to his belly button. "Put on some clothes, why don't you?" I teased.

He stretched, groaned and twisted his back, bringing out a loud popping sound. Then he grinned big. "Ahh. Ready for breakfast."

"How many do you want?" Mom asked the tone of her voice as cheery as a Disney character.

"I'm guessing he can eat ten." Dad raised his brows, taunting.

Luke pulled out a chair and sat, plopping both elbows onto the table. "I'll start with five. Abria, sit down."

Abria had one foot on the chair she was standing on, the other poised— as if we wouldn't notice—on the table. "Shurplesousdonshmalowya!" she screeched, then laughed.

"Mom and I thought it'd be fun to do something together today," Dad said.

"What's the weather supposed to be like?" I craned for a look out the window at the sky. White clouds. Patches of blue sky.

"Cold but no snow until tonight." Mom poured more batter onto the griddle.

We'd stopped doing family things about a year ago, when Abria's behavior meant she wouldn't sit still through a movie, would run away from us, or stand on tables or—horror of horrors—drink from other people's beverages at restaurants. Taking her anywhere meant we lived with our nerves exposed. Not a relaxing way to spend time together.

"I can't." Luke cut into his stack of pancakes. I wasn't surprised he was backing out—he hated being seen in public with Abria. "Gonna look for a job."

"On Saturday?" I asked. "Isn't that a Monday through Friday afternoon thing?"

"It's a whenever I can do it thing. I need a job. I'm going to go look today."

He'd tried holding down jobs before, but had flaked off, not sticking with anything for longer than a couple of months. I hoped that he wasn't pursuing work to support his habit. I tried to shove that idea out of my mind because it brought gnarly dark feelings with it and the morning had been pleasant.

"They're hiring at McDonalds," I suggested. I remembered seeing the sign posted when I'd eaten there with Britt, Weston, and Brady.

Luke nodded and filled his mouth with a bite. "Okay. Thanks."

I was still mulling over going to the party later at Weston's. I figured Britt was the one behind Brady's invitation. She probably envisioned us making up. Usually, I was the first one to extend myself when Britt and I argued. I swallowed pride easier than she did.

"Zoe, do you want to go with us to the zoo?" Dad asked.

I grinned at Abria. "Princess Abria's favorite place."

※ ※ ※

Hogle Zoo was a rather utilitarian home for exotic creatures. What the place lacked in natural atmosphere it made up for in efficiency. All of the exhibits were arranged in one long time-saving loop. Once you'd made the loop and taken each short offshoot, you were done. This was good for Abria because her attention span for any supervised activity ranged from five seconds

223

to five minutes.

So she wouldn't run away, we rented a heavy-duty plastic red wagon. The zoo had an entire fleet for toddlers and young children, pushed and pulled along by panting parents.

I got the job of pulling her.

She clung to the side, eyes wide, so excited to ride, she barely noticed our first stop: the monkeys.

Mom took her head in her hands and turned it so she'd see the black, swinging creatures. Still engaged in the novelty of riding in the wagon, Abria flicked her gaze at the squawking monkeys, flapped then gripped the sides of the wagon in a sign of: forget- the-monkeys, I'm-ready-to-go.

The elephants were my favorite pachyderm. The large, African beasts must have been a favorite for a lot of other people, because the crowd around their outdoor exhibit was large. Dad, Mom and I waited behind the five-people deep gathering for our turn to move to the front, so Abria could see.

As we inched forward, I saw that the wagon and its bulk were getting in the way. "I'll park the wagon over there with the others."

Dad took Abria into his arms. "Come on, Abria."

Her eyes locked on the wagon. In spite of Dad's gallant efforts to show her the elephants, Abria squirmed and writhed—her focus on the red wagon parked a few feet away.

We moved onto the next exhibit: polar bears. One massive beast lay sprawled near an icy cascade of water. The other was nowhere in sight. Sleeping bears are dull, so we moved on to the tigers.

The orange and black beauty roamed the "tundra" back and forth, back and forth, in a repetitive motion that caught Abria's eye—maybe she could relate to the animal's need for repetition. I wasn't sure. But she focused on the zigzagging tiger long enough for us to cheer once and describe in a short sentence that tigers were *big cats*.

When it was time to move on around the loop, Dad gingerly placed her into the wagon and pulled her down a slow decline. Abria flapped and laughed. Soon, Dad was at a jog, pulling her along, laughing with her. For the first time in as long as I could remember, Dad looked like he was having fun, too.

I was glad we'd come to the zoo.

We ate lunch near the playzoo—a sanded area surrounding an animal-themed play set with picnic tables where patrons could eat while children acted like animals. Abria forwent eating and ran to the gym, climbing without fear to the highest bars.

Abria's fearlessness always garnered a few stares of criticism. Like: *don't you care about how high she's climbing? Don't you see that can be dangerous? What's wrong with you?*

Usually, I glared brazen onlookers into deference. Today, the darts of criticism silently thrown our direction flew past me with little notice. I kept a smile on my face and my eyes on my sister. She was happy. Her sense of balance was rivaled only by birds. Pretty amazing.

Mom and Dad chatted over lunch while I stood near the play gym with Abria. Occasionally Mom dipped her head into the curve of Dad's neck. He wrapped his arm around her, held her. He even snuck a kiss.

Sweet.

I turned my attention back to the play set and didn't see Abria up on the top bar. My gaze swept the gym. So as to not alert my parents—they were enjoying themselves so much— I ventured closer. The panic I usually felt when I couldn't see Abria, snapped to attention. I searched for Matthias, didn't see his tall, erect form anywhere.

Immediately, I walked the circumference of the play area, searching for her. The sound of Mom's laughter caused me to whip my attention to where Mom and Dad were sitting. They stood now, talking to a grey-uniformed zoo worker who held Abria in his arms.

Matthias.

Relief poured into my system. I smiled and crossed to them, shocked. Thrilled. Awed. They could see Matthias. He was talking to them.

"There you are." My gaze met Matthias' deep blue glittering eyes.

"This nice young man found Abria." Mom looked effervescent. So did

225

Dad. Clearly, Matthias' soothing calm had engulfed them and any worries they might have had were gone.

"Well, hello there." Matthias held my gaze in an unspoken message of familiarity. "Is this your dazzling sister you were telling me about, Miss Abria?"

Mom's laugh fluttered out like a school girl's. She smoothed back her hair, her hands nervous. I couldn't stop grinning.

Dazzling? Heat flushed my face.

Yes, dazzling.

"She doesn't usually speak," Mom said.

Dad smiled at Abria. "She tries real hard, don't you beautiful girl?"

"Look how calm she is," Mom observed. "Do you have children?"

Mathias threw his head back in a contagious laugh. "No."

"You're very good with them." Mom eyed his name tag. So did I. How did he manage to get a tag with his name on it? "Matthias."

Matthias dipped his head. "Thank you."

"We usually don't bring her to places like this," I said. "She likes to run."

Dad lifted a shoulder. "But she loves the zoo, so we try."

"And we're so glad you brought her." Matthias gave Abria a quick squeeze.

Mom reached out for Abria. Matthias caught the motion out the corner of his eye and a flash of awkwardness crossed his face. I snapped my arms out. Smoothly, he passed Abria into my arms, mine brushing his, bringing our gazes together in a tight lock that sent warm flutterings through my body. Breath—his, mine—I wasn't sure who's, whooshed through my cells and it seemed as if my whole being took a deep sigh.

"I'll take her," my words whispered out. Abria's calm demeanor remained. "You do have a way with her."

"She's in her sister's arms now," Matthias' voice was soft. "She's safe."

I melted. Gathering my senses, I tilted my head at him. "Thank you."

"Yes, thank you so much." Mom held out her hand to shake Matthias.'

Without a hint of awkwardness, he clasped his hands behind his back and gave her an efficient nod. "My pleasure. Now, if you'll excuse me. I'm off to chase some hooligans down in the bird sanctuary. A pleasure meeting you all. Have a dandy day."

Mom, too enamored with Matthias to notice he'd purposefully declined physical contact, withdrew her hand. "A pleasure meeting you, too, Matthias."

"Thanks again," Dad said.

Matthias turned to me. *You take care, Zoe.*

At first I wasn't sure if I was really hearing his thoughts or my wild imagination was getting out of hand. My heart danced. *I will. You...too.*

"Stay close to your big sister now," Matthias spoke to Abria, but his blue eyes stayed with mine. A shiver of delight tickled my spine.

"Thank you so much for helping us," I said.

"Of course." *Goodbye, Zoe.* Matthias stole through the crowds, swift, smooth and efficient. I didn't take my eyes off of him—couldn't. My heart soared.

I love you. He was too far away to hear the exuberant thoughts of my heart, thankfully. *Yes, I love you. So much.* A rush of emotion engulfed me. I blinked back the beginnings of tears.

His form was nearly out of my vision, his halo of hair glistening in the distance, when he turned and looked at me. My heart pounded. His gaze held mine across the busy expanse of the lunch area. Seconds turned into minutes. Bodies flowing between and around us seemed to wind down to slow motion. Mom's voice. Dad's. Abria's chattering. Every sound softened, melting into the slow...pounding...beat...of my heart.

Zoe.

Time blinked. In a flash he vanished.

"Zoe?"

"Honey, are you all right?"

"Zoe?"

"What's wrong with her?" Mom's frightened voice echoed through my stalled brain. "Something's wrong."

Dad moved into my line of vision, his face taut. His hands were on my shoulders, warm, reassuring, firm. He gave me a shake. Where was Abria? She wasn't in my arms anymore. Mom held Abria's squirming body against hers.

The moment came into focus with the measured shift of a kaleidoscope. Matthias.

He'd heard the tender feelings of my heart. He'd looked at me.

And only said my name.

I stood hollow. Gouged. Empty.

"Abria, be still," Mom's tone held frustration—that old companion, the rock each of us carried perpetually in our shoes.

"I'm okay." I didn't recognize the fragile voice coming from me.

"You sure? You turned white as a sheet." Dad held me between his strong palms, eyeing my face. "You want to sit down a minute?"

"Can I ride in the wagon?" I whispered. I wasn't joking, but Mom and Dad thought I was. Smiles broke the tight worry on their faces. My legs—I couldn't feel them. My arms hung useless at my sides.

Hollow.

Gouged.

Empty.

Dad took Abria from Mom's arms and put her into the wagon. Mom followed Dad as he started pulling Abria to the next exhibit. How my legs moved, I wasn't sure. I trailed them, the sound of their chat about the animals drifting into one ear and out the other like a deafening vapor.

Matthias.

The words I'd uttered squeezed a merciless fist around my heart. Tight. *Tighter.* **Bursting.** Tears rushed behind my eyes. Mom and Dad were busy pointing out hyenas to Abria.

Too many tears to blink back. Streams. Down my face.

I turned away, my heart shattered.

Wiped tears.

Held back a sob.

Closed my eyes.

Took a deep breath.

More tears.

"Zoe?"

"Coming. Got something in my eye."

"We need to keep moving, she's getting antsy."

I nodded. "Be right there."

Sounds mixed with tears and puddled in my brain. I couldn't believe he'd heard the tenderest words of my soul and had only said my name.

Zoe.

Hopelessness.

Everything I knew and understood—the unbreachable gap of Heaven and Earth that stood between us.

In his tone.

I don't remember the rest of our visit to the zoo. Somehow, I was in the car, in the backseat next to Abria.

I stared out the window.

Cars raced by.

Cities passed.

Mom and Dad talked their voices a low murmur. Abria silent.

The hum of the engine.

"You're awfully quiet." Mom—wondering.

I hurt inside.

What did you expect? That you'd live happily ever after? That he'd come back to life? What did you think would happen, Zoe?

I closed my eyes, rested my head against the cool window. "Tired."

"Oh." Relief coated Mom's tone. "Rest honey."

Rest? I welcomed death. Anything but the cavernous blackness slowly seeping into the hollowed, gouged emptiness.

Matthias.

The car came to a stop. I opened my eyes. Home. I didn't want to move. I could have stayed in the car forever, disintegrated into the seat. What did it matter if I became part of an object? My heart—that which made me human—hurt too much.

Being an object would be easy. No pain. Just existence.

Abria had fallen asleep during the drive. Dad carried her inside. Mom followed. "You coming?" she mouthed to me from the porch.

I hadn't moved. The car door was still shut. Glass and steel separated us. Not Heaven.

I nodded, opened the door and willed my body inside.

Despair, desperation—both emotions swirled in a quiet storm inside of me. I took the stairs to my bedroom, shut the door, and fell onto my bed.

More tears.

Silent sobs, the kind that start at your core—like an earthquake—wracking your being as if an unseen hand has reached inside and is shaking you. Violent. Without mercy. Sobs that drown from the inside out.

Drowned.

Eyes open, bedspread wet beneath my face, I stared at the wall. Old photographs. Yearbooks. Desk. Bookshelf. Posters. Useless things. Objects I'd have given anything to trade places with.

Then I wouldn't hurt.

"Zoe."

Mom. Mortal comfort. Her arms wrapped tight around my body, offering a soft shoulder to weep on. Not the soul penetrating comfort Matthias gave me—like living in baptismal water.

"Honey, what's wrong?" Her hand caressed my head, my back, in loving strokes.

"Nothing. I'm fine. Really."

"You haven't been yourself since the zoo. Did something happen?"

Yes. I told the man I love that I loved him and he didn't say anything. Only my name. As if he stood on one side of the Atlantic and I on the other and there was no possibility of a bridge. Too far. Impossible to build, let alone cross.

"Nothing happened."

"Zoe. Please let me help you. I don't want you to feel like you…like you have to turn to another source."

"Don't worry Mom." Matthias had helped me with my footing whenever I climbed a mountain. My steps were surer now. I wasn't going to fall back.

"Is there anything I can do? I'd do anything to help."

"I know."

More soft strokes. I closed my eyes. Tired. And slept.

When I opened them again. Mom was gone. My head, my back, where her gentle strokes had caressed, was cold. My skull throbbed from weeping.

Had I dreamt the day?

My damp bedspread reminded me that, no, the tears I'd shed over Matthias were real. He'd only said my name.

Zoe.

The Atlantic. Me on one side, Matthias on the other.

Rattling of pots, pans, and the scent of dinner filled my senses with the temporary comfort of food. I rolled onto my back, not at all hungry.

I stared at the ceiling.

My cell phone vibrated in my pocket. I ignored it. It vibrated again. I pulled it out. Brady.

u comin 2nite?

The last thing I needed was a party. People getting what they wanted would only remind me that no matter what I did, I would never get what I wanted.

On the other hand, noise would smother the sound of Matthias' voice that kept playing in my head on a loop of hopelessness.

Zoe.

The silent storm of despair and desperation that had been swirling inside of me started to gain momentum. I sat up.

Frustration.

Anger.

Who did Matthias think he was? Someone who could come in and out of my life, tormenting me with something I couldn't have? How wrong was that?

I stood, took a deep breath and looked at my ravaged face in the mirror. What would a night of partying with friends do for me?

Laughing.

Playing.

Flirting, lots of flirting.

I could do some tormenting of my own. Unlike Matthias, I could touch and be touched by anyone I damn well pleased.

EIGHTEEN

Weston's house throbbed with heavy music. Cars lined the street. I looked for Britt's white mustang but didn't see it. Weston had probably picked her up.

I drove my silver bug onto the lawn, shot a grin at one stunned guy standing out front, and parked. The day's disappointments still clung to my heart, like gremlins picking, pinching, piercing.

I checked my face in the rearview mirror. It had taken hours of ice packs to get my swollen eyes back to normal. Even now, my cheeks were still flushed with scattered blotches.

Matthias.

I gazed at the house. No outside lights were on this time, and only a smattering of red and amber snuck from the windows. The place seemed darker than the last party.

Why was I nervous? I'd been to tons of parties. I knew the game, and I'd come to lose myself in harmless flirting and fun. There was nothing wrong with that.

I scanned my outfit: nice jeans, red knit top with *Playee* silk screened across the front. Silver earrings dangled from my ears and silver beads and bangles cuffed both wrists. I'd sprayed my favorite perfume behind my neck— just in case a hottie got close enough.

I left my bag in the car, tucked my cell phone and keys in my hand, got out and locked the door.

"You parked on the grass," the stunned jock observed.

"Yeah." I straightened my shirt. My palms were moist. Why?

I took a deep breath. There didn't seem to be as big a crowd at this gathering. And from where I stood, the forms I saw mingling through the window were mostly guys, fewer girls. *Nice odds.*

I took a step and heard my name.

Zoe.

My heart leapt. I whirled around.

Matthias stood five feet behind me, a soft beam in the dark night. His hands were in the pockets of his light slacks. The washed-white shirt he wore intensified the blue in his piercing eyes.

Joy filled me, and the joy spilled into the caverns he'd left behind when he'd said my name.

I couldn't melt. Couldn't let his comfort, his serenity, the essence of his being surround me and dissolve the frustration and hurt. He'd never be mine. I had to accept that.

I had to forget him.

Move on with my life.

It was then I noticed two others like him. One stood on the east side of the house, the other nearer the front window. Both were dressed similarly to Matthias, both beings illuminated an incandescent glow. *Guardians.*

How odd there were only two.

One was a young man, about Matthias' age. He stood by the front window, focused on someone inside. The other was an older woman with white hair. Her gaze was locked on an exterior wall of the house—as if she had x-ray vision and saw beyond brick, mortar and wood. Both guardians attention was riveted to people I couldn't see. My gaze slid to Matthias, whose attention was fastened to me.

"Don't go inside," he said.

The force of his warning rammed through me. My knees trembled in the aftermath, but I lifted my chin. "Why not? It's just a party. I've been to lots of them."

236

His gaze held mine in a tight line, unbreakable, boring into my soul. In that moment, I knew I should not go inside. To do so would put me in danger. He was there, after all, to protect me.

"Zoe."

"Stop saying my name!" Hopelessness ripped through fresh wounds. "Why do you care, Matthias?" I strode to him, then stopped. If I got too near him, he'd toss his aura over me like a comforting blanket. I wouldn't be able to think.

"Uh, are you okay?"

I jerked left. The jock who'd seen me park stood wide-eyed, watching. I glanced at Matthias, tense as a panther ready to pounce. Was this jock a threat to me? I took a step back.

"I'm fine."

His lip turned up in amusement. "You were talking to yourself. You high?"

"Yeah, actually, I am. Seeing things, too."

He nodded. "That's cool. You got any to share?"

I almost rolled my eyes. "I don't share."

"Oh." He shrugged. "No problem. Weston's probably got some stuff inside. You coming in?"

I slid a look to Matthias. "I sure am."

I turned around, fighting the urge to steal another glance of satisfaction at Matthias, and crossed the threshold.

Red lights. Bodies. Shadows. Pulsing music broke through the walls in a violent vibration, a rhythmic pound meant to seduce.

Just what I needed.

The jock I'd followed inside smelled good. Spicy and male. Deep down, a suppressed primal hunger wet its lips. The guy clicked looks over his shoulder at me; I sent him my best flirtatious smile.

A few familiar faces greeted me with nods. Girls scanned my outfit with curious jealousy. Guys eyed me with that same primitive hunger I had, their intentions clear by the way their eyes swept over me.

A lot of prospects. *Nice.*

I cruised through bodies creating a gyrating wave that pushed people together. I kept an eye open for Britt but didn't see her. I found Brady in the hall, laughing with a bunch of his and Weston's jock pals over a six pack.

When he saw me, he stopped talking and came over. "Hey. You came."

"Yeah. Where's Britt?"

He jerked out a nod toward the ceiling. "Upstairs with Wes. Want a drink?"

I looked around. "You got any soda?"

He laughed. "You're joking, right?"

"Actually, I'm not. Pepsi. Thanks."

His smile tweaked in that junior high mentality meant to humiliate. "Okaaay. Pepsi. I'll see what I can find."

"You do that." *What a retard.* I passed his buddies who gave me jock nods and I headed through the house in search of my first hottie for the night.

The halls were so dark I could barely see where to go, much less faces to choose from. In every corner, couples wrapped around each other, bumped, grinded or locked lips.

I had the fleeting thought of Matthias. To kiss him here in this dark, raw place. *Hot.* The sexy image didn't stay in my mind, for I saw something that stopped me in my tracks.

In the living room packed with laughing, talking, dancing kids there hovered countless black figures. My first thought was that I was hallucinating. But I was sober. The transparent black images moved like vapors of smoke, slithering in and out, around and on top, underneath and between the oblivious teenagers.

My heart jumped. Black spirits. Matthias had called evil black spirits and he was right. There was no light in them at all.

Their features were human, only their transparency lacked the substance of flesh and bone, or soul. Each was intent, focused—grinning as they swooped, slid and hovered. A cold sweat broke out on my skin. I'd never seen anything so disturbing, yet I was unable to stop watching as they wove around those gathered in the room.

Suddenly, two of them broke away and followed a couple coming toward me. My heart leapt to my throat. I stepped back and pressed myself against the wall of the entry hall.

The couple was twined together, their lips devouring each other, hands exploring. Shadowing them were the black spirits, snarling out silent laughs, their onyx eyes gleaming as they circled, like sharks.

I prayed they wouldn't see me. I didn't know what would happen. Would they come after me because I knew Matthias? Fear—fiery and scalding—raced through my trembling system. I closed my eyes when they passed, afraid if they looked at me, I'd dissolve. Or die. My heart pounded in my chest. Twenty beats. Then I opened my eyes.

I caught the backs of their sinewy blackness just before they vanished up the stairs, behind the couple, and followed them into a room. The door shut.

No. The image of those evil creatures watching the couple sent a cold, icy disgust through my body.

I had to get out of there.

Terrified, I now saw that what I'd thought were shadows when I'd first come into the house, were really dozens of these dark spirits, luring, enticing, beguiling each person in the place.

"There you are." Brady came out of nowhere. I jumped. "Didn't mean to scare ya." On a laugh, he handed me an open can of Pepsi.

My hand shook when I took it. "Th-anks."

"You okay?"

I couldn't stop shaking. Sweating. Fear ran loose like a thousand rats in my body. "F-fine." I tilted back my head and took a long drink. Closed my eyes. Leave now, Zoe, I thought. *This isn't a place for you...*Matthias' words echoed faintly in my head.

"Britt's upstairs. She wants to see you." Brady's eyes...had they always been that dark?

"Oh?" My hand trembled so badly, I could barely bring the can to my lips for another drink.

239

Brady eyed my fingers as I took a swig from the cold can. "I'm supposed to take you up there. Wanna go?"

Panic collided with fear inside of me, the frantic rats crashing into each other as the image of a gaping trap came into my mind. "Tell her to come down," I said.

Brady studied me for a second, then looked around. "You sure? Cause she's up there with Weston."

That didn't make sense. Last I'd heard, the two of them still weren't talking. "If she wants to talk to me, I'll be down here."

A flash of anger sparked Brady's eyes. He turned and that's when I saw the menacing black spirit hanging on his back. The translucent creature was a male, and straddled him as if Brady was a horse or some beast he was riding. His long arms stroked Brady's head, neck, chest, all the way down his body in an invisible seduction meant to excite.

Shocked, I stood frozen at the bottom of the stairs, watching. Couldn't Brady feel that? Was the invisible stimulation what enticed him into a state of hunger?

Suddenly, Weston appeared. He stood with Brady at the top of the stairs, both of them looking down at me. Black spirits whirled around them. Weston had two. One riding his back—a woman—her hands in a constant caress of Weston's body. The male danced and hovered around the female with his mouth twisted in a gaping laugh.

Brady and Weston started down the stairs. *Move. Run. Get out of here.* My feet started to tingle. Numbness followed. The deadening sensation inched up my legs like snakes, wrapping around and around. My pounding heart slowed. *Move, Zoe. Run!*

"Hey Zoe." Weston smiled when he reached me.

"I need to go." My voice—the snakes slithering around my limbs were closing in on my throat. "I..."

"You can't go yet." Weston stepped close. The musky scent of his body assaulted my weakened senses. He wrapped an arm around me, smiled. Dangling over his shoulder was the female, laughing—silently. Her hands

240

never stopped caressing him. Everywhere. In the air the hideous male slithered up and around in a sickening display of pleasure that rolled panic into a fear so terrifying, I was sure I would die.

"Zoe, you don't look so good," Brady's amused voice came at me in muted bubbles.

My head swam. My legs—noodles—my heart hammered. Blood rushed through my veins in a paralyzing scream.

Snakes covered my body now, I couldn't move. Their tingling squeeze immobilized me and I collapsed into Weston's arms. "What...did you...put... in my drink?"

Weston's lip lifted. "Something to loosen you up, baby."

Overhead, the black spirits' gazes latched on mine. Their onyx eyes glittered with victory.

NINETEEN

I opened my eyes and found myself in a dark room. In a strange bed. My head throbbed. I tried to lift my arms, to rub my face but my limbs were so heavy, I could barely move them. A sour residue thickened the inside of my mouth. Where was I? What had happened? Images pulsed through my mind: Faces. Laughter. Shadows.

How did I get here?

It took all my strength to lift my head so I could look around. Black corners. A shadowy door. A draped window.

I still wore jeans and long sleeved red tee shirt, but the cool air on my shoulder drew my fuzzy gaze to a jagged tear in the fabric, leaving me exposed.

On a groan, my head fell back against the pillow. Something was wrong. I was smashed, yet I hadn't had any alcohol. *What happened? Where am I?* Panic rolled through my system. I drew in a deep breath, determined to rise up to my elbows so I could make out this place, but the act was like lifting a cement slab.

That's when I saw him.

Felt him.

Like the sun raging behind a storm.

He sat in the chair like a warrior after battle, his long legs extended, arms out to his sides, palms up—as if battle had drained him. But that was impossible. The source from which his energy flowed was Eternal. The comfort I was accustomed to when he was in my presence was out of my reach, dancing around him in a soft glow. The only light in the room emanated from his being, beneath the soft ivory of his clothes. He didn't say anything. His clear blue eyes were fierce, locked with mine. A shiver trickled through my limbs.

His gaze held mine in piercing intensity, cutting my soul open as if he would dissect right then and there if I was innocent or guilty of the night's activities. I opened my mouth to defend myself, not sure what retribution I would face but my throat locked. Had I put us in danger? Would the heavens thrash and roar? Would he leave me? The thought filled me with a dread so black, my arms trembled. I nearly crumpled into the mattress.

"What happened?" I rasped.

His lock on my gaze held me captive, a blinkless stare I couldn't escape. Memories of the night dripped with a slow leak into my conscience and shame forced me to close my eyes.

Why did you go inside, Zoe?

I heard his question as clearly as if he'd spoken to me. But he hadn't. We could read each others' thoughts, that was the beauty, the miracle of our relationship.

I was angry. I'm sorry. I shouldn't have. It was wrong. I'm sorry.

Silence. Thick. Hot. Sticky.

Look at me.

I can't. Tears rushed behind my eyes and burst through my closed lashes. He'd saved me tonight. Whatever had happened had been treacherous, the magnitude something I could only measure by the intensity in his countenance—like the sun tearing through black clouds, claiming possession of the sky.

I managed to roll onto my side, desirous of nothing more than to avoid him. But he was next to the bed, looking down at me. I buried my face in the pillow.

Please. Don't stay. I don't deserve you.

Silence.

Tears burned behind my eyes. Then I felt Matthias' warm hands on my head. The wretched dark images trapped in my system drew out of me, up through the top of my crown. My eyes flashed. He stood over me, hands on my head, posture sure, illuminated in white, his face turned heavenward. In a brilliant flash of blinding white, the sheer blackness being drawn from inside of me whirled upward, around his body, like a furious twister snaking through the ceiling until it vanished.

My body, lightened now by the elimination of darkness, sighed. Awed, I lay looking at him—how beautiful he was. His brilliant countenance spread into the room and reached out to me, filling me with admiration. And love.

Thank you.

His hands gradually lifted from my head and went to his sides. His eyes met mine. *You're welcome.*

He'd come to my aid, ridded me of the lingering pollutants, the shame without reprimanding me.

Complete forgiveness.

"How?" My voice scraped out of my throat. Something in his gaze sent a thread of concern through my blood. *I thought you couldn't be where evil was.*

A moment passed. Two. Three. His unwavering gaze never strayed from mine. A heavy silence blanketed the room. Another taut moment passed. Three. Four. *Did you do something…wrong?* But how could he? In his refined state, was he still capable of doing anything wrong?

He closed his eyes in a ponderous tight expression and shook his head. "Don't worry yourself about this, Zoe."

"I should have listened to you. I shouldn't have gone in at all. That was…" I looked away. Closed my eyes. *Stupid.*

You're learning, like everyone must learn, how to choose.

If I'd only stayed outside. With you. I turned, met his caring gaze. "Those other guardians I saw. What about them?"

"There were two others who are safe now. Don't worry about them."

"I should have gone in and found them, told them—"

"You can't force anyone to choose something. Each must decide for himself." Matthias sat down on the edge of the bed. His closeness sent a warm wave of *him* through me, deep and penetrating. He studied me for a long moment, his gaze so comforting, I became relaxed. Sleepy.

Rest.

When I opened my eyes again, I was clear in body and soul. Matthias stood looking out opened curtains to a sunny, blue-sky Sunday. Where was my bedroom?

I sat up.

Matthias turned, smiled. "Feel better?"

"I'm in a motel room." He nodded. "How did I get here?" The night's events moved through my mind in gray clouds. "Brady?"

"And the other double-crosser."

Weston.

He crossed to the bed. The fierceness coloring his eyes sent me back. "What happened?"

Matthias tensed. "They brought you here to commit the most offensive of sins." His body bulged with contained rage. Then, he closed his eyes, let out a long breath and his body relaxed.

"What did you do? Matthias, tell me what you did to them."

After a long silence, his eyes opened. "Justice was satisfied." The feral look in his eyes thrust a shudder through my system.

"One of them spiked my drink. What if they try to do that to some other girl? I can't let that happen."

"I believe they learned their lesson, Zoe." The silent assurance is his words put to rest the injustice bubbling inside of me and I let out a breath.

"You should be getting home. Your parents are frantic." He held out my cell phone. I looked into his eyes, still curious about what he'd done to Weston and Brady but the look of the-subject-is-closed kept me from asking for more. The phone sat like a baby bird in his palm, the sight of it yet another reminder of what he'd done for me.

I took it and called home.

"Zoe?" Dad's tone was frantic.

"Dad, I'm okay. I'm sorry I didn't call you earlier, but I wasn't able to. I'll explain when I get home."

"Zoe, for heaven's sake." I bit my lip at the irony of his statement, and looked up at Matthias.

Dad sighed into the phone. "After our talk the other night, you can imagine how worried your mother and I were when you didn't come home."

"It wasn't on purpose, I promise. I'm really sorry. Just know that I'm okay and I'll be there soon."

"Are you here? In Pleasant Grove?"

"Yes. I'm…" I glanced at Matthias who gave me a nod. "With a friend."

"I want an explanation when you get here."

"Of course. Be there soon." I flipped my phone closed. "Wow. He was scared"

"He loves you."

Whenever Matthias said *love,* the word melted the air. "I know." I threw my legs over the side of the bed, stood and wobbled.

Matthias set his hands on my shoulders, steadying me, and captured my gaze. His tender touch drew the protected feelings of my heart out into the open. Gratitude—so immense words were insignificant, filled my soul.

I wrapped my hands around his wrists and closed my eyes against tears. "I…" *I told you I loved you yesterday. My heart…it hurt…you didn't say anything. Why? It hurt so much… I thought I would die.*

His gentle finger stroked my cheek, wiping away tears. I opened my eyes, searching the endless blue depths of his for the answers I sought.

"It's impossible, isn't it?" I whispered. "You. Me. I can see it in your eyes. I heard it in your voice yesterday when you said my name. I heard hopelessness." More tears slipped down the sides of my cheeks. I squeezed the warm flesh and delicate bones of his wrists. *Flesh. Bone.* I held him in my hands—yet he was out of my reach.

246

The sapphire flecks in his eyes sharpened. His aura whooshed through my system—a warm reassurance as peaceful as sleep. Every cell tingled and felt ready to burst with sweet contentment.

"I know how you feel." He lowered his head, closed his eyes a moment. His dark lashes fluttered against his alabaster skin. How I wanted to touch his face, feel his skin, trace his lips.

He opened his eyes.

You think I don't have feelings, Zoe. You're wrong.

A knot formed in my throat. What was he saying?

I'm saying that just because I am a guardian does not mean that I'm void of the emotions mortals have. I've been mortal. I've felt everything you feel. My feelings are like yours, Zoe. He stepped closer. I caught his sunlit scent. Felt the warmth of his body. *Only the love I feel for you is magnified.*

Love?

"I know you love me. You're here to protect me. That's what you do."

"No, Zoe. I'm *in* love with you."

His words wrapped joy around my bones. *What does that mean?*

I should think that was clear.

"No, I mean, are you going to die now for saying that to me? Are you in trouble?"

His smiled, and reached out, his fingers lightly skimming my cheek his touch so electric, I was certain I would burst with joy.

Only that I love you.

The force in his eyes left no room for doubt. The universe, as I knew it, wasn't capable of holding the magnitude of Matthias' feelings. Whatever sphere he dwelt in, wherever Heaven was, my mortal brain couldn't grasp the extent of his love.

TWENTY

Matthias walked with me out into the bone-chilling morning air, through the motel parking lot. I was perched in the heavens somewhere; the word *love* floating in my mind like a cloudy spot blocks vision, only this delightful cloud blocked my mind. I couldn't think straight. I stared at him. And stared. His smile submerged me. His aura engulfed me. *Love.*

I let out a content sigh.

We stopped at my silver bug, parked under a tall light post. The sight of my car was a reminder of what had happened the night before, and I took my first good look around at the run down freeway motel the boys had brought me to.

I met Matthias' hard gaze with my own look of astonishment.

Thank you. Again.

You're welcome.

Matthias had somehow gotten my car to the motel. He wouldn't say how, he just grinned.

"You mean my car zipped through the streets of Pleasant Grove without a driver?" I chided, unlocking the door.

He wagged his brows at me over the roof of the car, then dipped into the passenger seat, shutting the door behind him.

"Freaky." I started the engine.

"Jakey is more like it." He stretched out his legs and reclined the seat. "A nifty ride. And the most extraordinary thing—the seats move."

I sputtered out a laugh. "Yes, I know."

The morning was bright, the skies blue, with billowing white clouds. The perfect image of Heaven, I thought, pulling onto the road.

Enraptured as I was from his declaration, it took a moment for me to clear my thoughts. The motel was miles from home, next to the freeway in an industrial section of town. When I thought about what would have happened to me if Matthias hadn't stepped in, a cold shiver raced over my skin.

I caught my reflection in the rearview mirror and gasped. Mascara smeared beneath my eyes. Blush was gone. No lip gloss. And my hair was all over the place. *I look terrible.*

You're the cat's meow.

I glanced at him—and longed for him to be mine. Mortal. Alive. Someone I could spend the rest of my life loving. What was our connection? And what good was love if you couldn't live with it?

I sighed.

"You know, this machine is quite dandy. The round design is especially nifty."

I figured he was trying to change the subject and get my mind off of him. "Bugs are popular cars because they're cute."

"Bugs?"

"Nice try, Matthias." I held his gaze as long as traffic permitted.

"I'm not here to hurt you, Zoe."

"I know."

We drove in silence for a while. *Am I in danger? Is that why you're still with me?*

His blue gaze was unblinking. *No.*

I walked into the house smiling. Floating...out of this world—caught somewhere between Matthias' Heaven and my earth.

He loved me. As impossible as that was, it was true. A truth I couldn't deny or ignore simply because he was there and I was here.

I savored the knowledge.

Mom came running. Dad was right behind her. I heard Abria chattering in the kitchen. Luke followed Dad. Worry wracked their faces.

"Zoe!" Mom wrapped around me.

Dad buzzed like an angry bee. Luke hung back.

"What happened?" Dad asked.

"Nothing. I'm okay. Really."

Mom eased back, keeping my shoulders in her hands. Her concerned gaze swept me from head to toe. Thankfully, my jacket hid the tear in my shirt.

"I'm glad you're okay, Zoe. But I want an explanation," Dad said.

"I went to a party last night. At Weston's."

"Larson?" Luke asked.

"Later, I fell asleep at a friend's place."

Mom and Dad weren't buying my story. Both looked like I'd just told them that I'd eloped, was pregnant, and was going to work as a pole dancer for the rest of my life. I bit my lip. "And I didn't drink an ounce of liquor, I promise. I had a soda."

A long silence stretched in the air. "We just talked about this," Dad said.

"I know, and that's why I want you to trust me. I didn't drink. That's not part of my partying anymore, it's not."

"You should have come home," Dad scrubbed his jaw.

"Like I said, I fell asleep. I really am sorry to have worried you. I should have called at least."

"Look at it from our point of view," Mom said. "You're gone overnight without a word? As much as we want to trust you again, Zoe, the circumstances don't look good."

I nodded, sorrier than ever that I'd walked into the stupid party; put myself at risk even after Matthias' warning and I hadn't thought ahead about what the ramifications of my choice would look like to my parents. I blinked back tears. "I really am sorry."

Mom and Dad exchanged glances. I searched their countenances for forgiveness, swearing inside I would never do anything to endanger precious trust again.

Abria's laughter drew our attention to the kitchen, and we followed Mom in that direction. Abria stood on the table, reaching for the chandelier overhead.

"Abria, no!" Mom raced over and whisked Abria into her arms, then set her feet on the floor. "No chandelier."

"Chan!" Abria reached for it again. "Chan!"

Saved by Abria—at least temporarily. It was good to be home. Yesterday's baked bread smells, the pattering sounds of Abria. Family faces shot love straight to my heart: Dad. Mom. Luke. I smiled at Luke, who hadn't stopped staring at me.

Dad studied me, deciphering. What could I say? That a guardian angel had swooped down from Heaven and saved me?

"I'm gonna go get cleaned up." I said, backing toward the stairway. All eyes stayed with mine. "We've got church in—what—an hour?" I glanced at my watch, kept walking, and crossed my fingers that the mention of church was enough for a subject shift. I was glad nobody followed me with more questions.

※ ※ ※

Having Matthias in my life had opened windows. Windows with vista views I never dreamed I'd see, much less take a real good look at.

I wasn't sure what the future held for me. For Matthias. But a certain serenity resided in my heart now. Whatever the future brought, I could deal with it. No fear. Real joy. Endless hope.

After I showered, I dusted on some shadow and blush, and a little gloss. I slipped on a black skirt and fuzzy purple sweater that made my green eyes look like emeralds. Every few minutes I'd catch myself thinking about the miracle of Matthias' love—of what he'd done for me and where I was today because of him, and a rush of euphoria filled my system.

We drove—all of us in Dad's car— to the meeting house. I expected Mom and Dad to be pleased that we were all together, but they were unusually quiet. Tension in their expressions carried traces of unanswered questions—no doubt for me.

The crystal day was cold but the sky remained blue, clouds dotting the heavens in cottony white. I'd never noticed the canvas of the sky—how in one corner, the universe was puffed with soft white hope. In another, graying clouds stretched forth, threatening more storms.

Where are you, Matthias? I closed my eyes, picturing his glorious being surrounded by white mists, a smile on his lips, his blue eyes sparkling, hand reaching out. For me.

"What are you smiling about?" Luke whispered.

I opened my eyes. Heat flushed my skin, but the smile on my lips wouldn't go. "Nothing."

He eyed me. He looked amazingly clear.

"So nothing really happened last night?" Luke pressed.

Was he curious or mad? His even nature was hard for me to gauge. "Nothing happened."

He eyed me longer. Deeper. Then he turned his attention out the window, leaving me alone for the rest of the drive.

I toyed with telling him about Matthias, but my seeing angels wasn't something I took lightly. I understood that I needed to guard this special gift or it would be taken from me. And I would never jeopardize Matthias in any way.

I'd die first.

After Dad parked the car, we got out. Dad came around and picked Abria up in his arms. Gaze locked on Luke, he ticked his head toward the church. "Luke, let's take Abria inside."

Uh-oh. Mom lingered by my side and strolled slowly. "Zoe." Her heavy tone sent my defenses up. *Just take it as it comes. She loves you; remember that,*

I told myself. "Is there anything you want to talk about?" She hooked her arm in mine. I caught a whiff of her floral perfume on the cool breeze tickling my neck.

"Mom, you don't have to worry about last night." I squeezed my hand over her arm.

"I'm…I feel like I've spent so much time focused on Abria, you and Luke have suffered. I'll never forgive myself for that."

"That's not it at all." I'd felt my share of what I'd perceived was neglect. But, stepping out of myself, I could see that both my parents were doing more than their best with all of us. I'd only thought I was being overlooked.

"I don't want this to be a time when you turn to something else for help," she said.

How could she know that help had been Heaven sent? My eyes filled with tears at the mercy. I turned away, blinking them back. If she saw tears, she'd think she'd caused them. "I won't. Please, don't worry about me," I said.

"I just want to make sure." She squeezed me close. "I was lucky to have you first. I couldn't have been a mother without you."

"Aw. Mom."

"No, I mean it. Abria. Luke. You're my right hand."

"You're doing a great job, Mom. Don't be so hard on yourself. Everybody looks at you and says, *wow, how does she do it all?*"

"And I tell them I have the best daughter in the world. My helper. My friend." She reached up and touched the side of my face. "I just want you to know how much you mean to me. I forget to say it."

We were close to the front doors of the church. Mom's eyes glistened. I brought her against my side for another hug. Then my gaze lifted, searching blue and white sky in hopes of a glimpse of Heaven.

TWENTY-ONE

On Monday Pleasant Grove High School buzzed like a beehive. The strong current reverberated through my bones the moment I walked through the glass double doors on my way to class.

Laughter to my right. Whispering left. A cluster of girls in a pow-wow so tight, my curiosity peaked. None of the electric chit-chat was aimed at me, I was merely highly aware that something was going on. What, I didn't know.

I headed for my locker, waving at a few friends, nodding at others. Britt must not have let loose a rumor after all. I didn't care. What she or anyone else thought about me was not the arrow of my compass any more.

I wondered where Britt was. I hadn't heard from her over the weekend, but then, I'd only thought of her just now. Standing at my locker, I twirled the dial and opened the clanging door. I still didn't know whether or not she'd even been at the party. Matthias hadn't mentioned her. He'd only pointed the finger at Weston and Brady.

Britt probably hadn't even been there.

I grabbed the books I needed for first period and shut the door. That explained why she hadn't called or texted me all weekend. She was still mad.

I turned around and bumped into the molly-girl from history class. She stood—minus her guardian—looking at me with big brown eyes. She wore the same denim jumper she always did, and her hair was back in a pony tail. She held a pile of books against her chest.

"Hey," I said.

254

Overhead, the first bell shrilled. The halls started to empty.

"Can I talk to you?"

I glanced at the clock at the end of the hall. "Sure." I'd be late, but, oh well.

"I want to know why you talked to me the other day."

"You looked upset."

Her brown eyes deciphered my words. "I was."

Silence. Empty hall.

She took a deep breath, her fingers tightened around the books she clutched to her chest. "I just wanted to thank you." Her voice was soft, timid. Ashamed.

I reached out and patted her arm. "No problem."

"It really helped."

"Good. I'm glad."

She stuck out her hand, ready to shake. "Krissy."

I smiled. "Zoe."

✿ ✿ ✿

The buzz continued charging the halls with a vibe so intense that by the time I got to history, it was as if a million neon lights lined the corridors and classrooms. I looked for Britt, but she wasn't there.

I bit the bullet and texted her.

r u ok?

Nothing.

The weekend's events had taken me around the world of life's lessons and back. I felt like I'd leapt from high school senior to adulthood. Usually, I spilled my guts to Britt about everything. Now, I felt the urge to share, rather than spill, what I was going through. All that had happened. How life had changed.

I was a different person.

In journalism, Chase's gaze locked on me from the moment I entered the classroom. He looked studious in his khakis, striped polo and glasses. I waved him over and he was at my desk faster than Clark Kent could fly. "Did you hear what happened to Weston Larsen?"

My heart stopped. "No. What?"

Chase leaned close. He smelled like pumpkin muffins. "I thought you were friends with him."

I cringed. "Not really."

"Apparently, there was a party Saturday. He and Brady got into some trouble. No one knows exactly, but rumor has it they're both in the hospital."

"What?!"

He nodded. What had Matthias done? "Do you know anything else?"

"People are saying different things. I thought you might know, since you hang with them."

"I don't anymore."

Chase eyed me a moment. "You okay?"

I nodded. "They're both skeezebags. They probably got what they deserved."

"What goes around usually comes around."

"You're right."

"But your friend, the blonde, isn't she dating one of them?"

"She was. I…I don't know." Dazed, I lowered to my seat. "What are people saying? Did they get beaten up or something?"

Chased shrugged. "That's what enquiring minds want to know. There's the hospital rumor. Another I heard is that they got in a car wreck after the party. Yet another rumor circulating is they've got the plague. If you hear anything from your friend, let me know," Chase said, standing upright. "We could do a splashy article on the front page."

Nothing sounded more degrading than sensationalizing the horrific events of the weekend. "I wouldn't touch it."

"But you could get the inside scoop—"

"I'm not scooping anything, Chase." Fury rode my voice. "I hate those guys."

He blinked behind his glasses. "Sorry. I—I didn't mean to upset you."

"You didn't." I sighed. "Look, let's talk about this later."

Backing to his desk, he nodded. Curiosity and questions flashed in his eyes—questions about me and Weston and Brady.

With no recollection of the night other than the party and the motel, I had no idea how the events in between had played out. I sat at my desk, staring at my screensaver—a sunset—thinking about how Matthias had intervened.

He'd saved me.

Humbled, I sat a moment, trying once again to grasp the magnitude of Matthias' miracles. And, once again, my human brain wasn't capable. A slug of reality hit me in the stomach. Matthias didn't mess around.

My Yahoo IM popped up. Chase.

Starbucks? 2nite?

I grinned. An evening at Starbucks would be nice.

sure

The buzz about Weston and Brady started to die down after last period, the student body draining from the halls and classrooms taking the rumors along with them. I walked to my car, texting Luke.

u comin?

b there in a sec.

My phone vibrated with another, incoming text. Britt.

i need to talk to you

OK where?

can u come to my house?

sure b there soon

Had Britt heard about the weekend? Did she know I was involved? I sat in my car, waiting for Luke, and debated calling her, rather than going to see her. If she was still mad at me, I didn't need her flipping out.

I was over the weekend. From my perspective, I'd been in moral peril—placed there strategically by two sleaze bags. I didn't need to defend myself by rehashing what had happened that night to Britt's face. Matthias had assured me Weston and Brady had learned their lesson, I had no doubt he was telling me the truth.

The car door swung open and Luke bounded in. He actually had books tucked under his arm—a first. My mouth opened with intended drama. "Are those books I see?"

He grinned and slammed the door. "Shut up."

For the first time in a long time, the vibe between Luke and I wasn't hostile. The air was friendly, and the moment worth savoring.

"Did you hear about what happened to Weston and Brady?" Luke finally spoke.

"Yeah. Wild, huh?"

"They probably got what was coming to them."

"Uh, probably."

"I'm sick of those guys doing whatever they want and getting away with it. Everybody thinks they're all that because they're popular but they're slime. I get looked down on because I used to smoke pot and they—"

"Used to? Wait a second."

He bristled. "I'm trying, okay?" His tone was defensive. His eyes met mine, earnest commitment struggled with the pain of reality. "It's hard. The hardest thing I've ever done."

"I'm sorry."

He stared out the window, his frustration seeming to ebb. "I don't know. I want it so bad sometimes. I crave it."

I pulled onto the long hill that led to our street, not sure if I should go home yet. We hadn't talked like this in so long, he was opening up. I wanted to help.

"I used to feel that way for a drink. But, honestly? At Weston's, I was surrounded by the stuff and I didn't want a drop."

He turned, faced me. "So what happened?"

"To make me not want a drink?"

"At the party, Z. Come on."

"Brady spiked my soda."

"What?!"

"They're both skeezes." I didn't say anything more.

Luke spouted off, "You don't do that kind of thing and get away with it. Did you call the cops?"

"It was taken care of."

Questions still roved in his angry gaze. "I hope they both die or something."

I patted his arm. "I don't think they're going to be repeat offenders, bud. In fact, I'd bet my life on it."

🏵 🏵 🏵

After I dropped Luke at home, I drove to Britt's. I wasn't nervous to face her; I was curious and anxious to see where this rendezvous left our friendship. Were we still friends? *Could* we be friends?

In the western sky the sun's fiery rays melted through gray clouds stretching across the atmosphere in a futile effort at blocking its power.

Another storm on the way.

I parked out front and killed the engine. I wasn't even sure I'd tell Britt about what had happened. She might not believe me, with her feelings for Weston so strong and her head in the smog of his sleazy aura. How could Britt not see Weston for the snake that he was? But then, just a few weeks ago, I'd thought Weston was it too.

I got out and crossed the grass to her front door, knocked and waited.

When the door finally opened, Britt stood looking like she'd survived a hurricane. Her blonde hair sat like tumbleweed on top of her head. Her usually tan skin was pasty. The flowered flannel pjs she wore were stained and droopy.

"Hey," she grumbled. She stood back, holding the door wide open, so I went inside.

"What's up? Are you okay?"

She scuffled in bare feet across the wood floor toward the living room. "Lousy." She plopped onto one of two sleek deep gold couches that faced each other. I sat across from her.

"Something really weird is going on," she said, scrubbing her face with her hands. "Did you hear anything at school?"

Was she using me to find out what had happened at the party? "Why did you call me over here, Britt?"

"To—you know—talk."

"About what? Because if I'm not here about you and me, then I'm not staying."

"Don't be such a retard," she snapped.

I stood, ready to storm out. But she jerked to her feet, her dazed eyes blinking to sobriety. "Look, I'm sorry, okay? But you really pissed me off when you told my dad I was upstairs."

"He asked me where you were."

"And you knew Brady and Weston were with me!"

I crossed my arms over my chest. "Yeah, so?"

"That's it? That's all you're going to say?"

"What else is there to say? That was your mess, not mine."

Her eyes blazed. "What happened to you?"

"What're you talking about?"

"You used to watch out for me. Now you're this freaking narc."

"Your dad asked me a question. I answered him."

"With truth?" Britt spat. "Why didn't you just tell him I was out or something? He grounded me from going to senior prom! Weston and I are over! He forbid Brady and Weston from ever setting foot on our property again!"

Thick silence followed, broken only by Britt's erratic breathing.

I was ashamed that she still lumped me in with her—a lying, deceptive user. "You're better off without him."

"You're just jealous," she growled. "You've always been jealous."

I snickered. "Of you?" Had she really seen me as her jealous sidekick? What about friendship? Secrets? Was nothing sacred? I felt vulnerable now. Britt knew every dirty secret of mine. I'd shared with her my deepest, darkest dreams and fantasies. I'd also shared with her my deepest fears—and the tender spots of my heart.

She looked so weak, so pathetic and alone. Like a pretty cat, abandoned in the dirty street. The tender spot on my heart that she occupied tore open. "I'm sorry."

She stared at me for a moment, her rigid demeanor stony and cold. Her gaze searched mine. I hoped she could see that I was sincerely sorry. No one should leave a friend worse than they found them. She had feelings for Weston. Whether those feelings were based on lust or love, I shouldn't judge and I shouldn't condemn. She was human. Mortal. Just like me.

She shifted. "Yeah, well, I am too."

"You think?" I jested, smiling.

Her lips curved up a little. "Yeah. It was stupid, what I did." She fell back on the couch, grabbed a pillow and clutched it to her chest on a sigh. "I thought if Weston was jealous, he'd want me more."

"Yeah."

"He hated me for it. He told me he was going to get back at me. That was so junior high, you know?" Her face turned toward me. Tears crested her lashes.

"So what did Weston do?"

"He hasn't done anything—yet. I think he was going to do something at the party Saturday. He didn't invite me, of course. I'm pretty sure he was going to hook up with some loser so that I'd hear about it later. Only, he got sick."

My insides trembled. Memories of that night jumbled through my mind in gray clouds. *I was Weston's payback.*

"Sick?" I asked.

"I went to his house yesterday to see him, you know, to confront him about it. His mom said he was really sick. I told her it was an emergency, that

I needed to see him. At first, she wouldn't let me in. But I started crying and she let me upstairs to his room. Zoe, you wouldn't believe it." Clutching her pillow, she sat up, her eyes wide. "He was covered in these red, pustule things. It was so sick, I retched. Right there in his room, I puked. He looked like a gourd!"

An icy shudder rammed through me. I opened my mouth to speak, but shock closed a fist around my throat.

Britt stood, visibly upset from the incident, and paced. "I didn't know what to say to him. I don't know what those things are, but they were red and oozing like a million little volcanoes all over him. He started screaming at me to get out. Kind of poetic justice, don't you think?"

I couldn't respond.

"I mean, I guess his plan backfired. He won't be charming anybody into his bedroom looking like that."

I swallowed a knot. "Yeah."

"Brady has the same thing. Can you believe it? The two of them must have come down with one freaky virus. You think it's contagious?"

I took a deep breath. "Um. My guess is, *no*."

"Did you hear anything? I heard everybody was talking about him at school today."

"Yeah. But nobody knows anything."

"He'd die if anybody found out. *Die*. It's inevitable, though. Everybody will find out eventually. I only wish I'd thought to whip out my cell phone and take a picture of him. Humiliate him. Annihilate his overblown ego. Ha! Wouldn't that have been sweet?"

Revenge was as ugly and black as those evil spirits I'd seen at the party. I wanted nothing to do with evil ever again.

I lifted a shoulder.

"What?" she asked. "You don't think Weston should get what he deserves?"

"Sounds like he has already."

"I'm not sure it's enough." Britt threw down the pillow and started for the kitchen. I followed her. "I mean, as far as I'm concerned, he deserves to be scarred for life."

I didn't like how casually she tossed around something as potentially devastating as consequence. Where was her mercy? "I thought you wanted to make up with him?"

She pulled open the fridge. "I did, until you came. But I think you're right. I'm better off without him."

"So leave him alone."

She reached in for some orange juice. "Want some?" I shook my head. "He's not going to mess with me without severe punishment. If I stand back and let him get away with this, what am I saying to the rest of the female population?"

"He's covered in zits, Britt. What better punishment is there?"

"One that I enforce. I'm going to get a photo of him and spread it around school so every one of his fans can see how ugly he looks. That will cool his engines—for a little while anyway."

Britt poured herself a glass of orange juice and let out an "Ahh." Then she put the container back in the refrigerator. "I'll go back over and tell his mom another sob story so she lets me in—like I'm pregnant or something. Ha! Wouldn't that freak them out? They'd string him up by his—"

"Britt, that's cruel."

"So what. He deserves it. He's probably done this to more than one girl, Zoe."

"You really think you'll feel better making things worse for him?"

"Hell yes." She hoisted herself up on the counter top. "A guy who plays games deserves the hand he's dealt."

"What goes around comes around, you know," I said.

She cocked her head at me. "You have gone all narc on me. What's up, anyway? Is it that teacher dude? You still seeing him? I feel like it's been ages since we've talked."

It had been. Lifetimes. Sharing any part of my life now and how I saw things, felt things I'd never felt before: forgiveness, compassion, looking inside

263

someone else's heart—Britt wouldn't understand any of it. Britt drew her legs up to the counter and clasped them in her arms. "Is he hot? Have you hooked up yet?"

My stomach rolled with disgust. To label Matthias' beauty with a term used with the frequency of toilet paper demeaned who he was. But to ask about hooking up? Intimacy with Matthias was an act I had not allowed myself to dream of—the image blatantly sacrilegious.

"I better go." I turned and headed for the front door. I heard Britt run up behind me.

"So when are you going to tell me about him?" Her eyes glittered with the falling stars of gossip.

"Maybe later," I lied.

"Cool. I wanna hear all the juicy details, k?" She wrapped around me in a hug, and the transparent display of affection made me stiffen.

She opened the front door. "Looks like snow—again. That means I'll have to take Dad's car when I go back over to Wes's. Hey, you want to go? We could do some damage after the deed. You know, go find some hotties after I snap Weston's zit photo. Come on, it'd be fun. Like old times."

When I hesitated, she reached out and took my hand, swung it with hers. "You can put that teacher guy on hold for one night, can't you? For me?"

"Can't tonight." I started out the door, taking a deep breath, glad I was outside. "Sorry, hon."

"You sure?"

"Positive."

TWENTY-TWO

Starbucks was warm with the comforting scent of coffee, made even more inviting with patrons lounging in chairs, reading rustling newspapers or chatting with friends.

I scanned the place for Chase. He popped up from a chair at a window table. He had on the khakis I'd seen him in at school, only he'd added a navy cardigan. Adorably traditional.

I pointed to the menu and texted him: *u want something?*

It took him a few seconds to figure out that I was texting him. I waved my phone. He dug for his and then nodded at me.

hot chocolate, please. thx.

The guy had manners. I liked that. I ordered for us, waited while the server made our drinks, then took the two hot chocolates to the table. I sat and unloaded my purse.

"Hey."

"Hey."

"Thanks for the hot chocolate."

"No problem." Mine had hours to go before it was cool enough to drink. But it was a super hand warmer, and I kept my palms around the paper cup, savoring the heat.

"So."

"Next time, my treat," Chase said, bringing his drink to his lips.

"You bought the first time. Watch out, or you'll get burned." I nodded at the cup he held at his lips.

"Thanks." Without taking a sip, he set the cup down, his brown eyes fastened on me. "So, did you find out what happened to Weston and Brady?"

"I didn't." He'd never be able to resist running a story. I had the feeling most guys who didn't dwell in Weston's social circle took any opportunity to slug him in the gut if given one. And Chase had a journalist's mentality—go for the jugular no matter what. Though he'd been respectful enough of Matthias and Deity to draw the line when it came to Godly matters.

"Too bad. I was hoping you'd crack the shell on this case."

I fought a grin. "Case? We're getting a little too CSI here, aren't we?"

"My favorite show."

"How did I know that?"

He laughed. "Can I help that I'm a CSI geek?"

"You didn't hear anything else then? From anybody?" I was curious who knew what. There'd been at least fifty people at the party. Hadn't anybody seen Brady and Weston take me away?

"Nobody's talking. Weston's got to have some control over what's being leaked."

"Maybe you should just forget about it."

"I was so hoping that Brittany girl would tell you something."

"She and I aren't really close any more."

"Can I ask what happened?"

I shifted. "It's personal. We parted ways on amicable terms, though. Don't get the wrong idea." I had the impression that he might go ask her something, just to check out my side of the story. But then, a guy in Chase's social position—intelligent geek—would never have the guts to approach a social diva like Britt.

Except for a story.

A thread of panic wound inside of me. I sipped my too hot drink, just for something to do. If you throw a dog a bone, they usually go after it. "I do have something to tell you. I *did* go to the party."

"I knew it!"

"Keep your voice down."

"Did you see anything? Anything weird go down with Weston or Brady?"

"I didn't see anything happen to them. But I did see some weird stuff." He leaned on his elbows. "What?"

"I saw these black...creatures." Chase's eyes widened. "They were everywhere. Swimming in the air like...creepy apparitions. The scariest things I've ever seen. Matthias calls them black spirits. Have you ever seen them?"

His Adam's apple bobbed. He shook his head.

"Chase, these things were so evil, I..." A shudder quaked through me. "I can hardly talk about them."

"What did they look like?"

Even thinking about the black spirits caused a dread so great my insides trembled. If I talked about them, I was sure I'd invite the depraved creatures into Starbucks. Trying to find the words to describe the soulless creatures bound my tongue. My mind emptied of everything but their dark, slithering images. I opened my mouth, but nothing came. I had the strong impression that to talk about them wasn't a wise move. "I don't want to talk about it. All I can tell you is they hung on Weston's back."

Chase drove his hands threw his hair and sat back, digesting what I was telling him. "Man-oh-man. They hung on his back? They? How many were there?"

"Two. A male and a female."

"They're gendered?"

"Shh." I glanced around. No one was looking, thankfully. I leaned, he leaned. "Yes, they're gendered."

"Did you like, *see* something?"

"No of course not. And I wasn't looking. I'm telling you, it was terrifying. I got out of there."

"I'm blown away by this. Blown away." He stared at me, piqued interest in his eyes. "I have to know everything."

267

"Let's just say, I was at a party where people were drinking and getting it on, and that place was crawling with them. Like roaches. Two of them even followed one couple into a bedroom."

Chase gasped. He slapped a hand over his gaping mouth, then parted his fingers. "Serious?"

I nodded.

"Disgusting." He shuddered like he'd just downed a bottle of lemon juice. "That…that's depraved."

"Tell me about it."

"You said Matthias called them black spirits. Was he there?"

"Guardians can't be where evil is, remember?"

"Obviously, your life wasn't in danger then. Lucky for you. What made you decide to leave? I mean, besides being surrounded by a bunch of floating devils?"

"Evil isn't anything to make light of. If I hadn't seen them crawling all over everybody myself, I probably wouldn't take it seriously, either. But they are just as seductive as Matthias is powerful."

Chase's right brow lifted. He studied me for a few long moments. Then he sipped his drink. "Okay, I agree that guardians are powerful. But something else happened that night. What?"

"Why do you think something else happened?"

"Because your face is white. You really did have some kind of monumental encounter with those things. But you're here. You survived. So, what else happened?"

"I told you, I left."

"Just like that? They didn't see you or try to stop you or anything? You're *good*, for crying out loud. Didn't they try to do *something* to you?"

"They don't have bodies, Chase. They can't *do* anything. They can only entice. I saw it over and over."

"Huh." He thought on that a moment. "I'm almost tempted to do something evil just to see one." He grinned.

"Are you serious? If you'd do something that stupid, then—"

"Just kidding. Jeez. It's one thing to play with the light. It's another thing to play with the dark."

"You shouldn't *play* with either one. Both are forces that need to be respected."

"Okay, okay, I was only joking."

"Maybe if you'd looked hell in the face like I did you'd have more respect."

He propped both elbows on the table and clasped his hands. "You're not a very good liar, Zoe."

Nothing pleased me more than to hear that news. "Really?"

"Yeah. I like that about you."

After Britt shoveling me in with her pile of skanky friends, Chase's compliment, sincere as it was, vindicated me. "Thanks, Chase."

He crossed his forearms and leaned close. "I know you have feelings for Matthias, but…if that ever changes…"

"I don't. I can't." My heart started to pound. "I mean, anything with Matthias is impossible. So, what's the point?"

His lips lifted in a slow grin. "Like I said, you're a lousy liar."

Chase and I shared a slice of coffee cake and another round of drinks— his treat— talking about his little brother who had ADHD and Abria's autism. He was amazed at the similarities in their disorders, and wanted to come over and meet Abria sometime.

He walked me to my car, just as a light rain started falling. He held the door open for me and I got in.

"Thanks for the drinks and coffee cake," I said.

He held my gaze for a moment, then, suddenly placed a kiss on my cheek. A little buzz of shock tingled where his lips left their imprint. "Bye, Zoe. See you on Monday."

My mouth was open, but my voice wasn't working. I smiled, nodded. He shut the door and stood in the rain, next to my car, as I started the engine and backed out. I sent him a wave, keeping a curious eye on him through my rearview mirror as I navigated the parking lot toward the street.

Finally, he walked to his car.

Warmth trickled from my cheek where he'd kissed me, to my toes. How sweet. I drove through now-bulleting rain, my heart beating in time with the hum of the windshield wipers.

"He's a good chap, Chase is."

Thrill raced through my veins. "Hey. What are you doing here?" I was so pleased to see him. The car lit with his presence like a beam from the moon had dropped from the night sky.

"I think he has feelings for you, too."

"Yeah, he does. I can tell when a guy likes me."

Was that why he was here? *Is he—dare I think the word—jealous? Oh no. No.* I cringed. *You idiot. He can hear what you're thinking!*

I couldn't look at him, too embarrassed that I was thinking impossible thoughts. Matthias would never be jealous. He was better than that. A fact I loved about him.

I came to a stoplight and closed my eyes. *Get a hold of yourself, Zoe. Enjoy the time you have with him. Keep your thoughts real.* My eyes opened.

He smiled, and the car flashed with a brilliant light.

"You're going to blind me with your...your beams."

He laughed. "My beams?"

Beams, beams, beams. Beamdabeambeamer—anything to keep my mind off how hard my heart was beating.

The light turned green and I drove on, every cell in my body exploding with heat—as if I'd been plugged into the sun. I could hardly breathe.

"You're happy." His voice was mellow.

"Yes. I am."

"I'm pleased for you, Zoe. Your heart has always been good. You've accepted Abria for who she is, and your love for Luke has overcome your frustration."

My heart thrummed with truth. "Yes. It's…a miracle." I glanced at him. His blue eyes were bright patches of sky in the dark car. The image of him standing in a mist of fluffy white clouds against a sea of azure blue heaven came into my mind. His hand reaching out—for me.

I swallowed a knot of discomfort. God didn't waste time. Neither did Matthias. His visits had a purpose or he wouldn't be here.

"Don't be afraid." His eyes held mine in unblinking significance.

Up ahead, headlights from an oncoming car shone through the rain. I stopped at the crest of the hill, ready to turn left onto my street, and waited for the car to pass. Above the battering drops I heard the roar of the speeding engine. My heart throbbed. *Oh no.* I saw the flash of bright yellow and black—the wasp truck— racing through the downpour, heading toward me. I gripped the wheel.

Steel crashed into steel. A furious thrust. Windshield shattered. Screeching rubber. The car spun. I opened my mouth to scream. Nothing. Rain hit my skin. Stinging. Burning. Pain raked my limbs. The car whirled round, round, round, the screeching so loud it was as if the heavens screamed through the rain.

Black.

TWENTY-THREE

A soft beep jumps through the haze in my head. Continuous. Comforting, in a neutral, melodic way. Where is it coming from? I open my eyes to search for it.

White ceiling. With black dots. Voices. Soft voices. Muddled. Pain. Everywhere. My face—fire and ice. My limbs—heavy. Please take the pain away. I can't think. My head hurts too much. Like a million knives thrust into it.

"Zoe?" Mom's voice. Terrified.

Panic fights through my dulled system, pricking my nerves along the journey to my heart. I struggle to open my mouth and speak, but can't. *Why can't I talk? What happened?*

A warm hand on my arm, the touch familiar. Mom's whisper.

"Zoe." A sob.

Don't cry Mom. I'm here. I'm here.

Another hand. Strong fingers squeeze my fingers. *Dad.* Tears—One. Two. Drops on my arm. *Dad, don't. I'm okay. I'm going to be fine. Matthias told me so.*

Matthias. *Where are you?*

Rest, Zoe. His voice, serene and settling, falls over me, and my pain vanishes.

My eyes open. Black dotted ceiling. White walls. Beeping tone still there, like a ticking clock.

"She's awake." *Luke.*

"Zoe?"

"Zoe!"

My body aches, but I feel hands touching me, soft caresses of comfort that press pain more deeply into my body. I groan. My head still throbs. I blink, hoping my fuzzy vision will clear, but it looks like a coating of Vaseline covers my eyes.

I look for the faces of my family through the haze and see Mom's beautiful blue eyes. Her dark hair. She holds a tissue at her trembling lips. "Mom."

She tightens her grip around my arm. More pain. I close my eyes. But I have to see Dad. "Dad?"

Movement. Dad and Luke are there then, standing next to Mom. It's so good to see them—for our eyes to meet. I hope they can see how overjoyed I am seeing them, having them there. I want to reach out and put my arms around them, but nothing happens. I don't move. Too tired. Too much pain throbbing through my limbs.

"Abria?" My voice rasps, but I'm so happy to be able to communicate.

"She's at home, honey."

Home. Home flashes in my head: countless family dinners, laughing, talking, sharing each other. I can't wait to go home again. Abria smiling, running through the halls like a bird longing for freedom. My heart aches for her silly laughter. "I want to see her."

Mom weeps. Her squeeze on my arm intensifies. I hear Luke choke and look at him. He's sobbing, and turns away. *Aw, bud. Don't cry.* I want to put my arms around him. Wish I could move. Too tired.

"Hang on, Zoe." Dad's voice tries to cut through my aches with hope, but there's too much pain. I want to let go. *Where's Matthias?*

I'm here, Zoe. I hear his voice and something zings through my veins, deadening all pain. I look for him. He's standing in the corner of the room. White, pure, divine.

There you are. It's about time.

I've been here all along.

How come I haven't seen you until now?

Your family needs you.

They're so sad. Mom's crying. So is Dad. And Luke. What happened, Matthias? All I remember is you and me in the car.

You were hit by another automobile.

Shards of glassy memories glimmer in my mind. *Yes, I remember. Am I going to be okay? I want Mom and Dad to know.*

Matthias' serene blue gaze holds mine in an unblinking, silent message. *What does your heart tell you?*

A steady beat of comfort reverberates in my chest.

"Zoe? Honey, Abria's here." Has time passed? I'm not sure. One moment I am talking to Matthias, the next I am looking at Mom. Her lips quivering up in a smile. Her eyes shadowed with fear, skin ashen with worry. In her arms, she holds Abria.

My heart flies with delight. "Hey…baby." Words work from my tongue, like pulling a sinking ship with a rope.

Abria is amazingly calm, staring down at me. I long to touch the soft curls in her hair and hold her, smell her little girl scent. My arms are too heavy to lift, and when I manage to raise them an inch, Mom and Dad break out in shocked smiles.

Dad moves next to Mom. "Don't tire yourself, Zoe. You need all the rest you can get."

But I want to hold…"Abria…"

"She's right here." Tears stream from Mom's eyes again. Abria reaches one hand out to me for a treasured second, then it's gone, back at her side. She feathers her fingers against the palm of the opposite hand.

Mom clutches Abria close. "Say hello to Zoe, Abria."

"O."

"Good...girl." Words are harder to pull out, drifting as they are further out to sea. *Where is Luke?* "Luke."

Dad glances toward the door. "He's out in the hall." His pause is long, heavy. His face tight. "Do you want him?"

I close my eyes and try to nod. My head barely moves. I hear the whoosh of the door, prattling from the hall—a moving cart, a droning voice on the intercom. Then the door whooshes again.

I open my eyes. Luke is next to the bed, Mom, clutching Abria to her chest, is behind him, hiding her sobs in Abria's neck.

Luke's blue eyes are blotchy and red. *My little brother, crying.* His face battered by anguish. I need to hug him, tell him everything is going to be all right. *Matthias?*

Yes, Zoe?

They're so upset. They can't see that everything is going to work out, that I'm fine.

"Bud..." With effort I squeeze out the word. He lays his warm hand on my arm. Less pain this time.

"Yeah?" Luke's voice hitches.

"Glad...you...re..." *here. So glad to see you again. I'm going to miss you.* I close my eyes against tears, but they spill down my cheeks.

I'm going to miss you. All.

A whirling tunnel of flashing images sucks me effortlessly toward a blinding white light. My life. Pictures both live and still, move before my vision in a vibrant history of the last eighteen years, three months, two days and eight hours of living. My life. Childhood. Luke, Mom, Dad. Abria. Friends, relatives, neighbors, school mates. Faces I know well, others I haven't thought of in years, now remembered with bold clarity. Good. Bad. Secrets. Truths. Kindnesses. Cruelties. Joy. And regret.

Mom and Dad. Weeping at the hospital. Luke. Abria.

The last moments. Ten seconds. Three.

Final breath.

My soul aches and reaches back, yearning to do something for my family. *I'm sorry for everything. Anything I ever did that hurt or disappointed you. Please forgive me.*

Forgiveness. The only thing I want.

My last wish.

Everything will be all right.

Where the words come from, I don't know, but the ache I have inside vanishes, replaced by a soothing calm more potent than the calm I feel whenever I am with Matthias.

I know my family will be in good hands, and I let go, submitting myself into the light.

Zoe.

My heart fluttered open. I blinked, my eyes struggling to adjust to the brilliant colors surrounding me. A meadow. Soft blades of grass tickled my bare feet. The crisp scent of greenery muted the scent of rose, carnation and lily. Flowing against me, a silky barely-pink dress, so comforting the fabric was unlike anything I'd ever worn—the garment as much a part of me as skin.

I twirled, the freedom to move without pain inexplicably satisfying. A weightless peace filled my soul. I smiled, marveling. I was fresh. New.

"You're the cat's meow."

My head whipped up. Matthias stood a few feet away, surrounded by radiant daisies, wildflowers and roses—in every color and variety. He didn't look a day older than twenty, the age at which he'd died. Young. Eager. He wore a pale shirt and ivory slacks, the luminescent shades radiating a soft white light from his being, a radiance which spread out like beams of sunlight to me.

He reached out a hand, his long fingers extended.

I wanted him—wanted to feel his flesh and bone. To immerse in the comfort surrounding him, comfort that reached out in invitation and promised completion.

I ran to him.

He caught me in a tight embrace that joined us from chest to toes. Warm, sweet, fusion.

I can't believe I'm here. With you!

At last.

"Is this Heaven?"

"A place in between."

I eased back, locking my gaze with his. "What do you mean?"

His hands gently traveled from my waist to my shoulders. "It's called Paradise."

"Sounds perfect." I grinned.

"Almost. But it's not Heaven—that's perfect. This place, Zoe, is a temporary place for mortals who still hang in the balance of life."

"So Paradise is a place to chill? Before I cross through the big golden gates."

Matthias threw back his head in laugh. "Something like that." The warmth of his hands caressed my arms as they moved down to my hands. We linked fingers and he drew me closer.

Don't let me go.

Asking for wishes already?

"So you're going to grant me three wishes?"

"Only three? I thought a bearcat such as yourself would want a dozen— at least."

I shook my head. His body felt so strong and alive next to me, an electric current bounced between us. *I don't need dozens of wishes fulfilled. I'm with you. There's nothing else I want.*

Matthias pressed his forehead to mine. "I've been waiting for this moment." His silky voice poured into me. "I want to savor it." He lifted his fingers to my face, tracing the contours of my cheek.

So this is our connection, isn't it? No wonder you couldn't tell me.

Because I didn't know.

"You didn't?"

"I was there to watch over Abria. That was my assignment. And then I fell in love with you, Zoe."

The way he said my name turned my heart inside out. *Another wish.*

Anything.

Kiss me.

With aching intensity, he lowered his face. His mouth joined mine in starlit heat, sparking thrill and joy, spreading love through my soul in a consuming brushfire.

I locked my arms around his neck. *I love you.*

Ah, Zoe. He broke the seal of our lips, still cradling my cheeks in his hands, and he eased back in a sparkling grin. "I liked that wish," he whispered against my mouth.

HEAVENLY - JENNIFER LAURENS

Hands linked, he urged me to the sweet grass beneath our feet. The rushing urge to be one with this place caused me to lie down, close my eyes and take a deep breath.

The temperature was comfortably warm, the grass not too prickly under my back. I lay looking skyward at the deep blue atmosphere above. The sun appeared closer, more fiery and powerful, as if to say I'm still here providing you light, yet its heat was even.

Matthias was propped on his side next to me, his gaze pressed into the skin of my face. *You're staring.*

I can't help it. You're radiant. He brought my fingers to his mouth. I closed my eyes. My heart fluttered, waiting.

Kiss me.

Warm lips. A soft, subtle heartbeat against my fingers. Joy coursed through me with each of my breaths. I opened my eyes, savoring the liquid highlights in his hair underneath the sun's beams. "Is that the sun?"

He nodded. "I told you. God doesn't waste anything. Each creation has infinite capabilities." He leaned close and kissed the tip of my nose. "Including you."

I wanted to wrap around him and simply lay there in his comforting, complete embrace. He grinned. "That's a wish I can grant." Then his arms slipped around me and he pulled me against him.

This really is paradise.

"Yes."

Just a second ago, I'd been in pain. The complete freedom I was experiencing brought the tormented faces of my family into my mind and an old echo of my flesh sent an ache through me. "My family...it was hard leaving them."

They'll be all right, Zoe.

Surety filled the air around me. Matthias' words were true, each one settled inside of me, taking hold of my soul in such a way that all doubt vanished with my next breath. *I'll miss them.*

That love you carry with you.

I closed my eyes, the yearning, the missing not gone—but tucked away, placed in a constant vivid display of happy moments—like photographs—at the forefront of my thoughts offering me comfort.

I've never felt anything like I feel now. Here. For you.

I wish I'd known you in life. I closed my eyes holding back a sudden surge of tears. *I wish we could have been together.*

We're together now. His arms wound around me, an eternal encirclement of completion.

ABOUT THE AUTHOR

Jennifer Laurens is the mother of six children, one of whom has autism. She lives in Utah with her family, at the base of the Wasatch Mountains.

Other Titles:

Falling for Romeo

Magic Hands

Nailed

Visit the website: www.heavenlythebook.com

Read a sneak peek at the exciting follow up book to Heavenly:

PENITENCE

I was awake.

But I was dead.

Was the vast gouging ache in my heart or in my soul? It didn't matter. I writhed in agony trying to escape, willing to do anything—even hurl myself from a rocky cliff, or into a turbulent black sea to rid myself of the dread spreading throughout my being.

Just seconds ago I'd been cradled in the arms of the man I loved. Complete comfort had surrounded me. Joy. Peace. Safety. All of those gifts eluded me now.

Now, a fierce fire raced through my veins. Bruised muscles screamed. My heart pounded out each difficult breath.

Flashing images of the accident blared into my consciousness. More vibrant and real than any memory I'd ever recalled when I'd been alive. Jarred, I gasped. My heart sped. I reached for Matthias.

Concern flashed over his face. "Zoe?"

"I…" I gulped for breath. Night. Pouring rain. The yellow and black truck. Scraping steel. Blinding headlights. "I see the accident."

"Look at me." His hands reached out in urgency for me, but he was disappearing—being sucked away. "Zoe. Look at me."

I'm trying! Through the blast of crashing images, I strove to keep my gaze locked on his. I could barely see his face through the collage of the accident whirling in my mind. My body felt weighed down, as if I'd taken in a breath of leaden air. Like a tornado the sensations stormed, tearing apart Matthias' face, ripping him further and further from my view until he shrunk, devoured in the vortex.

I strained, reaching back. Screamed for him. Kicked and clawed as though I'd been dropped into the dark abyss of an open grave. *Please! I don't want to go. I want to stay with him!*

ISBN: 978-1-933963-84-6

Printe
2133 7B

9 781933 963846